Who was Brian's father?

Gabriel Serrano knew.

Madelyn St. James *thought* she knew.

But sometimes there was a difference between the facts and the truth.

Gabriel and Madelyn shared a secret—and a past they would both rather forget. Yet out of their darkest hours blossomed a love neither one could ever have predicted…

Dear Reader,

Welcome to the latest selection of six, sizzling romantic suspense novels from Silhouette Sensation!

I'm thrilled to announce the start of a twelve-book series this month, A YEAR OF LOVING DANGEROUSLY. Sharon Sala, a best-selling, award-winning, absolutely incredible writer, launches things with *Mission: Irresistible*. Every book in A YEAR OF LOVING DANGEROUSLY features a complete romance, along with a piece of an ongoing puzzle, and enough excitement and tension to fuel your entire year! Try it out!

Reader favourite, Justine Davis, is back with us this month, with a reformed bad boy, so look for *The Return of Luke McGuire*. But if you prefer the more usual policeman hero, you can still indulge yourself with *Gabriel Is No Angel* by Wendy Haley and *A Stranger Is Watching* by Linda Randall Wisdom, both are wonderfully tense and sensual stories.

Finally, we have two very different stories of heiresses about to claim their inheritance: Fiona Brand's *Blade's Lady* is a classic woman-in-jeopardy story, while *Daddy by Default* from Nikki Benjamin deals with secrets from the past.

Enjoy them all!

The Editors

Daddy by Default

NIKKI BENJAMIN

™ SILHOUETTE
SENSATION
®

Silhouette, Silhouette Sensation and Colophon are registered trademarks of Harlequin Books S.A., used under licence.

First published in Great Britain 2001
Silhouette Books, Eton House, 18-24 Paradise Road,
Richmond, Surrey TW9 1SR

© Barbara Vosbeirn 1997

ISBN 0 373 07789 0

18-0701

Printed and bound in Spain
by Litografia Rosés S.A., Barcelona

NIKKI BENJAMIN

was born and raised in the Midwest, but after years in the Houston area, she considers herself a true Texan. Nikki says she's always been an avid reader. Her writing experience was limited, however, until a friend started penning a novel and encouraged Nikki to do the same. One scene led to another, and soon she was hooked.

When not reading or writing, the author enjoys spending time with her husband and son, needlepoint, hiking, biking, horse riding and sailing.

Prologue

With a muttered curse, Ethan Merritt sat back in his chair, pressed the heels of his hands to his forehead and closed his eyes, blocking out what little he could see of the small, sparsely furnished room where he'd slept the past four weeks. The sharp, stabbing pain shooting through his skull was almost unbearable, but soon now, he would finally have some surcease.

Outside the open window, a chorus of frogs peeped and croaked, rhapsodizing melodically, while myriad night-flying insects, drawn by the light, thunked and fluttered against the fine mesh of the screen. Familiar sounds underscored by the whisper of waves upon the sandy shore a few hundred yards from the wood-frame house he shared with his assistant, Madelyn St. James. Sounds he had grown accustomed to during their stay in the Bay Islands of Honduras. Sounds that soothed his soul when daylight faded into darkness and he had no choice but to sit alone and contemplate his fate.

He was only forty-five, and he was known internationally for the excellence of his outdoor photography. Until six months ago, he'd believed he had everything to live for. Now he was going blind. And worse, he was slowly, surely succumbing to a creeping paralysis that would eventually leave him as helpless as a newborn.

He could have dealt with the loss of his sight, and he would have. But the prospect of ending up dependent on the kindness of strangers for the simplest of his wants and needs was more than he could countenance. And considering what a bastard he'd been all his life, who but a stranger—a highly paid stranger, at that—would look after him?

His half brother? Ethan mused. Or his lovely assistant?

Gabriel would hardly welcome him with open arms, but neither would he turn him away. He had already proven himself to be the kind of decent man who willingly did what he believed to be his duty. But Ethan had no right to burden Gabe again. No right at all after what he had done to him ten years ago.

Madelyn, too, had proven to be a decent person. She had already indicated her willingness to stay with him as long as he wanted, and she would. She was good and kind and capable, and lately, so damned dependable. But Ethan couldn't allow himself to take advantage of her, either. She had put up with enough of his guff, standing by him long after someone less principled would have walked away without a backward glance.

Poor girl. She'd had no idea what she was getting herself into when she agreed to hire on as his assistant. Either she hadn't heard or had chosen not to believe the rumors going around about him.

Ethan could only imagine how dismayed she must have been when she finally realized what a jerk he could be. Yet she hadn't cut and run. Rather, she had given as good as she got, putting him in his place whenever necessary, treating him much as she must have done the more obnoxious of the adolescents she'd taught in junior high school.

Against all odds, her skill with a camera had also surpassed his wildest expectations. As the virus he'd contracted in South America half a dozen years ago began to take its toll, robbing him of his sight, more and more of the work he'd sold as his own had actually been hers.

She'd probably go on letting him use her indefinitely, but he couldn't do that. Unfortunately, neither could he get her to leave of her own accord. For the past few days, he had done his damnedest to drive her away. Ignoring his foul mood, she had quietly completed the photographs he'd been hired to do for *Travel International*. Then, having read about a doctor in Houston who specialized in the treatment of rare tropical diseases, she had made arrangements for them to fly there the day after tomorrow.

With a weary sigh, Ethan dropped his hands to his lap and opened his eyes again. Despite the bright light shed by the bare bulb hanging overhead, he could make out little more than vague shapes and shadows.

He wanted to share Madelyn's belief that there could be a cure for him, but he knew better. And he wasn't about to use the money he had left on what would only prove to be a futile effort to save himself. Not when he had the boy to consider.

Thus, he had made arrangements of his own. Arrangements meant to benefit the three people involved. More than likely, they wouldn't realize that at the outset. But maybe one day… Maybe Gabriel, Madelyn and the boy would—

"You're up later than usual. Having trouble sleeping again?"

Caught off guard, Ethan turned toward the sound of Madelyn's voice. He wished he could see her clearly one more time. Tall and slim and young and lovely—her auburn hair falling thick and straight to her shoulders, her gray-green eyes bright with interest, a wry smile tugging at the corners of her mouth.

But he couldn't allow her to come any closer. Her concern for him was almost palpable. All too easily, albeit unknowingly, she might tempt him to hang on a little longer, and that he simply couldn't do. Not with his window of opportunity closing more rapidly than he'd originally anticipated.

"Actually, I was just on my way to bed." He stood, tugged his T-shirt over his head and tossed it on the chair. Arching an eyebrow, he added sardonically, "I don't suppose there's any chance I can induce you to join me?"

"Ethan, please, give it up, will you?" she replied, her exasperation evident despite her teasing tone.

"Come now, Maddy, admit it. You'd be hurt if I didn't hit on you at least once a week." He favored her with a slight smile, turned and moved toward the bed, the weakness in his legs slowing his progress.

"Not necessarily," she answered. Then, more seriously, she asked, "Are you sure you're okay? You've been kind of quiet all day."

"Just thinking about all I have to do before we head back to the States. I don't want to leave any loose ends."

"You never do," she assured him.

"Mostly, thanks to you." He paused, then glanced back at her, adding before he could stop himself, "I really do appreciate all you've done for me."

"In your own churlish way?" she responded with the barest hint of sarcasm.

"I'm not always a boor, am I?"

"Not always," she conceded. Seeming to hesitate, she shifted in the doorway. "Ethan—?"

"As you said, it's late, and I'm tired," he cut in, unwilling to allow their conversation to take a maudlin turn.

"Then I'd better let you get to bed."

"I'll probably sleep late in the morning."

Casually, he slid one hand into the pocket of his khaki shorts and curled his fingers around the vial of pain pills he'd been hoarding for almost two months.

"Sounds like a good idea to me. I'll probably do the same."

She lingered a few moments longer, then finally murmured a quiet "good night."

Barely resisting the urge to call out to her, to beg her to stay, Ethan stood still and silent until he heard the door close. Then he sat on the edge of the bed, took a deep, steadying breath and eased the vial from his pocket.

Chapter 1

"**Y**ou're not serious, are you, Cullen? Please, tell me you're not serious," Gabriel Serrano demanded as he shot to his feet, almost overturning the sturdy leather armchair he'd been sitting in.

Making no attempt to hide his anger, he leaned forward, braced his hands on the desk and glared at the lawyer.

"I wish I could, Gabe. But in this addendum to his will, Ethan bequeathed his half ownership of the house the two of you inherited from your mother to a woman by the name of Madelyn St. James."

Obviously caught off guard by Gabriel's immoderate behavior, Cullen Birney eyed him uncertainly as he held out a small sheaf of papers.

His fury mounting, Gabriel grabbed the papers, crumpled them in his fist and tossed them on the desk.

"The bastard. The dirty, rotten, stinking bastard."

Turning away, he paced across the office, paused,

shoved his hands in the pockets of his suit pants and stared at the floor.

Over the years, Ethan had taken great pleasure in letting Gabriel know just how little he meant to him, treating him unconscionably on more than one occasion. That he had chosen to do so from beyond the grave, as well, was almost more than he could bear.

There had been many times when he'd had good reason to damn his older brother to hell. But lately there had also been times when Gabriel had hoped the two of them might one day reconcile. Not so much for their sake, but for Brian's.

Now he realized what a fool he'd been to consider such a possibility. Ethan wouldn't have been interested. In fact, he probably would have laughed in his face had Gabriel found the courage to suggest it. And then, knowing Ethan, he would have taken even greater delight in the little…surprise he had been planning for his younger brother.

How could he have done it? How could he have left his half of the house to some *bimbo?* Had his brother hated him that much? Or had he fallen under the woman's spell? Considering his brother's track record, Gabriel found that hard to believe. She'd have to be one hot little piece of—

"I'm sorry, Gabe," Cullen said. He stood, crossed to Gabriel and placed a hand on his shoulder. "I know how much the house means to you."

"You've made sure the damn thing's legit?"

"I've gone over the will as well as the addendum, looking for loopholes, but there aren't any. I also took a look at the copy of your mother's will I found in my father's files. I had hoped that she'd left instructions regarding the disposition of the house should one of you die, but unfortunately, she didn't. So, yes, as far as I can see, the addendum is legitimate, and thus, legally binding.''

''Is there any way I can challenge it? Maybe prove that he wasn't in his right mind or that he was coerced?'' Gabriel asked, eyeing his friend hopefully.

''You could, but I'm afraid you'd be wasting your time and your money,'' Cullen advised. ''I contacted Gerald Goodson, the New York lawyer who drew up the addendum for Ethan before he left for Honduras. Goodson indicated your brother was of sound mind and body when he signed the papers. He also told me, in no uncertain terms, that he was prepared to say as much in court. I gather Ethan must have expressed some concern that you would try to interfere—''

''And he wanted to make sure his lady love wouldn't have any trouble collecting the payment he obviously promised her for services rendered,'' Gabriel cut in bitterly.

''Actually, Madelyn St. James was his assistant,'' Cullen replied, his tone placating.

''Oh, yeah. I can just imagine how inventively she saw to his…needs.''

''When I talked to her earlier, she sounded quite nice. A little young maybe, but nice.''

''Of course, she would be. Nice and young. That's the way Ethan always liked them,'' Gabriel muttered.

For one long moment, he recalled what a nice, young woman Lily had been the day Ethan had taken a fancy to her ten years ago. Then, realizing Cullen had indicated he'd spoken to the St. James woman, Gabriel shoved that sad memory aside and rounded on the lawyer.

''You talked to her? When?''

"Yesterday afternoon," Cullen replied, returning to his desk.

"You called her?"

"Actually, she called me. Then I called you and, as you may remember, insisted we meet today."

"Why did you wait until now to tell me you'd talked to her?" Glaring at the lawyer, Gabriel stalked back to the leather armchair and sat down again.

"I thought we ought to go over Ethan's will and the addendum first."

"Well, we've done that," Gabriel shot back impatiently.

"Yes, we have," Cullen agreed. "And, as I've told you, both documents appear to be legitimate. Consequently, you and Madelyn St. James now share ownership of the property located at 15 Alameda Road."

Sitting back in his chair, Cullen seemed to hesitate.

"And?" Gabriel prodded.

Had he any choice at all, he would rather not know what had given his friend pause. But he was afraid that where the St. James woman was concerned, avoiding the inevitable—even for a short time—would put him at a disadvantage.

"She would like to take a look at the house sometime later today."

"Oh, really?"

Unable to ignore the flicker of worry edging around his anger, Gabriel eyed Cullen narrowly. Having to allow a stranger access to his house made him feel powerless. But what could he do about it? According to Cullen, she had just as much right to be there as he did.

"She arrived in Santa Fe yesterday afternoon," his friend offered by way of explanation. "Apparently, she found a letter addressed to her among Ethan's personal papers. In it he advised her to contact me about the house. From the little she said during our conversation, I gather she hasn't seen a copy of Ethan's will or the addendum, and she doesn't seem to know about you or…your son.''

''So she thinks she's inherited sole ownership of the house?'' Gabriel muttered.

''Yes.''

Ethan had always been good at throwing monkey wrenches into the works, but he'd really outdone himself by adding that addendum to his will. With what amounted to little more than the stroke of a pen, he had turned Gabriel's life upside down, and more than likely, Madelyn St. James's, as well.

Gabriel could have almost felt sorry for the woman. But then, he reminded himself, she had chosen to associate with his half brother of her own free will. And any woman foolish enough to do that deserved to suffer the consequences.

''Did you set her straight?''

''I thought it would be wiser to explain the situation in person,'' Cullen said.

''When are you planning to do that?''

''She's agreed to meet with me at three o'clock this afternoon. I'll go over Ethan's will with her, and then…'' As he had earlier, the lawyer hesitated. Glancing down, he straightened the papers Gabriel had tossed aside as he added, ''John Santos will be joining us at my request.''

''John Santos? The real-estate agent? Why?'' Gabriel asked, momentarily confused.

''As executor of the will, it's my duty to take into consideration the best interests of all those named as beneficiaries,'' Cullen replied, meeting Gabriel's gaze once again. ''I've already mentioned that Ms. St. James has a right to take a look at the property.''

''I know, but why—?'' Gabriel began, unable to hide his impatience.

''She also has a right to know how much it's worth,'' Cullen stated matter-of-factly.

''How much it's worth?'' Still puzzled, Gabriel sat back in his chair and stared at his friend. ''A lot, I imagine. But I'm not planning on selling. Not to her or anyone else. Unless—''

Stopped by a sudden thought, he frowned.

''Unless what?''

With a sinking feeling in the pit of his stomach, Gabriel gripped the arms of his chair so tightly, his knuckles turned white. ''Unless there's some way she can force me to do it.''

''Only if you choose not to buy her out. In that case, she can insist the house be sold to a third party. Then the two of you would split the proceeds equally.''

''But the house is easily worth half a million dollars,'' Gabriel snapped.

''Easily,'' Cullen agreed.

''And I'm a junior high school principal living paycheck to paycheck. Aside from a modest savings account, my half of the house is all I have of value. Buying her out isn't going to be all that easy for me to do.''

''Then I suggest you try to be as cordial to her as you can. Maybe she'll be willing to work something out.''

Overwhelmed by a sudden sense of desperation, Gabriel stood and walked to the window overlooking the Plaza. The house meant so much to him. Always had, and always would. He couldn't lose it. Not to satisfy the whim of some moneygrubbing woman who had probably done nothing more than service his besotted brother sexually.

"Like what?" he asked, glancing over his shoulder at Cullen.

"I'm not sure," Cullen replied. "Let me give it some thought. With luck, I should be able to come up with something you'll both find agreeable. But you're going to have to mind your manners in the meantime. She'll be a lot more amenable if she doesn't feel she's being bullied."

"Whatever you say," Gabriel muttered, staring out the window again.

He and Cullen had been friends for a long time. Trusting him came naturally. But there was a good chance Madelyn St. James had arrived in Santa Fe with an agenda all her own. An agenda that could end up costing him his home no matter how conscientiously Cullen worked on his behalf.

"When I meet with Ms. St. James this afternoon, I'll explain the situation to her as best I can. Then I'll let John Santos give her an idea of how much the property is worth. After that, I'll bring her over to the house. Probably around four-thirty or five o'clock. Unless you would rather I wait...."

"I can be home by four. Come anytime after that," Gabriel said.

Luckily he didn't have any meetings scheduled that afternoon, and his assistant principal could handle any problems that might arise later in the day.

"You'll be hospitable, won't you?"

"I'll try."

"I'd try hard if I were you," Cullen admonished. "You want Madelyn St. James working with you, not against you. Right?"

"Yeah, right," Gabriel agreed reluctantly as he moved away from the window.

"Hey, I'm on your side, you know."

"I know." Dredging up a smile, Gabriel paused in front of Cullen's desk. "And I appreciate it," he added as they shook hands. "Really, I do."

"Hey, isn't that what friends are for?"

As Gabriel walked down the flight of steps leading from Cullen's office to the street that bordered one side of Santa Fe's central Plaza, he glanced at his watch. Almost one o'clock. He had been gone longer than he'd thought he would when he left the school almost two hours earlier. But then, he hadn't thought Ethan's will would contain any surprises, either. Fool that he was, he had assumed his half brother—for once in his life—had simply done what was right.

And in all fairness, at least to a certain extent, Ethan had. A generous sum of money had been deposited in a trust fund for Brian. All things considered, that was only just. Ethan's money should have gone to the boy, and had.

But to bequeath his half ownership of the house to a stranger...a stranger who could turn their lives upside down on impulse...

Why had he done it? To remind his younger brother—one last time—of how much antipathy he bore him?

Try as he might, Gabriel had never been able to break through the wall Ethan had insisted on erecting between them. For years, he had worshiped the ground his older brother walked on. But Ethan had wanted nothing to do with him, and he'd had no qualms about letting Gabriel know it.

Eventually, Gabriel had learned to give him a wide berth. The two of them had hardly spoken on the rare occasions Ethan had come home from college. Then he'd graduated and moved to New York. Years had passed without a visit from him. Gabriel had finished high school, then college, and had begun to teach.

Then their mother and Gabriel's father had been killed in an automobile accident. Ethan had come home for the funeral, and once again, Gabriel had found himself hoping they might finally be friends.

Instead, Ethan had driven one final, hurtful, hateful wedge between them.

As Gabriel paused on the sidewalk, a blast of cold air sent a shiver down his spine. Despite the bright sunlight, the temperature hovered in the low forties—not unusual for mid-January in northern New Mexico.

Tipping his face to the sun, he slipped into his wool overcoat, dug out his gloves and put them on, then headed across the street. Nuestra Junior High School was only a few blocks away, an easy walk on a day like today. He was glad he hadn't brought his car. He needed the time to clear his head and calm down before facing whatever awaited him back at the school.

Gabriel exchanged greetings with several people, then turned a corner, leaving the hustle and bustle of the Plaza behind. With only the occasional whoosh of a vehicle passing to disturb the quiet of early afternoon, he strode along purposefully.

He had been sorry to hear of Ethan's death almost a month ago. Truly sorry. There might not have been any love lost between them, but along with Brian, Ethan had been all the family Gabriel had left.

The letter he'd received from Ethan's lawyer—via Cullen—had advised that Ethan had died of complications from a virus he'd contracted, and that according to his wishes, his body had been cremated and his ashes scattered along a beach on the island of Roatán.

Gabriel hadn't had any problem accepting the circumstances of his brother's death. Nor had he had any concerns about Ethan's will. The lawyer had forwarded a copy to Cullen along with the letter, but Gabriel hadn't been in any hurry to have it read. He'd wanted to wait until after the Christmas holidays, and reluctantly, Cullen had agreed.

Now Gabriel could only curse himself for being so unconcerned. Had he known about Ethan's bequest to Madelyn St. James a few weeks ago, he would have had time to prepare for her arrival. As it was, he'd be meeting the woman face-to-face in a matter of hours, and those hours would be filled with the wants and needs of several hundred unpredictable preteens and adolescents.

Formulating a plan of action in the midst of what he often considered barely controlled chaos would be impossible. Luckily, Brian had been invited to a friend's house after school, so he would have a little time to himself then. Not enough to do him much good. But he'd take what he could get.

Once again, the thought of all he was going to have to deal with before the day was done had Gabriel reeling. Having someone with whom to share the burden would have been a help. But as he'd done each time a problem had come up in the eight years since Lily had run off, he was going to have to cope alone.

"Ah, Gabriel, get out the violins, why don't you?" he muttered, just barely containing the urge to feel incredibly sorry for himself.

And not a moment too soon, he added to himself as he rounded another corner and spied Ricky Montoya and Fred Grimes huddled half under a bush alongside the front steps of the school building, each puffing away on a cigarette.

"Aren't you supposed to be in class?" he asked, his voice laced with amusement as he gazed down at them.

Talk about begging to be caught. But then, the two of them thrived on any attention they could get. Which wasn't surprising considering their family backgrounds.

"Mr. Serrano," Ricky yelped. "What are *you* doing out here?"

"I was just about to ask you the same question."

Sitting beside Cullen Birney in his aging Jeep Wagoneer as he pulled out of the parking garage a block from his office, Madelyn St. James wondered if she had ever felt quite as stupefied as she did at that moment.

Yes, once before. And then—as now—all thanks to Ethan Merritt.

Dazzled by his praise of her work and desperate to get away from her overbearing parents, her egocentric brothers, their wives and children, she had eagerly accepted his offer of a job as his assistant. She had resigned from her teaching position, given up the tiny garage apartment she'd rented three blocks from her parents' house, put her meager belongings into storage and gone off to South America with him, only to realize she'd jumped from the frying pan into the fire.

On her own, hundreds of miles from home, she'd been in a state of shock. But not for long. Much too proud to admit what a mistake she'd made, Madelyn had pulled herself together then dealt with Ethan as best she could.

She'd had to put him in his place umpteen dozen times, but eventually they had reached a level of mutual understanding and respect that had made leaving him impossible for her to do.

Finding him dead—more than likely by his own hand, though he hadn't left a suicide note, and the aging, overworked island doctor hadn't seen any need for an autopsy—had saddened her greatly. And learning that he had remembered her in his will had touched her deeply.

Now she realized she should have known there was more to Ethan's leaving her a house in Santa Fe, New Mexico, than she could have ever guessed. She had seen for herself how slyly scheming he could be, often just for the fun of it. Setting up one last rather clever ruse would have been right up his alley.

Not that suspecting the worst of him would have kept Madelyn from traveling to Santa Fe to claim her inheritance. After almost a month back home in south St. Louis, she had known that if she stayed there permanently, inevitably she would end up acting as the St. James family dogsbody once again.

Moving to what she had assumed would be her own home in New Mexico had been an acceptable alternative as well as an affordable one—just barely, considering how little she had left in savings after buying a small car.

Blissfully unaware of what awaited her in Santa Fe, Madelyn had loaded several boxes of clothing and camera equipment into the car, bid her disapproving family farewell and headed west, sure that no matter what state the house was in, she could soon turn it into the home of her own she'd always wanted.

Her only real concern had been finding a job. But with her teaching credentials in order and several letters of recommendation in hand, she hadn't thought that would pose too great a problem. She had known she was going to need a regular paycheck coming in to afford the upkeep of a house. And she'd been willing to go back to teaching rather than work at her photography to guarantee she would.

Now her careful consideration seemed all for naught.

She didn't actually own a house after all. She had inherited only Ethan's half of a house that also belonged to his younger brother. Or rather, half brother. A man Ethan had never mentioned in all the time she had worked with him.

Why, Ethan? Why? she wondered, her shock gradually turning to dismay as Cullen Birney guided the Jeep along first one street rimming the Plaza, then another.

"We probably could have walked the distance to the house just as fast as driving," Cullen said, interrupting her thoughts. "But once the sun sets, the temperature is going to drop fifteen or twenty degrees. That would make the walk back a little chilly even for a native like me."

"I'm not in any hurry," Madelyn replied, offering the lawyer a slight smile.

True enough. She could have waited a good long while to meet Gabriel Serrano. And though she knew hardly anything about him, she suspected the feeling was mutual. But as co-owners of what real-estate agent John Santos had indicated was a very valuable piece of property, she and Gabriel had quite a lot to discuss.

Cullen had made it clear that Mr. Serrano wasn't interested in selling. Madelyn certainly didn't have any problem with that. Obviously, Gabriel had a personal attachment to the place while she did not. And with her limited funds and lack of collateral, she couldn't very well afford to buy him out.

In fact, considering her current financial situation, Madelyn had to admit she'd be more than happy to accept the quarter of a million dollars Gabriel Serrano was going to have to pay her in order to gain sole ownership of the house. She would be able to buy a more modest home of her own and have enough left over to support herself while she worked on her photography.

As Cullen had advised, the sooner they could come to terms, the better.

She should be thrilled with her good fortune. But in all honesty, Madelyn couldn't say that she was. Truth be told, she was filled with an inexplicable sense of dread.

She would have found it creditable had Ethan bequeathed her a small, run-down house somewhere on the outskirts of town. But to leave her something of such value…

Why had he done it? Out of the goodness of his heart? No, not the Ethan Merritt she had known. While he had never been truly hateful to her, neither had he been especially kind or considerate. More often than not, he'd been ill-mannered and overbearing. In addition, he'd been one hell of a wily rascal, delighting in all sorts of tomfoolery. Which led Madelyn to believe that very soon now the other shoe was going to drop.

"Have you had a chance to look around town?" Cullen asked.

A stocky man of medium height, probably in his mid- to late-thirties, with shaggy sandy-colored hair and mild blue eyes, he seemed nice enough. However, despite his rumpled clothing and laid-back manner, he also seemed remarkably adroit.

"Just a little," Madelyn admitted.

After arriving yesterday afternoon, checking into a small hotel a short distance from the Plaza and calling the lawyer as instructed in the letter Ethan had left for her, she had gone for a walk. Unfortunately, spending months at a time living in one tropical location or another for the past couple of years had left her more susceptible to the cold than she'd realized.

She had walked only a few blocks, then scurried back to the warmth of her hotel room. Venturing out again late that morning, she had gotten as far as the Plaza. There she had browsed in various shops until her appointment with Cullen Birney.

"This time of year it's kind of quiet, but there's still a lot to see and do," he said.

"I gathered as much from the guidebook I bought."

"I hope you'll have time to look around before you leave." Glancing at her, the lawyer smiled congenially.

"Oh, I'm sure I will," Madelyn replied, a hint of amusement creeping into her voice.

Mr. Birney seemed to believe her stay in Santa Fe would be decidedly short. Of course, he wouldn't know she hadn't anywhere else to go but back to her autocratic family, and she wasn't about to tell him as much.

She might not have a home of her own yet. But that didn't mean she couldn't start making a life for herself in Santa Fe. She had liked what she'd seen of the city so far. Liked it a lot. But she'd just as soon keep her plans to herself for the time being.

As executor of Ethan's will, Cullen seemed to be going out of his way to treat her fairly. Still, Madelyn couldn't help feeling that if he were forced to make a choice, he'd put Gabriel Serrano's best interests ahead of hers.

Of course, she couldn't blame him. Evidently, he had known Ethan's brother for years. However, that gave her all the more reason to keep her own counsel.

"You said you stopped in St. Louis to visit with your family over the Christmas holidays. Are you from there originally?"

"Yes," Madelyn answered easily.

The lawyer seemed to want to talk and she didn't mind telling him a little bit about herself. She certainly didn't have anything to hide. No bad debts, no warrants out for her arrest, not even a speeding ticket to her name.

Until two years ago, she had led a very dull life. And though her time with Ethan had been quite…interesting, she hadn't done anything to be ashamed of while they were together, either. Well, *almost* anything—

"How did you meet Ethan?" Cullen continued.

Surprised that the lawyer seemed so attuned to the trail her thoughts had taken, Madelyn hesitated. Then, realizing her relationship with Ethan *would* be of interest to him, she answered matter-of-factly.

"Some of my photographs were included in a show at one of the more reputable galleries in St. Louis's Central West End. Ethan was in town on business of some sort and came to the opening. He admired my work, the gallery owner introduced us and before the evening was over, I'd agreed to quit my teaching job at the end of the month—it was June and the school year was almost over—and sign on as his assistant."

Gazing out the window at the unique Southwestern-style adobe homes lining the winding residential street onto which they had turned, Madelyn wondered where she had ever found the courage to do something so totally out of character. Ethan *had* been charming, not to mention very persuasive. Still—

"And you were together how long? Just two years?"

"Actually, a little more than that," she replied, her manner toward the lawyer chilling at the way he had used the word *just*. His tone had been dismissive, as if he considered the time she had spent with Ethan negligible at best.

"Had he been sick for a while before he died?"

Suddenly wary, Madelyn turned to look at Cullen Birney. With the deepening twilight casting his face in shadow, his expression was unreadable.

Maybe he was simply curious. Then again, maybe he

was hoping to find a way to blame her for Ethan's death, which would, in turn, enable him to have her cut out of the will.

In truth, Madelyn had done everything she could for Ethan, trying to keep his spirits up in the face of what they had both known was an increasingly hopeless situation. Perhaps she hadn't yet convinced herself that she'd been right to leave him alone that last night. But she hadn't committed a crime by going along with his wishes, either. And she wasn't about to defend herself as if she had.

That the lawyer seemed to be considering the possibility that she might have allowed Ethan to die so she could inherit a quarter of a million dollars left a bad taste in her mouth. So bad that she was tempted to tell him thanks, but no thanks.

As far as she was concerned, Gabriel Serrano could have the house free and clear. Only the fact that Ethan had never made any mention of his half brother, yet had included her in his will knowing she would inevitably come face-to-face with him, kept her quiet.

Ethan had never done anything without good reason. And Madelyn wasn't about to walk away until she found out why he'd wanted her to make this trip to Santa Fe. Even if he had only been having one last laugh at the expense of those he'd left behind.

"According to what he told me, Ethan contracted the virus several years ago, but he didn't start exhibiting any serious side effects until last summer. After that, he declined fairly quickly," she stated simply as she gazed out the window again.

Then, determined to get a few answers of her own before they arrived at the house, she asked rather pointedly, "Am I right to assume that Ethan and his brother weren't...close?"

"What makes you think that?"

Aware that he was hedging, Madelyn bristled inwardly. She had as much right as he to ask questions and be given honest answers.

"In all the time I worked with Ethan, he never once mentioned he had a half brother living in Santa Fe. Nor did he ever mention anything about a house. I don't know about *you,* but that certainly leads *me* to believe they must have been estranged," she snapped, unable to hide her irritation.

"I think *estranged* is a little harsh," Cullen replied in a mild tone. "Ethan was twelve years older than Gabe. He had finished college, made New York his home base and begun traveling around the world taking pictures long before Gabe was out of grade school. They never really had much of a chance to get to know each other."

Madelyn suspected there was more to Ethan's distancing himself from the only family he had, especially when he had known he would soon be wholly dependent on others for his every need. But Cullen had slowed the Jeep and switched on his turn signal as they approached a narrow drive cutting through the high adobe wall edging the roadside on the right.

Apparently they had reached their destination. Aware that Cullen would probably use that as a reason to avoid answering any further questions, Madelyn sat quietly as they made the turn.

No doubt Gabriel Serrano himself would provide some clue as to why Ethan had led her to believe he was all alone in the world. Cullen hadn't told her much about him. She knew that he was the principal of Nuestra Junior

High School, he had a nine-year-old son, Brian, and he was divorced.

Not enough to judge what kind of man he was. At least not with any accuracy. But she would be meeting him very soon now. Maybe she'd be able to determine whether he had given Ethan good cause to stay away, or if Ethan had somehow made himself unwelcome.

"Here we are," Cullen said as he guided the Jeep along the drive.

At Madelyn's first glimpse of the house, her breath caught in her throat. Set back on a wide expanse of manicured lawn, surrounded by several towering pine trees and lit by the soft glow of lamplight, the old adobe house looked warm and welcoming. A place to come home to, she thought, suddenly wistful. How had Ethan ever managed to stay away?

"Since it's almost dark, you won't be able to see much of the grounds tonight, but I'll be happy to bring you back tomorrow morning if you'd like to take a better look around then."

"Oh, yes, I would," she answered eagerly.

Even though the house wasn't really hers and never would be, she wanted to see it, *really* see it, at least once.

After parking behind an old pickup truck, Cullen came around to the passenger door, helped her out of the Jeep and led her up the short walkway.

Resisting a sudden urge to hang back, Madelyn wished she could feel as if she had a right to be there. Instead, she continued to be oddly ill at ease. Number 15 Alameda Road was more than a valuable piece of property, half of which she had inherited. Number 15 Alameda Road was somebody's *home,* and she was about to intrude.

Suddenly she wished she could creep back to the safety

of her hotel room. But it was too late for that. Much too late.

As she stood off to one side, the lawyer rapped on the heavy wooden door. She heard faint footsteps followed by the click of a bolt lock being drawn. Then the door swung open and a tall, dark man stood before them.

"Cullen." His deep voice less than hospitable, he offered his hand to the lawyer.

"Gabe."

The two men shook hands. Then Gabriel Serrano turned to look at her.

Her lips slightly parted, Madelyn stared at him, unable to hide her surprise. Not only was he tall and dark, but handsome, too. Yet he looked nothing at all like his half brother. In fact, he was the absolute antithesis of Ethan Merritt.

Granted, Ethan had been about the same height as Gabriel. He'd also been attractive in his own way. But he'd had long, shaggy blond hair, and bright, often icy, blue eyes, and he'd been slender to the point of seeming almost effete.

By contrast, Gabriel had neatly trimmed black hair combed back from his forehead. His eyes were a warm, rich shade of brown. And the navy pullover and tight-fitting, faded jeans he wore only served to emphasize his powerfully masculine build.

"Gabe, this is Madelyn St. James," Cullen said by way of introduction. "Ms. St. James, Gabriel Serrano."

His eyes narrowing slightly, Gabriel looked her over with what she could only call hostility.

"Ms. St. James," he said, no warmth at all in his voice.

He neither offered her his hand nor invited her into the house. He gazed at her a few moments longer, insolence now also evident in his dark eyes. Then he spun around and headed down the hallway, his boot heels beating a rapid tattoo on the tile floor, leaving her and Cullen Birney, sputtering apologetically, to trail after him.

Blushing to the roots of her hair, Madelyn wanted nothing more than to fade into the woodwork. That being impossible, she squared her shoulders, reminding herself, as she had earlier, that Ethan had wanted her there for a reason. And no matter how rudely Gabriel Serrano behaved toward her, she was going to find out what that reason was.

Not only for Ethan's sake, but for her own, as well.

"What a lovely house," she said, her voice cheery, as she and Cullen joined Gabriel in the living room.

Unbuttoning her black wool coat, she crossed to the fireplace and held out her hands for a few moments, savoring the fragrant warmth radiating from the burning logs. When neither man replied, she slipped out of her coat and tossed it, along with her purse, on a nearby chair. Then, tucking her hands in the pockets of her calf-length denim skirt to hide their trembling, she glanced over her shoulder and forced herself to smile brightly as she met Gabriel Serrano's angry gaze.

"I can't wait to see the rest of it."

Chapter 2

"I just bet you can't," Gabriel muttered, ignoring the warning look Cullen shot his way.

Though Madelyn continued to meet his gaze, the blush already staining her cheeks darkened perceptibly. For one long moment, he thought she would say something more. Instead, she turned away again, tipping her chin up wordlessly as she stared at the flickering firelight.

He was behaving badly, and he knew it. Yet Gabriel couldn't seem to stop himself. He had thought he'd prepared himself for her arrival, but he hadn't. Not by a long shot.

After dropping Brian off at his friend's house, Gabriel had come home alone, taken a hot shower, then dressed in jeans and a sweater. With time to spare, he'd lit a fire in the fireplace and grabbed a cold beer from the refrigerator. Then he'd settled into his favorite chair—the chair *she* had so casually draped with her coat and purse—and had a little talk with himself about the wisdom of accepting what he couldn't change.

By the time Cullen's knock had sounded at the door, he had been feeling reasonably cool, calm and collected. And he had stayed that way up until the moment he'd laid eyes on the St. James woman.

For some inexplicable reason, Gabriel had expected her to be part little girl lost, à la Lily, and part scheming seductress, and he had braced himself accordingly. Finding that she wasn't at all what he'd imagined her to be had thrown him totally off balance.

She was tall, at least five-seven, perhaps five-eight, and though she was slender, there was a strength about her, a…sturdiness, that he couldn't help but admire. Her auburn hair hung smooth and straight to her shoulders and her wide, gray-green eyes seemed to hold no hint of guile. Modestly dressed in a white turtleneck sweater, a long, slim skirt and black boots, and wearing only the barest hint of makeup, she looked…honest and… dependable. Too honest and dependable for the likes of his brother.

She also seemed poised and self-confident. Yet Gabriel sensed a certain vulnerability about her. A vulnerability that called out to him in a way that had him wanting to reassure her everything would be all right, when *he* was the injured party here.

Was it any wonder his first instinct had been to lash out at her with a churlishness that now had him cringing inwardly with embarrassment? Never in his life had he treated a woman so rudely without any provocation. But what else could he have done to distance himself from her as he'd known he must?

No matter how attractive he found her to be, Gabriel couldn't afford to harbor any fond feelings for Madelyn

St. James. Not when Ethan had already given her the power to turn his life upside down.

Nor did he have any intention of allowing history to repeat itself, either. He had cleaned up the mess Ethan had left behind ten years ago. He wasn't about to be suckered into doing it again.

Of course, he could be way off base. But studying Madelyn as she stood quietly by the fire, Gabriel had the sneaking suspicion that his beloved brother had left another naive young woman in the lurch.

This time, however, *he* wasn't about to come to the rescue. He had taken on the thankless task of serving as Ethan's stand-in once already. And as far as he was concerned, once had been more than enough.

He could sympathize with Madelyn St. James all he wanted, and though he really ought to know better after Lily, he did. But that didn't mean he had to bend over backward for her. He was going to do what he was obligated to do by law, nothing more, nothing—

"If this isn't a good time for you after all, Gabe, I'm sure Ms. St. James won't mind waiting until another day to see the house," Cullen said, his voice filled with reproach.

"Actually, this is as good a time as any for me to show her the house," Gabriel replied, attempting to sound more congenial than he felt.

As Cullen had warned, his hostility toward the woman would only make it that much harder for them to come to an agreement on how best to settle Ethan's estate. Also, having the chance to show her around the house without his inquisitive young son underfoot had been an unexpected stroke of luck—one he had only begun to appreciate fully when he thought of all the questions he would have had to answer if Madelyn and Brian crossed paths.

"What about you, Ms. St. James? Are you still agreeable to seeing the house tonight?" Cullen asked.

"Yes, of course," she answered, turning to face them again after only a moment's hesitation.

"Would you like something to drink first? A soft drink, tea, a cup of coffee?" Gabriel offered as he should have done in the first place.

She met his gaze for several seconds, a wary look in her eyes, obviously trying to determine what had caused his sudden change in attitude. A frown creasing her forehead, she finally looked away.

"No, thank you."

"Cullen?"

"Maybe later," he replied as he set his briefcase on the coffee table then shrugged out of his overcoat.

"Well, then, why don't we get started?" Gabriel suggested with a heartiness he could only hope didn't sound quite as false to Madelyn as it did to him. "As you've probably guessed, this is the living room."

While it was a little late to start acting like a gracious host—as the expression on Cullen's face reminded him— it was the best he could do to make amends for his earlier behavior. He had only been trying to protect himself as well as what he considered his, and for that he had no intention of apologizing.

"Very nice," Madelyn murmured as she moved away from the fireplace.

She paused to run a hand over the dark red fabric finely striped with gold covering the sofa. Then she continued on her way around the wide, open room, surveying the mix of antique furniture that had belonged to Gabriel and Ethan's mother and the more modern, yet complementary pieces he had made himself, her gaze appreciative rather than avaricious.

As Gabriel led her through the small formal dining room then into the airy, well-lit kitchen, he had to admit his first impression of her seemed valid. She *was* a decent woman. Yet he couldn't allow himself to forget how she'd come to be there.

The longer he observed her—as he found himself doing with growing interest—the harder it was for him to believe she had been the latest in Ethan's ever-changing string of women. She just didn't seem like the type to have been taken in by his handsome face or his famous name.

Of course, Ethan had always loved a challenge. And surely she had done a hell of a lot more than change the film in his camera to be remembered so generously in his will. As she'd had every right to. She was an adult, after all, and as far as Gabriel knew, unattached. Why shouldn't she have shared his brother's bed?

He had no reason to be concerned about her relationship with Ethan. No reason at all. She wasn't anything to *him*. Not personally. He was going to have to buy her out regardless. Beyond that, nothing else about her should matter to him.

Still, Gabriel couldn't seem to quell his curiosity.

"So how did you hook up with my brother?" he asked as he leaned a hip against the kitchen counter and crossed his arms over his chest.

Pausing in her perusal of Brian's artwork that decorated the refrigerator door, she glanced at him, her annoyance at his choice of wording plainly evident.

"I didn't *hook up* with Ethan, Mr. Serrano," she replied. "As I explained to Mr. Birney earlier, your brother hired me to work as his assistant after seeing a display of my photographs at a gallery in St. Louis. But then, you would have known that if you'd been in touch with him over the past two years." Still holding his gaze, she added pointedly, "But you weren't, were you?"

"No," Gabriel admitted, albeit grudgingly, feeling as if he'd been called on the carpet and issued an unwarranted reprimand.

She had no right to make him sound like the guilty party where Ethan was concerned. Unfortunately, he couldn't say as much to her without going into a detailed explanation of exactly what Ethan had done to *him* ten years ago, something he had neither the time nor the desire to do.

"Why not?" she prodded.

"We were never close."

She eyed him skeptically for several moments, but much to his relief, she didn't press him any further. Turning away, she crossed to the French doors that opened onto the patio, cupped her hands on the glass and peered into the darkness.

"What's out there?" she asked.

"A cottage," Gabriel answered, aware that she must have spied the small adobe building tucked in a far corner of the lamplit courtyard.

"Is it part of the property?"

"Yes."

"Can I see it?" She glanced at him hopefully.

After a moment's hesitation, Gabriel nodded. "Yes, of course."

He didn't want to take her out to the cottage, but he couldn't refuse without giving her a reason. And he wasn't about to do that. Why he'd prefer to avoid the place really wasn't any of her business.

"I'll get your coat," Cullen offered.

He had trailed along behind them, saying very little. But every time he had caught Gabriel's eye, the lawyer had shot him a warning glance, reminding him wordlessly of the risk he would be running by alienating Madelyn St. James.

"Thanks." She watched him leave the kitchen, then turned her attention to the cookbooks lined up on a shelf of the wrought-iron baker's rack off to one side of the French doors.

Without Cullen to act as a buffer between them, Gabriel felt oddly uncomfortable. He wasn't sure why. They were in *his* house. If anyone should be ill at ease, it should be her. But she seemed quite…content.

Wordlessly, she took a cookbook from the shelf and thumbed through it. Gabriel wondered if she was really interested in the recipes or was only pretending to be. Then he wondered why he cared.

Highly annoyed, he fished a set of keys from one of the drawers under the counter. Crossing to the laundry room, his boot heels clicking on the tile floor, he grabbed his faded denim jacket off the hook on the wall and shrugged into it.

Carrying Madelyn's coat over his arm, Cullen hurried through the kitchen doorway.

"Here you go," he said, offering her a beneficent smile.

Murmuring her thanks, Madelyn allowed him to help her into her coat.

Reminding himself yet again that he wouldn't be helping matters any by letting her get to him, Gabriel took a deep, steadying breath. He could stomp around in anger and frustration all he wanted once she was gone. But for now, he was going to have to mind his manners.

"Ready?" he asked, moving to the door as Madelyn finished buttoning her coat.

"As I'll ever be," she quipped with a slight smile.

Admiring her spirit in spite of himself, Gabriel led the way across the courtyard. She was certainly proving capable of holding her own. Which did nothing to put his mind at rest. Were she a meeker, humbler sort, he would have had a much easier time dealing with her. Unfortunately, it didn't seem as if he was going to be that lucky.

He unlocked the cottage door, reached inside and flipped the light switch, then ushered Madelyn and Cullen into the large L-shaped room that doubled as both bedroom and sitting room, a freestanding fireplace separating the two areas. Dustcovers had been draped over the few pieces of furniture, and with the heater turned down, it wasn't much warmer inside than out.

"As you can see, the place has been closed up for a while," Gabriel pointed out.

Madelyn gave the room a cursory look, then crossed to the galley kitchen. Standing in the doorway, she eyed the compact area with interest.

"You don't use it?" she asked.

"Not me," he retorted.

"Why not?"

Her attention obviously caught by the bitterness that had edged into his voice inadvertently, Madelyn paused in the bathroom doorway and glanced at him.

Mentally cursing himself for not being more circumspect, Gabriel shoved his hands in his pockets as he shifted from one foot to the other. A simple "no" uttered nonchalantly would have sufficed. Instead, he'd let his feelings show. Now he was going to have to offer some sort of explanation to satisfy her curiosity, or run the risk of being rude…again.

"I've never felt it was mine to use," he admitted, opting for honesty.

"But I thought you said it's part of the property."

"It is," he assured her.

"Then why…?" she prodded, a frown creasing her forehead.

"Ethan's father worked as a photographer, too, but his specialty was portraits. He had the cottage built to use as a studio. After he died, it sat vacant for several years. Then, about the time he turned sixteen, Ethan moved out here. He said he needed some *space.* He'd been such a pain in the butt, our mother didn't argue with him, even when he declared the place off-limits to all but a chosen few."

"And you weren't among them, huh?" Madelyn asked, a mischievous glint in her eyes.

"The pesky younger brother?" Gabriel snorted derisively. "Not hardly."

"But that was years ago," she chided quietly.

Evidently, she found it hard to believe he had been influenced by Ethan's dictates so far into adulthood. Of course, there was much more to his avoidance of the cottage than that. But he wasn't about to go into the details with her.

"Hey, what can I say?" he retorted. "I learned to give this place a wide berth early on, and some habits are harder to break than others."

"And I thought my brothers had sibling rivalry down to an art form," she murmured as she turned to peer into the bathroom that had been set up to double as a darkroom.

"You have brothers?" Gabriel asked.

After the way she had snapped at him when he'd asked her how she'd hooked up with Ethan, he had been hesitant to question her further about her background. Now he couldn't resist jumping into the opening she had given him. He figured the more he could find out about her, the better it would be for him in the long run. And he would just as soon turn their conversation away from his relationship with Ethan.

"Two—both older, both married with children and both as determined as ever to prove they're numero uno every chance they get," she replied.

"What about you?"

"I learned at a very young age to keep my mouth shut and stay out of their way. As luck would have it, the only thing they've ever agreed on was making sure I remained low *man* on the totem pole."

"Two against one, huh?"

"Yes, two against one."

"What about your parents? Didn't they intervene?"

"Not really. I was just a girl, after all, and in our house that meant second-class citizen."

Surprisingly, Madelyn didn't sound resentful. In fact, Gabriel got the impression she had resigned herself to the situation for as long as she'd thought she had to. And then Ethan must have come along with a job offer that promised to take her away. Had he been in her shoes, Gabriel wouldn't have had to think twice about what to do.

Again, he suffered a momentary pang of sympathy for her. Then, almost instantly, he realized how unwilling she must be to return to such a situation. Hit by the likely possibility that she could very well be thinking of staying in Santa Fe, Gabriel eyed her somewhat askance.

"Surely, it wasn't that bad," he said.

"Probably not," she admitted, though her tone seemed sadly lacking in conviction.

"Seen enough, Ms. St. James?" Cullen interjected brightly.

He had been standing off to one side so quietly that Gabriel had forgotten he was there. Now he glanced at the lawyer gratefully. They had dawdled in the cottage long enough as far as he was concerned.

"Yes, of course."

With a sidelong glance at Gabriel, she headed out the door. Then, leaving him to lock up, she walked back to the house with Cullen. By the time Gabriel joined them in the kitchen, they had shed their coats in readiness for the remainder of the tour.

Looking at the clock on the wall above the refrigerator as he shrugged out of his jacket and tossed it on a chair, Gabriel realized he was going to have to make it fast. Otherwise, she would still be there when Brian got home.

"The bedrooms are this way," he said, moving toward the hallway that opened off the far side of the breakfast room. "There are four altogether. The master bedroom, my son's room, a guest room and my study, and two bathrooms—one off the master bedroom and one here in the hallway."

Since he and Brian made their beds each morning and put their dirty clothes in the laundry hamper each evening, Gabriel hadn't had much tidying up to do. The floor of Brian's room was littered with plastic building blocks and an assortment of small-scale cars and trucks, and the desk in his study was buried under stacks of paperwork and professional journals. But since the clutter didn't bother him, Gabriel hadn't really cared what Madelyn thought of it.

He kept the house as clean as he could with a little help from his son, and twice-weekly visits from their housekeeper, Millie Richards. The place might be worth half a million dollars. But first and foremost, it was their home, and it was definitely lived in.

Obviously in no hurry, Madelyn looked into each of the bedrooms. A smile played around the corners of her mouth as she paused in the doorway of Brian's bedroom, then again when she paused in the doorway of his study. She spent the least amount of time standing in the doorway of the master bedroom, as if her intrusion into his private domain made her uncomfortable. Though he did notice that her gaze seemed almost longing when she caught sight of the fireplace tucked in one corner.

Probably thinking of how cozy it would have been to curl up in front of it with Ethan, Gabriel thought sourly.

Almost instantly, a wave of guilt washed over him. Ethan was dead, and he hadn't any right to resent the fact that Madelyn might be missing him.

Whether he liked it or not, she and Ethan had been together for two years, and obviously they'd had a close, personal relationship. One that must mean something to her still.

At least she didn't come across as the gold digger he had initially imagined her to be. For which he was secretly sorry. She would have been a lot easier to dislike if she didn't seem to be such a nice person. Although they hadn't talked money yet. Maybe she was waiting until then to show her true colors.

"That's about it for the main house," Gabriel advised as she moved away from his bedroom doorway. "There's also a two-car garage and a workshop out back at the end of the driveway."

"A workshop?" she asked, eyeing him with interest.

"I like to do carpentry in my spare time."

"He's being modest," Cullen chimed in. "Actually, he makes furniture—lovely pieces like these." As they returned to the kitchen, he gestured toward the round, gateleg table and four ladder-back chairs in the breakfast room. "Unfortunately, getting him to part with any of his creations is almost impossible. Believe me, I've tried."

"It's just a hobby, which is probably why I enjoy it so much," Gabriel said. "I'm not so sure I would otherwise."

"More's the pity," Cullen muttered.

"I have to agree with Mr. Birney," Madelyn added. "Especially if the desk in your study and the wardrobe in the living room are your work, as well."

"They are," Gabriel admitted, more pleased than he had any right to be by her recognition of his work. Then, after another glance at the clock, he turned to Cullen. "I've made an appointment to talk to one of the loan officers at the bank on Tuesday. That's the soonest someone could meet with me. Until then, I won't know exactly when I'll have the funds available to buy out Ms. St. James's half of the property." Shifting his attention back to her, he added, "I'm sorry for any inconvenience that this will cause you."

Gabriel wished he could settle up with her that very minute, but he didn't have on hand one-tenth of the money he owed her. However, he was more than willing to mortgage his soul if that was what it took to hang on to his home.

"I'm not in a hurry, Mr. Serrano," she replied.

"I thought you might want to get back to St. Louis."

"Oh, really?"

"Cullen mentioned you'd been visiting your family there."

"I had been," she agreed. "But I'm not planning on going back anytime soon."

"You're not?"

He shouldn't be surprised. Not after what she'd told him about her family. Yet he was. Surprised and somewhat dismayed. If she wasn't going back home, where was she planning on living?

"I've gotten too independent for their liking," she admitted with a hint of pride.

"So you're going to strike out on your own? Maybe do some more traveling?" he asked, hoping she had chosen *that* alternative rather than the one he most feared she had.

"Actually, I've done all the traveling I want to do. At least for a while. I'm ready to settle down, and since I like what I've seen of Santa Fe—"

The chiming of the front doorbell echoed through the house, halting Madelyn in midsentence. As she looked toward the living room, the sinking feeling Gabriel had begun to experience as he got the gist of what she was considering deepened tenfold as he realized his son was home.

Excusing himself, he crossed the kitchen and headed down the hallway, aware of Madelyn and Cullen trailing along behind him. Since there was no way to get Brian past them, Gabriel girded himself for the worst.

Madelyn St. James didn't seem like the kind of woman who would blurt out anything awkward or indelicate in front of a young boy. But he had learned long ago he wasn't any judge of women.

He opened the front door, caught Brian in his arms as the boy launched into the entryway, then waved to Carol Murphy, mother of Donny, Brian's best friend. Waving back, Carol shifted into reverse and backed down the driveway.

"Hi, Dad," Brian said, returning Gabriel's hug, then squirming to get loose. "Who's here?"

"Mr. Birney and…a friend of your uncle Ethan's."

Aware that it wouldn't be much longer before his son decided he'd outgrown hugs and kisses, Gabriel savored the physical closeness Brian still allowed, breathing in the crisp, cold air the boy had brought in with him.

"A friend of Uncle Ethan's?"

Brian's eyes widened with delight as he pushed past Gabriel and hurried toward the living room. Though he had never met Ethan, he knew all about his famous uncle. He also had albums full of Ethan's photographs, as well as a budding interest of his own in photography.

Despite his animosity toward his half brother, Gabriel had felt duty-bound to make Ethan as much a part of the boy's life as he possibly could. And, of course, the boy had been fascinated by him and the exciting life he had seemed to lead.

"Hi, Mr. Birney," Brian greeted the lawyer.

"Hi, Brian. How's it going?"

"Okay." The boy shifted his gaze to Madelyn. "Hi."

"Hi," she replied, her voice barely above a whisper, staring at him as if she'd seen a ghost.

Pausing beside his son, Gabriel draped an arm over the boy's shoulders protectively.

"My dad said you're a friend of my uncle Ethan's."

"Yes, I was," she said, her gaze still locked on the boy.

"Madelyn, my son, Brian," Gabriel offered by way of introduction. "Brian, this is Ms. Madelyn St. James."

Her expression one of utter confusion, Madelyn looked up at Gabriel. He eyed her steadily, willing her not to say aloud what she was so obviously thinking.

She blinked once, then again, as understanding slowly dawned on her. For just an instant, Gabriel saw a flash of sympathy in her gray-green eyes, sympathy edged with a compassion that caught him completely off guard. Then she turned her attention back to Brian and, offering him a gracious smile, extended her hand.

Sensing that she would say just the right thing, Gabriel released the breath he'd unconsciously been holding.

"I'm very pleased to meet you, Brian."

Giggling, Brian took her hand and gave it a vigorous shake.

"I'm very pleased to meet you, too, Ms. St. James. Did you know my uncle Ethan a long time?"

"About two years."

"I never got to meet him and now I never will," Brian advised her, his tone suddenly somber. "He died, you know."

"Yes, I know."

"But I have lots of pictures of him." He hesitated, then smiling once again, he added, "I look like him, don't I? Just almost exactly like him."

"Yes, just almost exactly like him," Madelyn murmured, risking another glance at Gabriel.

Some of his tension seemed to have eased, but he still watched her warily, as if he wasn't quite sure what she might say or do next. She wished there were some way she could reassure him without alerting the boy.

Granted, she had realized almost immediately that Gabriel Serrano wasn't the biological father of the child he so proudly and protectively referred to as his son. Ethan Merritt had that distinction. But she wasn't totally insensitive. She would never speak her supposition aloud. At least, not in the boy's presence.

While Brian acknowledged his resemblance to his *uncle* Ethan, he obviously wasn't old enough to question it…yet. But all too soon, he would be. Then what would Gabriel tell him?

Instinctively, she knew he wouldn't want to hurt the boy any more than absolutely necessary. Yet she felt sure he'd be as honest as he could, depending on the circumstances.

And under what circumstances *had* Brian Serrano been conceived? Madelyn wondered. Had Ethan even known of his existence? And if so, why was Gabriel raising him as if he were the child's father?

As if he had been reading her mind, Gabriel frowned warningly. Admitting that she'd probably never know the answers to her questions, Madelyn offered him what she hoped was a reassuring smile, then looked back at the boy as he spoke to her again.

"How did I meet your uncle Ethan?" She repeated his query, buying a few seconds to collect herself. "Well…"

For the third time that day, Madelyn recounted how she had come to know Ethan Merritt. Brian listened with such obvious acceptance that she wanted to hug him. After the skepticism with which Cullen Birney and Gabriel Serrano had greeted her story, his reaction was a refreshing change.

"So, you're a photographer, too?" he asked when she'd finished.

"I'm not nearly as accomplished as your uncle was, but yes, I'm a photographer, too. Unfortunately, I haven't gotten to the point where I can support myself with the pictures I take. So I'm going to go back to teaching school until I can."

"My dad used to be a teacher. Now he's the principal of Nuestra Junior High School," Brian stated with no small amount of pride. Then, not giving her a chance to comment, he veered off on another tangent. "Did you come to Santa Fe just to see us?"

From the corner of her eye, Madelyn saw Gabriel shifting nervously. She assumed he hadn't told his son about her claim to half of the house they called home, and she could understand why. He wouldn't have wanted to worry the boy. And neither did she. Though Gabriel didn't seem capable of giving her that much credit.

"Actually, I came to Santa Fe so that Mr. Birney could help me take care of some personal business," she replied, choosing her words carefully. "When I met with him, he told me about you and your dad. He asked if I'd like to meet the two of you. I said yes, of course, and… here I am."

"Yeah, here you are," Brian chortled agreeably. "How long are ya gonna stay?"

Madelyn made a show of glancing at her watch.

"Well, it's getting late, so not too much longer."

"*No,*" the boy protested. "How long are ya gonna stay in Santa Fe?"

"Oh." Madelyn hesitated, shifting her gaze to Gabriel again.

He was watching her intently, waiting for her answer.

Somehow she had a feeling he wasn't going to like it. But her mind had been made up before Brian had bounded into the living room. Seeing the boy had only strengthened her determination to stay in town.

More than ever, she believed Ethan had wanted her here for a reason. And she no longer thought that reason had anything to do with his having a last laugh at his half brother's expense. Ethan had been a lot of things— some good, some not so good. But he had never struck her as being truly hateful.

Maybe she was being overly fanciful. Yet she sensed that whatever had happened here ten years ago, Ethan had lived to regret it. He hadn't considered coming back here because he hadn't felt that he could. So he'd sent her in his place.

Again, Madelyn wondered why. Certainly not to make amends. Not when he had left her half of a valuable property that should—by all rights—have gone to Gabriel.

"A long time?" Brian prodded, reminding her that she had yet to answer him.

"Yes," she agreed. "I'm planning on staying a long time. In fact, as I was about to tell your father just before you got home, I think I'd like to live in Santa Fe permanently."

"Oh, wow, that's great." Brian whooped. "Then you'll have way enough time to tell me what it was like to work with my uncle Ethan. And maybe you could teach me some of the things he taught you about taking pictures, too. Where are ya gonna live?"

"I'm not sure yet, but as soon as I know—"

"What about Uncle Ethan's cottage, Dad?" Brian whirled around excitedly and eyed his father with unabashed eagerness. "She could live there, couldn't she?"

Madelyn gaped at the boy, then shot an embarrassed glance Gabriel's way.

"Brian, I don't think—" Gabriel began, his displeasure at his son's suggestion more than evident.

"But why not?" Brian demanded. "She was Uncle Ethan's friend and she needs a place to live and you always said the cottage was his special place. So it would be *perfect.*"

Having had a few moments to consider Brian's idea, Madelyn had to admit it wasn't all that outrageous, after all. What the boy had said was true. She *had* been Ethan's friend, she *did* need a place to live and the cottage *would* be perfect, at least temporarily.

Considering half the property was rightfully hers, she

could demand a lot more than use of the cottage. Especially since she'd already indicated she was willing to give Gabriel all the time he needed to arrange to buy her out.

"You know, that sounds like a good idea to me, Brian," she ventured, ignoring the glaring look Gabriel gave her.

"But it's been vacant for years. It's musty and dusty—" Gabriel growled.

"I wouldn't mind cleaning the place, and I wouldn't stay long. Once I've finished my business with Mr. Birney, I'll be able to buy a little house of my own." Meaningfully, she met Gabriel's gaze.

He seemed to understand what she was saying. However, he was anything but pleased. She would have preferred to have his cheerful cooperation. Lacking that, she was almost tempted to back down. Almost...

She had agreed to go along with what he wanted as far as settling Ethan's estate was concerned, and he owed her something in return. All things considered, allowing her to live in the cottage was little enough to ask of him.

"You know, Gabe, that sounds like a fair deal to me," Cullen said.

Looking as if he were caught between a rock and a hard place, Gabriel shoved his hands in his pockets. He glared at Cullen, then at Madelyn. But when his gaze rested on Brian, his anger seemed to dissipate.

"All right," he agreed. "Ms. St. James can use the cottage."

"Yippee," Brian shouted, dancing around exuberantly.

"When would you like to move in?" Gabriel asked, his tone icy.

"Saturday," Madelyn replied after only a moment's hesitation.

That would give her tomorrow—Friday—to get some of the cleaning done.

"Fine." He eyed her grimly, then added, "I'll get the key…and your coat." Turning on his heel, he headed back to the kitchen.

Obviously pleased to have gotten his way, Brian followed after him. Madelyn heard him ask what they were having for dinner. Gabriel muttered something about leftovers, something more about homework, then the two of them vanished down the hallway.

Left alone with Cullen, she stared into the fire, now burning in a desultory fashion. She wanted to believe she'd been right to insist on staying in the cottage. Still, she had her doubts.

She had never been one to go where she wasn't wanted, but she couldn't afford to be too proud. She had a lot of thinking to do in the days ahead. And considering the direction her thoughts had already begun to take, she was going to need what was left of her savings to see her through a much longer period of time than she had originally planned.

Suspecting what she did about Ethan's relationship to Brian, Madelyn felt more and more uncomfortable about claiming her inheritance. Yet she wasn't quite ready to walk away. She had no idea why, but she wasn't.

"Don't mind Gabe," Cullen advised, interrupting her reverie. "He's fairly laid-back most of the time. Hearing that Ethan left you half the house came as quite a shock to him, but given a few days, I'm sure he'll get over it."

"I don't blame him for being upset. In his place, I would be, too," Madelyn said as she turned to face him. "I don't mean him any harm, though. And I won't make a pest of myself. In fact, I'm quite good at minding my own business."

"I had a feeling you were," Cullen replied.

"Were what?" Gabriel asked as, sans Brian, he joined them again.

"Good at minding my own business," Madelyn answered unabashedly, taking her coat from him.

"Oh." Looking somewhat disconcerted, Gabriel tossed Cullen his jacket. Then he dangled a set of keys in front of Madelyn. "One of these fits the front door of the cottage and the other fits the garage door. You can park your car in the space on the right if you want."

Madelyn took the keys from him with a murmured, "thank you."

"There's a telephone on the kitchen counter. It's connected to the same line as the house. I don't mind your using it as long as you pay for any long-distance calls you make."

"Of course I will," she assured him.

"There are dishes, pots and pans, and silverware in the kitchen. Also sheets and towels in one of the bathroom cabinets. I imagine they're going to have to be laundered, but you're welcome to use my washer and dryer tomorrow morning. My housekeeper, Millie Richards, will be here then. If you'd like, I'll tell her to expect you."

"Yes, please," Madelyn responded.

He wasn't any happier about the situation than he had been ten minutes ago. Yet he seemed to be going out of his way to make her move into the cottage as easy as possible. She realized he had his own best interests at heart. More than likely, he figured that if he kept her happy, she would go along with anything. But she was grateful all the same.

"And please don't use the fireplace until I have the chimney cleaned."

"I won't."

"I can't think of anything else at the moment, but if something comes to mind later, I'll leave a note with Millie. She'll be here about eight o'clock."

"Fine."

Madelyn slipped into her coat, then retrieved her purse from the chair by the fireplace.

"If you need anything once you're settled, just let me know," Gabriel advised as he started toward the front entryway.

"I will."

"I'll be in touch," Cullen said.

"Thanks." Gabriel shook the lawyer's hand, then opened the front door. Turning to Madelyn, he added, "Have a good evening, Ms. St. James."

"You, too, Mr. Serrano."

She met his gaze for a moment longer, wishing they could be friends. He was the kind of man she would have liked to have on her side. But there wasn't the slightest hint of affability in his expression.

Sadly, she looked away as Cullen Birney took her arm and led her out into the cold, clear night.

Clutching the keys Gabriel had given her in one hand, Madelyn sat beside the lawyer, saying nothing as he backed the Wagoneer out of the driveway and headed toward her hotel. She had at least half a dozen questions she wanted to ask, but she had meant what she'd said about minding her own business.

Still, there was one answer she felt she had a right to have. One answer that would help determine her future course of action.

"Tell me something, Mr. Birney," she began.

"If I can," he hedged, much as she'd had a feeling he would.

"Am I correct in assuming Ethan was Brian's biological father?"

The lawyer drove on in silence so long, Madelyn wondered if he'd heard her. Finally, in a soft voice, he answered her quite simply.

"Yes, you are."

Without commenting further, Cullen pulled up in front of her hotel. Immediately, the doorman moved forward to open the car door for her.

"Well, here you are, Ms. St. James," the lawyer said, not quite meeting her gaze.

He seemed so relieved to be done with her before she had a chance to give him the third degree that Madelyn couldn't help but smile.

"Thank you, Mr. Birney. I appreciate all you've done for me."

"You're welcome, Ms. St. James." He hesitated a moment, then finally looked her in the eye as he added, "Why don't we plan to talk again next week after Gabe's had a chance to meet with his banker?"

"Sounds good to me," she agreed as she stepped out of the Wagoneer.

Inside the hotel, Madelyn started toward the bank of elevators. Halfway there, however, her attention was caught by the quiet ambience of the little restaurant off the main corridor. She realized she was hungry. She also realized she had no real desire to order room service again tonight.

She would be spending more than enough time alone in her room, as it was, mulling over the events of the day. Now, however, she wanted company, even if only that of strangers sitting at other tables.

Pausing in the arched doorway of the restaurant, she smiled at the maître d'.

"Table for one, miss?" he asked without the slightest hint of disparagement.

Madelyn nodded agreeably, then followed him across the elegantly appointed dining room. To her surprise, he seated her at a lovely little table near the fireplace. The kind of table meant to be shared with someone special.

For just an instant, she thought of Gabriel Serrano and how enjoyable it could have been to have dinner with him there by the fire. He was an attractive man in more ways than the most obvious. He seemed so solid, so...trustworthy. And she'd seen for herself the kindness and consideration he was capable of showing those he loved.

With a rueful shake of her head, Madelyn accepted the menu the maître d' offered her. Talk about fanciful.

Gabriel had made it plain he didn't even *like* her, and with good reason. Not only had she dropped down out of the blue to screw up what he had probably considered a very nice life. She had also had a close, personal relationship with the half brother who had somehow done him a great wrong.

Imagining that he would ever think of joining her for a romantic tête-à-tête was downright silly. He was far more likely to give her the widest berth possible until he could be rid of her once and for all.

Which was just as well, she told herself. Then, and again much later, as she lay alone in bed, just as she'd done every single night of her life.

Chapter 3

"Looks like Ms. St. James is all moved in," Brian said, halting just outside the garage.

"Yes, it certainly does," Gabriel agreed.

As he paused beside his son, he eyed the cottage with a strange sense of déjà vu. On an early-summer evening ten years ago, he had stood in almost exactly the same place. Then, he had been drawn by the warm glow of lamplight slanting through the wide wooden blinds—only half-closed—on the windows. Now, in the chill of a winter night, with painful memories he thought he'd put to rest suddenly all too fresh in his mind, he found the cozy little scene unbearably heartrending.

"Maybe we should go and say hello," Brian suggested hopefully.

"No."

Obviously surprised by his father's harsher-than-usual tone of voice, the boy gazed up at him, wide-eyed.

''But we've been gone all weekend,'' he protested. ''Shouldn't we let her know we're home again?''

''Our whereabouts aren't really any of Ms. St. James's business,'' Gabriel stated succinctly.

''But Dad—''

''No more buts, young man. It's getting late. We haven't had dinner yet. And unless I'm mistaken, you still have homework to do, don't you?''

''Yes, sir.''

''Well, then…''

Placing a hand on Brian's shoulder, Gabriel urged his son toward the house.

Had almost anyone else been staying in the cottage, more than likely he would have advised that person of their return. But Gabriel had spent the past forty-eight hours putting as much distance as he could between himself and his son and Madelyn St. James. He saw no reason to ruin all that hard work by going to see her now.

She hadn't been at the cottage when he and Brian had finally gotten home from school Friday night. Of course, they had been much later than usual, thanks to a stop at the boy's favorite pizza parlor. And then, very early Saturday morning, the two of them had set off on an impromptu trip to Taos for a little father-son bonding on the ski slopes.

Granted, Gabriel had known better than to think he could avoid Madelyn indefinitely. And he certainly had no intention of trying to keep Brian away from her in the days ahead. But he would just as soon not see her again yet. She stirred up too many conflicting emotions in him. Emotions that could get him into trouble of one kind or another if he wasn't careful.

He hadn't liked the idea of Madelyn living in the cottage even for a short time. Yet he had seen the wisdom of allowing her to do so. As Cullen had reminded him over and over, having her cooperation was of the utmost importance. And while she hadn't seemed like the type to cause trouble, you never knew what someone would do when a large sum of money was at stake until the situation actually arose.

However, making Madelyn happy, or as happy as possible under the circumstances, hadn't been Gabriel's only reason for acquiescing to her wishes. Despite the grace period he had insisted upon for all of them that weekend, he wanted Brian to be able to spend some time with her.

Gabriel believed he could trust Madelyn not to say anything untoward. And, in the long run, he thought it would do Brian good to learn as much as he could about his "uncle" while he had the chance. Especially from someone who held Ethan in higher regard than Gabriel ever had.

Somewhere in the back of his mind, he had to admit he'd also had a more personal motive for agreeing to let Madelyn use the cottage. Put simply, he had been... intrigued by her. Whether because she had been involved with Ethan, or in spite of it, he wasn't quite sure. But he intended to find out.

Otherwise, he would have no peace.

He had gone *years* without being the slightest bit interested in a woman. With a young son to raise, as well as a demanding job, he hadn't had the time or the energy necessary to maintain a sexual relationship.

Of course, now that Brian was older, and he had a few years of administrative experience under his belt, it was understandable that he'd begin to seek female companionship. And he had, on rare occasions, dated several very nice women. But none of them had sparked any desire within him for...intimacy.

Not that he was *lusting* after Madelyn St. James. But he *was* interested—

"Can we have macaroni and cheese for dinner?" Brian asked as Gabriel unlocked the French doors.

"Sure thing," he agreed, dropping their overnight bags on the laundry room floor, then leading the way into the kitchen.

"Guess I'll get started on my homework."

"Good idea." Noting the dejected slump to the boy's shoulders as he headed toward the hallway, Gabriel hesitated, then added, "You can visit with Ms. St. James tomorrow after school."

"I can?" Brightening considerably, Brain glanced at Gabriel for confirmation.

"As long as she doesn't mind having company," he temporized.

"She won't," Brian stated with complete confidence.

"Pretty sure of yourself, aren't you?"

"She likes me. I could tell." Grinning proudly, the boy turned away, paused, then looked back at Gabriel again, his blue eyes twinkling merrily. "Bet she'd like you, too, if you were a little nicer to her."

"I *was* nice," Gabriel protested.

"Not 'cause you wanted to be. I could tell that, too."

"Oh, really?"

"Yes, really."

"Well, I'll try to do better in the future," Gabriel vowed, somewhat disconcerted by how well his astute young son had read his behavior.

"That would be good."

Seemingly satisfied that he had gotten his point across, Brian turned and skipped happily down the hallway.

"I'm glad *you* think so, but *I* have my doubts," Gabriel muttered.

By eight o'clock, Brian was tucked into bed, sound asleep. Worn out by two full days of skiing, his son had barely been able to keep his eyes open during dinner. After assuring himself that the boy had finished his homework, Gabriel had suggested he make an earlier than usual night of it and Brian had readily agreed.

Now, alone in the kitchen, Gabriel finished loading the dishwasher, wiped down the counters, then moved on to the laundry room where he shifted a load of clothes from the washer to the dryer. That done, he headed back across the kitchen toward the hallway leading to his study.

He had bills to pay, a checkbook to balance and a pile of never-ending, school-related paperwork to sort through. More than enough to keep his mind occupied. Still, he couldn't seem to stop himself from pausing at the French doors yet again. Nor could he keep his gaze from lingering on the cottage.

Since the lights were on, he assumed Madelyn was there. Her car had been parked in the garage when they'd arrived home, and he hadn't heard her leave. He also assumed she'd had no problems moving in. Of course, after being away all weekend, then returning home unannounced, he couldn't know for sure. And wouldn't until sometime tomorrow when their paths would surely cross.

Unless…

As he had found himself thinking on and off all evening, Brian had been right. He really *should* have gone over to the cottage and checked on her. Out of common courtesy, if nothing else. In a way, he was her host. And her landlord, as well. Which also gave him the right, not to mention the responsibility, to see what she'd done to the place in his absence.

Probably nothing more than wipe up the layers of dust

that had accumulated over the years. But he should take a look, just in case.

And while he was at it, he really ought to run interference for Brian, too. He could tell her that the boy wanted to visit with her after school tomorrow, and make sure she didn't mind.

As for what she might say about Ethan when she and Brian were together…

He would have to leave that up to her. Bringing up the subject himself would only offer her an opening to ask questions he would rather not answer. He would have to trust that she'd continue to be as tactful as she had been Thursday evening.

Having given himself just the excuses he needed— ones that very nicely overrode his desire simply to *see* Madelyn St. James again—Gabriel grabbed his denim jacket and stepped out into the moonlit night.

He wouldn't stay long. Not with Brian alone in the house. He would make sure she had everything she needed in the way of household items. He'd also find out if the chimney sweep he'd contacted had come as requested Saturday afternoon. And he would advise her of Brian's impending visit. Then, his duty done, he would leave her in peace.

As for himself…

Striding across the courtyard, Gabriel sincerely hoped he wasn't going to stir up any more inner turmoil than he was already experiencing.

The distress he'd suffered over the bad memories that had surfaced earlier had faded as he'd gradually gotten used to the idea of someone living in the cottage again. Actually seeing how that someone had put her own personal stamp on the place might be exactly what he needed to erase certain incidents from his mind once and for all.

At the cottage, Gabriel hesitated just a moment, then drew a deep, steadying breath and rapped on the door.

"Just a minute," Madelyn called out.

As he stood waiting, Gabriel heard the faint strains of classical piano music drifting from within. He also caught a whiff of something that made his mouth water. A hearty soup or stew seasoned to perfection, he thought, surprised that she would go to so much trouble for herself alone.

If she *was* alone, he amended.

Shifting impatiently, he raised his hand to knock again just as the door opened.

She was dressed in faded jeans that clung to her slim hips and long legs like a second skin; a hunter green, nubby-knit, pullover sweater; thick wool socks and fleece-lined, brown suede moccasins. With her face bare of makeup and her hair pulled up in a sassy ponytail, she looked about sixteen. Sweet sixteen, yet sexy…too darned sexy for his peace of mind.

"Oh…hi," she greeted him, her wide, welcoming smile filled with such warmth and sincerity that he was momentarily taken aback.

He didn't want her to be happy to see him, and he certainly didn't want to be happy to see *her*. But how else could he describe the sudden buoyancy of spirit he had experienced the moment he'd laid eyes on her?

"Ms. St. James," he growled, frowning ominously.

"Yes, Mr. Serrano?"

Her smile replaced by a look of concern, she straightened her shoulders and met his gaze as if prepared for whatever bad news she expected him to deliver.

Realizing that he was on the verge of getting off to a

bad start with her yet again, Gabriel drew in another deep breath and pasted a smile on his face.

"I hope I'm not disturbing you."

"Not at all." Eyeing him even more warily, she hesitated, then added, "Would you like to come in?"

"Yes, please. But I won't stay long," he promised, moving past her as she stepped aside.

"No problem."

A few feet from the doorway, he paused and glanced around the room. He couldn't help but be impressed by all she had accomplished in just three days. What he could see of the place was now spotlessly clean, and the musty smell had been replaced by a combination of more pleasant scents: lemon oil and evergreen, a hint of cinnamon—probably from the bowl of potpourri he spied on one of the end tables—and, of course, whatever she was cooking in the little kitchen.

The few pieces of wood furniture—the end tables on either side of the sofa and the small, round oak table and pair of Windsor chairs in the living area, as well as the dresser and chest of drawers in the sleeping area—gleamed under a rich coat of polish.

She had also added homey touches of her own. Several throw rugs in shades of rose and blue covered strategic areas of the Saltillo tile floor. A similarly colored, floral-patterned afghan had been draped over the plain but serviceable navy blue sofa. A pair of blue place mats graced the round table along with a basket of silk flowers and several chubby candles also in shades of rose and blue. And from what he could see beyond the fireplace dividing the sleeping area from the living area, the bed also sported a new coverlet striped in the same colors.

"You've done a lot in the past few days," he acknowledged.

Actually, more than he would have thought necessary for what he had intended to be a very short stay.

"I got started and couldn't seem to stop," she admitted sheepishly. "I know I'm only going to be here temporarily. But after living in one anonymous room after another the past couple of years, I wanted to make this place feel as much like a real home as possible."

"Well, you certainly did a good job of it."

In fact, she had transformed the cottage so completely that—just as Gabriel had hoped—hardly any trace of Ethan's prior inhabitance remained.

"Thanks." She eased past him and headed toward the kitchen. "Would you like something to drink? I have cold beer and hot coffee on hand."

Cold beer?

Watching her walk across the room, Gabriel realized he shouldn't have been surprised. There was an earthiness about her, after all. And a lack of pretension that appealed to him.

To be honest, having a beer with her would have been quite enjoyable. Only, he wasn't there to socialize.

"Maybe another time," he replied.

"Of course."

She paused in the kitchen doorway and faced him again, the questioning look in her eyes reminding Gabriel that he had yet to tell her why he was there.

"Since we were gone yesterday and today, I just wanted to make sure you got moved in all right."

"I did."

"Also, I wanted to make sure the chimney sweep came yesterday as promised."

"He did."

"You're welcome to use the fireplace whenever you want, then."

"I will."

The merest hint of a smile played around the corners of her mouth and amusement lingered in her eyes.

Aware that his manner had once again grown more brusque than he'd intended, Gabriel willed himself to relax. Just because she had offered him a beer—a beer he had wanted to accept—he didn't have to react so defensively. She had only meant to be hospitable.

"If you'd like, I could start a fire for you now," he offered in what he hoped was a friendlier tone.

All trace of humor vanished from her face as she gazed at him uncertainly. Realizing that his sudden change of tack was making her uncomfortable, Gabriel hastened to offer reassurance.

"It won't take me more than a few minutes. Then I'll have to get back to the house."

"A fire would be nice," she conceded after hesitating a few moments longer.

"Consider it my housewarming gift," he suggested.

"All right." Nodding agreeably, she smiled once again.

More pleased than he should have been at being given the opportunity to do her a favor, Gabriel smiled, too.

"I'll get the wood, then."

"Need any help?"

"You can move the fire screen out of the way and open the damper. Also, there should be some matches in the kitchen. Want to see if you can find them?"

"Sure."

Almost as disconcerted as she'd been when she first saw Gabriel standing on the stoop, glowering at her, Madelyn watched as he turned and walked out the door. For the few moments it had taken her to realize his call wasn't exactly a friendly one, she had been glad that he'd come over. Then she'd been afraid he had found a reason to put her out.

That he had only wanted to assure himself that she'd had no problems moving in had been a relief. And his businesslike manner, while somewhat off-putting, had seemed quite appropriate.

However, just as she'd begun to feel as if she was getting with the landlord-tenant program he'd evidently been intent on establishing, he had started acting the part of gracious host.

For the space of a heartbeat, she had been grateful for his sudden kindness. Then, realizing that his gesture had been on par with throwing a dog a bone, she had been angry at herself for being so gullible.

All too aware of how vulnerable she was, physically and emotionally, she had retreated behind a much less amiable facade of her own.

No matter how attractive she found Gabriel Serrano, she couldn't afford to let him lure her into feeling too sympathetic toward him. He hadn't made any secret of how he felt about *her*. He considered her a thorn in his side; one he intended to rid himself of as quickly as possible.

But he had been so gently insistent about starting a fire for her that she hadn't had the heart to refuse him completely. And, of course, honest person that she always tried to be, she had to admit she was glad she was going to have his company for a little while longer.

Even realizing—as she had done Saturday night—that Gabriel and Brian must have gone away for the weekend, she had been too busy cleaning the cottage to feel lonely. But about an hour ago, with most everything done, including the pot of stew that was now simmering on the stove, she had experienced more than a twinge of regret for her solitary state.

Tweaking the blinds open, she had seen lights on in the house, and had assumed Gabriel and Brian were home again. Briefly—*very* briefly—she had considered inviting them to share her supper. But she had been so sure her offer would be rejected that she hadn't been able to work up the nerve to walk across the courtyard and ask.

Now she was glad she hadn't. Appearing too eager to develop anything more than the most casual relationship with Gabriel and his son would not serve her in good stead. She wanted nothing more from them—*needed* nothing more from them—than what she was entitled to, according to Ethan's will.

Especially not the heartache that went hand in hand with caring for someone who had such a hard time hiding his anger and disdain whenever he caught sight of her.

Better to let him come to her whenever he had good reason, she thought as she crossed to the kitchen and retrieved the matches she had come across earlier while cleaning out the drawers under the counter. That way she could avail herself of whatever companionship he offered without any cost to herself.

Returning to the living area, she walked over to the fireplace, moved the screen to one side, then opened the damper as Gabriel had requested. As if on cue, he came through the door, carrying a canvas sling filled with large chunks of wood as well as an assortment of odd bits and pieces to be used as kindling.

Though Madelyn hurried to move out of his way, the cold, smoke-scented air that clung to him enveloped her in an almost intimate way, drawing her into his personal space. For just an instant, she thought of how nice it would be to put her arms around him and offer to chase away the chill. Then, her face warming with embarrassment, she gave herself a firm mental shake.

"Got the matches?" he asked as he sat on the edge of the hearth and stacked the wood on the grate.

"Right here."

Not daring to move any closer, Madelyn extended her hand, offering him the box.

"Thanks."

The wood in place, Gabriel added the kindling, then reached over and turned the knob embedded in the outer wall of the fireplace. As a hissing sound came from the narrow pipe running under the grate, Gabriel lit a match and held it out. The gas caught with a slight puff, the flame flickering low, then leaping to lick at the firewood when he gave the knob another turn.

"How's that?" he asked, glancing up at her with a proud smile.

"Very nice," she complimented, relieved to have her wits about her once again.

"Think you'll be able to manage on your own the next time?"

"Actually, I think I could have managed on my own *this* time," she retorted, sending a wry look his way.

"Point taken," he replied repentantly. "The wood is stacked under a tarp out by the garage. There should be more than enough for the two of us, so help yourself whenever you want."

"I will, thanks."

Gabriel nodded once. Then, his expression growing serious, he focused his attention on the fire once again. Seeing that the wood had begun to burn on its own, he turned off the gas. But instead of taking his leave as Madelyn expected, he stayed where he was, staring at the flickering flames.

He had something more to say to her, something that seemed to be giving him pause. Madelyn wasn't sure she wanted to know what it was, but she had a feeling she was going to find out anyway.

"Brian asked if he could come over to see you after school tomorrow," he began at last. "I told him he could, but only as long as you don't mind."

"I don't mind at all," she assured him without the slightest hesitation.

She had liked the boy. He was bright and funny. Having him around would be enjoyable. Especially if he was as interested in photography as he had seemed to be.

But Gabriel had some reservations. She could tell by the way he glanced at her, then away again, a frown creasing his forehead.

"More than likely, he's going to ask about Ethan," he said, making no effort to hide his concern. "As you've probably guessed, there are some things about him Brian doesn't know yet. Things I would rather he didn't find out until he's a little older."

"I promise not to say anything imprudent," Madelyn replied.

"I would appreciate that." Replacing the fire screen, Gabriel grabbed the canvas sling in which he'd carried the wood, stood and started toward the door.

The way he avoided her gaze, Madelyn assumed he had said all he intended to say about the matter. No excuses, and certainly no explanations. Just a request for her compliance, no questions asked.

Talk about unfair. Her curiosity was more aroused than ever. Yet she didn't feel she had the right to pry. At least not as deeply as she'd like. Still, there was one point she wanted clarified, and she was annoyed enough by his attitude to risk his wrath by bringing it up while she had the chance.

"I was wondering…" she started as she trailed after him.

"What?" Finally facing her, Gabriel tipped his chin up defensively, the look in his eyes anything but encouraging.

Reminding herself that it was now or never, Madelyn took a breath, then continued. "Obviously, you've told Brian quite a bit about Ethan…."

"I thought that would be the best way to prepare him for what I'm going to have to tell him a few years from now."

"Yes, of course." Madelyn nodded, signaling her understanding. "But did Ethan…did he…know about Brian?"

"Oh, yes, he knew," Gabriel replied quietly, the anger in his voice heavily laced with a bitterness that seemed to speak of grievous disappointment. "As to whether or not he cared…" He shrugged and shook his head. "I can't really say. I wrote to him occasionally over the years, even sent him some photographs. But he never bothered to respond. Not once in nine years. He did set up a trust fund for the boy in his will, though." Again, Gabriel shrugged. "Guess that was better than nothing, huh?"

"I suppose," Madelyn murmured, lowering her gaze.

How sad that Ethan had chosen to disassociate himself from Gabriel and the boy, especially when he knew he was dying. No matter what Ethan had done to warrant Gabriel's animosity, Gabriel would have looked after him. She might not know all that much about him, but she knew enough to believe *that*. And surely, spending his last days with Brian would have given Ethan some comfort, even considering what a reprobate he'd been.

Yet, to her knowledge, Ethan had never considered the possibility of coming here. Instead, in his own round-about way, he had sent *her,* for reasons she was growing more and more hesitant to delve into.

"Anything else you want to know?" Gabriel challenged, drawing her attention back to him.

Quite a bit, Madelyn thought, but hadn't the nerve to say so in the face of his icy stare. By now, he must have realized Ethan had never mentioned the secrets of their past—the past they'd shared—with her. Since he seemed averse to doing so, as well, why provoke him? He would only end up resenting her even more than he already did. While she doubted he would ever be her friend, she certainly didn't want to go so far as to make an enemy of him.

Crossing her arms over her chest, she shook her head.

"Then I'd best be going." He reached out and grasped the doorknob, then glanced back at her. "We'll talk again after I meet with the bank Tuesday afternoon."

"Fine."

A moment later, he was gone, leaving her alone in the cottage, a whirl of cold air wrapping around her ankles, the fire, now crackling cheerily, warming her back.

Oddly bereft, Madelyn stared at the door for several seconds. Then, scolding herself for being such a ninny, she headed back to the kitchen. She had too much to do to waste time mooning over Gabriel Serrano.

She had been in the process of dishing up a bowl of stew for herself when he arrived. After she ate, she'd have to put the leftovers away. Then she really ought to bake some brownies. Brian would probably enjoy a treat after school, and thanks to her own sweet tooth, she had bought all the necessary ingredients while she was at the grocery store earlier in the day.

She still had to sort through some of her photographs, as well. She wanted to start putting together a portfolio to show several of the gallery owners around Santa Fe who featured such work. And she had to find the manila envelope with copies of her college degrees, teaching certificates and letters of recommendation, all of which she'd need to have on hand when she applied for a substitute teaching job with the local school district.

The sooner she could start bringing in a little money, the more secure she would feel. Then she could decide what to do about the inheritance she found herself wanting less and less the more she knew about Ethan Merritt and the brother and son he had abandoned.

Chapter 4

"So, now what am I going to do?" Gabriel demanded, pacing the length of Cullen Birney's office.

After spending over an hour with Sid Tuckerman, a loan officer at United Bank of Santa Fe, Gabriel had realized he was going to have a much harder time paying off Madelyn St. James than he had ever anticipated. In desperate need of advice from someone he could trust, he had called Cullen. When his friend had insisted they meet at once, Gabriel had readily agreed.

"First, you're going to stop doing your damnedest to wear a hole in my carpet. Sit, take a few deep breaths and try to calm down," Cullen instructed.

"Sorry." Offering the lawyer an apologetic smile, Gabriel flung himself into one of the chairs in front of Cullen's desk. "I know histrionics never help matters any. But I feel like I'm about to come apart at the seams. There has to be some way to get out from under my debt to Ms. St. James, aside from selling the house to a third party.''

''While that does remain an option, I think we should look upon it as a last resort,'' Cullen advised.

''Fine. I'd like nothing better. But then, how am I going to get the two hundred and fifty thousand dollars I owe her? While the bank will gladly accept the house as collateral for a second mortgage payable over a maximum of fifteen years, I'm not earning nearly enough to make the payments, much less have anything left to live on.

''The most I figure I can borrow under the bank's terms is one hundred thousand dollars. Even then, she will still be due a hundred and fifty thousand I have no way of paying.''

''Maybe she would settle for the hundred thousand.''

''I can't ask her to do that.''

''Why not? Too proud?'' Cullen asked.

Talk about hitting the nail on the head.

''I just don't want to be beholden to her,'' Gabriel muttered, looking away as the heat of a blush warmed his face.

''What about talking to some of the other banks or savings-and-loan companies around town?''

''I suppose it's worth a try. But it's going to take time to set up appointments. Added to the time it's going to take to actually be approved for the loan, we're talking months instead of weeks before I have any cash in hand. She may not want to wait that long.''

''She didn't seem all that anxious to get her hands on the money when we talked on Thursday,'' Cullen said. ''Seemed to me her biggest worry was finding an inexpensive place to stay, and since you're letting her use the cottage, she's all set.''

"But I only meant that to be a temporary arrangement—*very* temporary," Gabriel argued.

"So she stays a couple of months instead of a couple of weeks. What could it hurt?"

Gabriel had no answer to that. At least not one he could give his friend without revealing how Madelyn St. James's presence in the cottage had already begun to threaten the emotional stability he had worked so hard to regain after Lily finally left him.

By his own choosing, he had spent as little time as possible with Madelyn. Just a couple of hours on Thursday when Cullen had brought her to the house, and another thirty minutes or so Sunday night.

Yet, thoughts of her crept into his mind constantly, day or night, whether he was alone or with others. And some of those thoughts—the sensual, *sexual* ones that teased him at the oddest moments—he had no right thinking about a woman he hardly knew. Especially a woman who, until quite recently, had been involved with his half brother.

He had tried following Ethan's "act" once already. But, compared to him, Gabriel had been a grave disappointment to Lily—as she had made a point of telling him any number of times.

Granted, Madelyn St. James seemed more sensible, not to mention much more steadfast, than his ex-wife. But that didn't mean she would be less likely to find him a poor substitute for the "real thing" she'd once had.

Setting himself up just to be shot down would be a truly foolhardy thing to do. And the best way of avoiding that was avoiding *her.* Which he would be able to do much more easily if they weren't living in such close proximity to each other.

Frustrated, Gabriel stood and walked to the window.

The sun had set half an hour ago, and down below, the sidewalks lining the Plaza were empty. But only momentarily so. A couple came into view, wandering hand in hand along the storefronts, window-shopping, followed by a laughing, chattering group of teenagers.

"I suppose you're right," Gabriel responded at last, his lack of conviction evident in his tone of voice.

"I *am* right. One way or another, you're going to have Ms. St. James around longer than you expected. Wouldn't you rather use that time to get the loan you need with payments you can manage over a reasonable length of time than put the house up for sale?"

"What I would really like is another choice altogether," Gabriel retorted with more than a hint of his normally good humor.

"Oh, please. Give me a break, will you?" Cullen chided. "Having Madelyn St. James living in the cottage can't be *that* bad. She's young, she's lovely, she's intelligent, and best of all, she doesn't seem to be out for herself at your expense. You could do a lot worse, and not only tenant-wise, if you know what I mean."

Even without the suggestive wink Cullen used to punctuate his words, Gabriel knew exactly what his friend meant.

"Yeah, well, I didn't want or need a tenant. And I'm certainly not in the market for whatever else you think she might have to offer."

"That's a shame, Gabe. I have a feeling she could be good for you—real good—in more ways than one. You've been alone a long time. Too long, if you ask me."

"Well, I'm not," Gabriel shot back. Then, making a show of glancing at his watch, he added, "Oh, wow, I didn't realize it was so late. Brian's Scout meeting is almost over, and it's my night to drive the car pool.''

"Coward," Cullen muttered good-naturedly, pushing away from his desk and standing as Gabriel slipped into his overcoat.

"Really, I have to go."

Though he tried to sound contrite, Gabriel heard only relief in his own voice.

"Do you want me to call Ms. St. James and explain the situation to her, or do you want to talk to her yourself? Personally, I think you ought to do the honors, but if you're as eager to avoid her as you seem to be, I guess I can—"

"Damn it, Cullen, cut the crap," Gabriel interjected, laughing in exasperation. "I'll talk to her, all right?"

"That really would be best," his friend agreed in a solemn tone belied by the merry twinkle in his eyes. "Just be sure to let me know how she responds."

"I will."

With a wave of his hand, Gabriel let himself out of Cullen's office, hurried down the stairs and headed toward the side street where he had parked his truck. The drive to Brian's elementary school—where the four rambunctious boys waited for him under their leader's supervision—took less than five minutes.

His son's friends all lived within a few blocks of the Serrano house, so dropping them off was quick and easy. They themselves arrived home just after six-thirty.

Brian noted that Madelyn's car was already parked in the garage and the lights were on in the cottage. He also suggested they stop to say hello, an idea Gabriel swiftly nixed.

"But Dad—"

"You were over there almost two hours yesterday," Gabriel said. "Give the lady a rest, okay?"

"She didn't mind my visiting," Brian reminded him for the umpteenth time since he'd come back from the cottage last night.

"That was yesterday and she was expecting you. We can't just barge in on her whenever we feel like it, you know?"

Actually, Gabriel was planning on doing just that after Brian went to bed, but he would just as soon his son not know about it.

"She said I could come back anytime."

"But she's not really expecting you again until Thursday," Gabriel pointed out as patiently as he could.

According to Brian, he had an invitation to return after school on Thursday, the soonest he could make it since he'd had a Scout meeting today and a prior invitation to spend Wednesday afternoon at Donny's house.

"As a courtesy to her, I think you should abide by that agreement, okay?"

"Okay."

Reluctantly, Brian headed across the courtyard with Gabriel following a few steps behind him.

By nine o'clock Brian was finally in bed asleep, and Gabriel realized he had put off his visit with Madelyn as long as he could. He wasn't all that eager to share the news he'd had that day. Nonetheless, he shrugged into his denim jacket and let himself out of the house.

As he walked across the courtyard, he wished he had told her to have a telephone line of her own installed. That way he could have called first to let her know he was on his way.

Granted, he had said they would talk again tonight. But by now, she could have given up on him. It was still fairly early. However, if she wasn't planning on going out again, she could have already changed into her night-clothes. Alone in the cozy cottage, *he* would have made himself comfortable.

He would have started a fire in the fireplace, as he could see she had done by the smoke swirling into the darkness above the roofline. And he would have turned on some music, as the faint strains of a string quartet drifting into the night indicated she had done, as well. Then he would have turned the lights down low, poured himself a glass of wine and stretched out on the sofa.

In his mind, Gabriel could picture her in a long, white nightgown, ruffles at her wrists and throat, her hair loose around her shoulders—

What brought him up short, cursing under his breath, was that he had pictured himself there with her, as well. Stretched out beside her, holding her close.

Damn Cullen for stirring him up. He'd had a hard enough time schooling his thoughts on his own. Then his friend just had to go and give him even more ideas.

Dragging in a gulp of icy air, Gabriel slowly counted to ten. Finally, having regained a modicum of his emotional equilibrium, he rapped sharply on the door.

If she wasn't completely clothed, he wouldn't set foot inside the cottage. He would make some excuse and walk back across the courtyard just as fast as he—

"Just a minute," Madelyn called out.

As had happened Sunday, the music ceased, and a moment later the door swung open.

Though her smile wasn't quite as wide or as welcoming as it had been the other night, she seemed reasonably glad to see him. And much to Gabriel's relief, she was fully dressed in oversize, charcoal gray sweats that did almost too good a job disguising her luscious figure.

Actually, with her hair caught back at the nape of her neck with a gold clip and her face devoid of makeup, she should have looked plain as a brown paper bag. But he doubted she could have looked any more alluring to him had she come to the door wearing only the slinkiest of silk undergarments.

Groaning inwardly, Gabriel shoved his hands deep in his jacket pockets as he inhaled another deep breath of frigid air.

"Sorry I'm so late getting over here," he began. "But I thought it would be best to wait until Brian was asleep. Otherwise, he would have insisted on coming with me."

"No problem." She stood aside and gestured for him to enter. "How about some coffee? It's decaf, but I just brewed a fresh pot."

"Sounds good."

He would have really preferred one of the beers she'd mentioned the other night, but didn't have the nerve to suggest it. At least with coffee, he'd be more apt to keep his wits about him.

"How do you take it?"

"Just black."

"Make yourself at home." She nodded toward the sofa, adding, "I'll be right back."

Gabriel slipped out of his jacket, hung it on one of the pegs by the door, then sat in a corner of the sofa. As he stretched his booted feet out to the fire, savoring the warmth radiating from the gently flickering flames, he glanced around the cottage.

She had set out several framed photographs along the wall behind the oak table and chairs. He couldn't tell what they were of at that distance, but all appeared to be black-and-white rather than color prints.

More artistic than what he'd seen of Ethan's work, he

thought, wishing there were some way he could take a closer look at them without being obvious about it. He would also like to get a look at the photographs scattered on the table.

She had shown Brian some of her pictures yesterday afternoon. *Really* great shots she had taken of *really* beautiful birds somewhere in Central America, he had said. Gabriel wanted to see for himself just how good they *really* were. But he didn't want to risk getting caught nosing around in what was essentially her business.

"How did your meeting with the bank go?" she asked as she stepped out of the kitchen, carrying a small tray upon which she'd set two steaming mugs of black coffee, a plate of the brownies Brian had all but swooned over and a stack of napkins.

So much for small talk, Gabriel mused, watching her as she moved toward him. Maybe she was more avaricious than he had wanted to believe. But there was no greedy gleam in her eyes, and her mild tone had been that of someone making polite conversation.

"Not as well as I'd hoped," he admitted.

No sense prevaricating. The bottom line would have to be broached eventually, and he'd prefer to do it sooner rather than later.

"Oh?" She sat down on the opposite side of the sofa and set the tray on the center cushion separating them.

"Getting the loan may take a little longer than I'd anticipated."

He was hedging a bit, but he saw no reason to go into worst-case scenarios just yet.

"I'm not in any real hurry for the money." Picking up one of the mugs, she offered it to him, then waved a hand at the brownies. "Help yourself."

"Thanks."

Unable to resist, Gabriel set his coffee mug on the end table and took one of the thick, moist brownies—chock-full of chocolate chips and slathered with a layer of fudge frosting—along with a napkin. One bite assured him Brian had not exaggerated when he'd said they were the best he had ever eaten.

"Of course, it would be a help if I could stay here until everything has been settled."

"You're welcome to use the cottage as long as you want," he assured her.

"I hate to impose," she said, fixing her gaze on the fire as she sipped her coffee. "But until I find a job—" With a rueful shake of her head, she halted in midsentence. "Sorry. I'm crying poor when I'm not really that bad off. I'll probably be able to sell a few of my photographs through one of the galleries I've seen around town. And I've applied for a substitute teaching job with the local school district. One way or another, I'll have money coming in soon. Then I'll be able to move into a place of my own."

"Well, there's no rush as far as I'm concerned," Gabriel replied, and to his surprise, realized he meant it.

She was being more than generous toward him in her willingness to wait for the money he owed her, and having her around wasn't proving to be a burden. So why chase her off?

"Thank you."

"You're welcome." Finished with his brownie, he wiped his fingers on his napkin, then reached for his coffee. "Have you talked to anyone at any of the galleries?"

"No, not yet."

"I went to school with Henry Martin, the owner of Martin's Gallery on Palace Avenue. I'll give him a call tomorrow morning and tell him to be on the lookout for you. He's honest and dependable. He also has a reputation for showing high-quality work. Normally, he accepts pieces from local artists only. But since you worked with Ethan and will be living here now, I imagine he'll make an exception.''

''Especially with you to vouch for me?'' Madelyn asked only half-teasingly as she glanced at him.

''That *will* help. But only if your work measures up.''

''Maybe you ought to take a look at some of my photographs before you go out on a limb like that for me.''

Actually, he had been hoping she would suggest he do just that. Still, he didn't want to seem too eager.

''As long as you're sure you don't mind....''

''Not at all. A few of the ones I like best are already in frames. The rest are on the table. Go have a look while I get more coffee.''

Standing, she took his mug from him, then headed toward the kitchen. Snitching another brownie before he could talk himself out of it, Gabriel stood, too, and followed her across the room.

''Feel free to tell me which ones you think will be most likely to impress your friend.''

''I'm not really much of a judge where photographs are concerned,'' he admitted.

''But you know what you like, don't you?'' she asked, glancing over her shoulder at him and flashing him a smile that went straight to his heart.

Oh, yes, he knew what he liked, Gabriel thought, holding her gaze for half a second longer than absolutely necessary. He liked *her*. More than he had any right to. And if he didn't scare up some alternate female companionship soon, he was going to end up saying or doing something he would end up regretting...mightily.

''Most of the time,'' he answered at last.

"Then just tell me what works for you," she advised as she stepped into the kitchen.

Gabriel knew she was talking about her photographs. But that didn't stop him from thinking a truly lascivious thought or two before he finally turned his attention to the photos she had taken.

Though he had no idea how her work measured up to the accepted standards—whatever they were—he liked everything he saw.

The framed black-and-white photographs were of people rather than the places and things Ethan had seemed to favor; an old man asleep in a rocking chair on the porch of a dilapidated old house; a group of young women, two cradling babies in their arms, one holding the hand of a toddler, another hugely pregnant, all seeming to be laughing and talking at once; a young couple standing on a balcony, gazing at each other with a longing that tugged at Gabriel's heart.

On the table, interspersed with another half-dozen black-and-white photos were several color prints including the ones of birds Brian had mentioned and several market scenes so vibrant, Gabriel expected the people in them to glance up at him and speak.

To one side, he also saw a folder. Curious, he reached over, opened it and stared, in sudden dismay, at the four black-and-white photographs that slid onto the table.

A man…his cheeks hollow, his body emaciated, a haunted expression on his face as he leaned against a palm tree and looked out at the waves washing against a sandy beach. A dying man…a man who reminded him of…Ethan—

"Oh, God," Gabriel muttered, running his fingers over one of the photographs as if his touch on its glossy surface could somehow comfort the brother he had both loved and hated.

He hadn't known…hadn't *known*—

With a thunk, Madelyn set the mugs on the table, then reached out to gather up the folder and the photographs it had held. She hadn't meant for Gabriel to see them. Unfortunately, she had forgotten that she had left the folder on the table.

"I'm sorry, Gabriel," she murmured. "I should have put those away. They're…personal."

He caught her hand with surprising strength, and though he didn't hurt her, he held her still.

"They're of Ethan, aren't they?" he asked, his gaze still fixed on the photographs, both pain and anger evident in his voice.

"Yes."

She eyed the photographs, as well, her heart aching for Gabriel. Regardless of what had come between him and his brother, he had never stopped caring about Ethan. But had Ethan known that?

Madelyn could only hope so.

"When were they taken?" Gabriel prodded.

"A few days before he died."

Ethan hadn't been aware of her, lurking nearby, camera in hand. Had he been, he would have never allowed her to photograph him. And normally, Madelyn would have never considered intruding on his privacy without permission.

Even now, she wasn't quite sure what had prompted her to ignore her own code of conduct by taking those pictures on the sly. But she had been glad she had. At least until a few moments ago when she'd seen how they affected Gabriel.

"I never realized he was so sick," Gabriel said, glancing at her with growing bewilderment.

Madelyn didn't really want to tell him the truth about Ethan's illness. All that would do was add to his anguish. But if she tried to put him off, he would wonder what she was hiding, and more than likely, press her even harder.

Sooner or later, he would wring it out of her. So why cause him more upset in the process? After all, as Ethan's brother, he did have a right to know. And having seen the photographs, he was already somewhat prepared for what she would say.

Still, hoping to spare him the very worst, Madelyn chose her words carefully. She told Gabriel the barest facts about the virus Ethan had contracted years ago and the resultant blindness and creeping paralysis that had slowly but surely sapped him of his vitality.

"When did he start having problems?" Gabriel asked when she halted her recitation.

"About three or four months after I went to work for him, his vision began to fail. The paralysis started to affect him about six months ago. By the time he died, he was almost completely blind, was tiring more and more easily, but he could still get around on his own most days."

Gabriel had already let go of her. Now he turned, walked to the fireplace and rested his forearm against the narrow strip of wood that served as a mantel.

"But he was supposed to be in Honduras on an assignment when he died. How would it have been possible for him to continue taking high-quality photographs if he was going blind?" he demanded. "Or was that really why you had him down there, Ms. St. James?"

Madelyn couldn't blame Gabriel for being suspicious,

but that didn't make his questioning any less painful for her to bear.

She had begged Ethan not to go, but he had been insistent. So insistent that she had fully believed he would go without her. Looking back, she now realized he could have been planning to make Roatán his last stop here on earth, even then. But she wasn't about to try to explain that to Gabriel.

She would rather allow him to believe what he wanted about her than so much as hint at the possibility that Ethan might have committed suicide.

"Ethan arranged for us to go to Honduras," she stated matter-of-factly. "And, as had been the case for more than a year, I took the photographs he then sold under his name."

Facing her again, a frown furrowing his forehead, Gabriel studied her for several seconds.

Uncomfortable under his probing gaze, Madelyn turned her attention to the photos of Ethan, finally gathering them into the folder again.

"You let him use you like that?" Gabriel asked at last, his voice filled with dismay.

"I never felt that he was using me," she retorted defensively. "He taught me more than I could have ever learned on my own or from anyone else. He also gave me an opportunity to work at something I truly enjoy. And I was paid much better than most novices are. Without his name on the photographs, none of that would have been possible."

"Ah, so *you* used *him,* going along with whatever he wanted to keep your job instead of seeing to it that he got the medical attention he so obviously needed," Gabriel drawled, his manner taking an accusatorial turn.

"Considering your reward, I suppose that wasn't such a difficult course of action, was it?"

Her first instinct was to grab one of the coffee mugs and hurl it at him. But she refused to let him know just how deeply he had angered her. Giving any credence at all to what he had implied was beneath her dignity.

"Believe whatever you want, Mr. Serrano, but Ethan was an adult. He made his own choices. I did what I could for him, especially when it became obvious he was having a harder and harder time looking after himself.

"Unfortunately, I had no idea he had a half brother who cared about him as you seem to have. Otherwise, I would have contacted you. Maybe you would have been able to talk some sense into him. Then again, maybe not. As for me, I did the best I could with what I had without any expectation of a *reward*."

Averting her gaze, Madelyn tucked the folder under her arm, then picked up the coffee mugs and moved calmly toward the little kitchen. She'd had just about all she could take from Gabriel for one night. She could only hope he would take the hint and show himself to the door.

"I'm sorry, Ms. St. James. I was way out of line," he said.

The touch of his hand on her arm halted her in midstep.

"I thought I had dealt with Ethan's death, but hearing about it in a matter-of-fact way and actually seeing how much he suffered are two different things," he continued, his voice strained. "I realize that I reacted badly, jumping to the wrong conclusions, blaming you when you weren't the one at fault."

"No one was at fault, except maybe Ethan, and if so, it was his mistake to make," she replied, not wanting Gabriel to shoulder a burden that wasn't really his to bear, either. "He lived his life the way he wanted, and he faced death in a similar manner—on his terms."

"How was he toward the end?"

Hesitating, Madelyn glanced over her shoulder at Gabriel. The probing look in his dark eyes spoke volumes. He needed her reassurance that Ethan hadn't really been as bad off as the images in her photographs suggested. And she could give it—by hedging just a little.

For Gabriel's sake, and for her own, she wouldn't reveal how sad and alone Ethan had seemed those last few weeks on Roatán. She didn't want Gabriel to dwell on the possibility that Ethan might have committed suicide any more than she wanted to herself. Nor did she want Gabriel to wonder, as she did herself, if she might have been able to prevent it happening if she had only read the signs correctly.

"He was as full of the devil as ever," she said, smiling slightly. "Ordering me around just like always."

Gabriel nodded, his gaze softening.

"I have a feeling you were good for him."

"We were good for each other," Madelyn replied.

"I'm glad...for both of you."

"So am I."

"Well, I've stayed longer than I planned." Turning away, Gabriel walked to the door, took his jacket off the peg and put it on, then added, "I wish I'd had better news for you."

"Maybe next time," she said, forcing herself to smile brightly.

"Yeah, maybe next time."

"Thanks for stopping by."

"I said I would," he reminded her.

"Yes, you did," Madelyn agreed, wincing inwardly at how grateful she must have sounded.

Even though his only reason for visiting her had to do with the settlement of Ethan's estate, she had been looking forward to seeing him all day. As the evening had worn on, and he had failed to show up, she'd begun to think he had either forgotten or found something better to do.

Which was exactly what *she* should try to do, she thought. Find something better to occupy her time than waiting for Gabriel Serrano. Pinning any kind of hope at all on him—especially the hope for companionship—was bound to end in disappointment.

From the first, he had been all too eager to think the worst of her, and apparently, he still was. He had misjudged her yet again where her relationship with Ethan was concerned. And while he *had* backed off, she doubted that was the last time she would have to defend herself to him.

"I'll call Henry Martin first thing in the morning. When shall I tell him to expect you?"

"Thursday morning, say around eleven o'clock?"

"Sounds good to me," Gabriel replied as he opened the door. "If there's a problem, I'll let you know tomorrow evening. Otherwise, plan to be at the gallery on Thursday at eleven. Oh, and be sure to take the framed black-and-white photographs and the market scenes with you. They're very good."

"Thanks. I will."

With a nod of acknowledgment, Gabriel stepped outside, pulling the door closed after him with a quiet click.

Madelyn stood there a few moments longer with what was surely a silly smile tugging at the corners of her mouth. Her pleasure at the way he'd complimented her work was all out of proportion, but she allowed herself to bask in it anyway.

Finally she continued on her way into the kitchen, emptied the mugs and set them in the sink. Then, before she could forget again and leave the folder out, she crossed to the sleeping area and tucked it under the pile of sweaters she had folded into one of the dresser drawers.

Back in the living area, she added several pieces of wood to the now-smoldering fire, retrieved the leftover brownies and returned them to the cookie tin in the kitchen.

That done, she glanced at her watch. Just after ten. She should be feeling tired. She had been out most of the day, applying to do substitute teaching, then learning her way around town on foot. Instead, she was oddly restless. And the cottage she usually considered cozy suddenly seemed claustrophobic.

What she needed was a nice, brisk walk. The cold night air would clear her head of maudlin thoughts, and the added exercise would surely tire her out.

She wouldn't go far, she decided, taking her long, black wool coat from the closet. While it had seemed safe enough to wander around Santa Fe on her own in broad daylight, she knew that a woman alone in any town faced a much greater likelihood of running into trouble after dark. Especially when she was still unfamiliar with the area.

Locking the door after her, Madelyn paused just outside the cottage, allowing her eyes to adjust to the moonlit night. Across the courtyard, the house was dark. Evidently, Gabriel wasn't having any trouble sleeping, she thought with the barest hint of resentment.

Oh, that *she* could be that inured to *him*.

Annoyed with herself, she strode down the driveway. At the sidewalk, she turned right, heading away from town, choosing to stay in the residential area. That way, if she had a problem, she could go to one of the houses lining the street and ask for help.

Although the sidewalk angled uphill, and she wasn't quite used to the altitude yet, Madelyn managed to keep up her pace. No one else seemed to be about, and except for the muted thud of her sneakers on concrete, all was quiet.

She had gone about half a mile or so when she suddenly realized she was no longer alone. Without breaking stride, she glanced down at the little dog gamely keeping pace with her, and frowned.

She had no idea where the creature had come from. Maybe one of the houses along her route. Or maybe not, she reconsidered, slowing to a halt and gazing down at…him, she realized as the animal lifted one leg, marked a tree, then sat on its haunches, gazing up at her expectantly.

He was shaped a lot like a dachshund—long body with short, stubby legs. But he had a blunt nose and a docked tail. And his brown-and-white-and-gray coat was a scraggly mass of wiry curls. He didn't seem to be starving. However, he didn't appear to be well fed, either. And he wasn't wearing a collar.

"Well, hello," she said, not quite sure what to do next.

He wagged his little tail ever so slightly and scooted a few inches closer.

"Where do you live?"

As if giving her question serious consideration, he cocked his head to one side and his short, floppy ears perked up.

"Come on, then. Let's see if we can find your house," Madelyn said.

She turned and started back the way she'd come, and

he readily fell into step beside her. At the first driveway, she stopped and pointed toward the house.

"Go home, boy. Go home."

He stood, looking up at her, obviously confused.

"Okay. Wrong house."

She started off again, then stopped at the next driveway, and the next, and the next, each time repeating her "go home" routine. And each time, the little dog set off with her once more until they reached the cottage.

"All right, you're lost," she admitted. "And there's nothing more we can do about it tonight."

With the temperature already below freezing, Madelyn also decided it was too cold to make him stay outside. Unlocking the door, she stepped into the cottage, and after only a moment's hesitation, gestured for the dog to do likewise. He scampered across the threshold, then sat, gazing up at her inquisitively.

In the light of the lamp she'd left burning, she could see that he was in worse shape than she had thought. One of his ears had a nasty cut on it, and his coat was matted with bits of dirt and dried leaves.

"You're a mess, aren't you?"

Cocking his head to one side, he whined softly, as if in apology.

"A bath first," Madelyn stated as she hung up her coat and headed for the bathroom.

The dog trailed after her, sniffing the air hopefully. Aware that he must be hungry, she paused beside the bathtub and bent to scratch his head.

"Then a bowl of leftover stew," she promised.

To her relief, the animal put up no fuss at all when she lifted him into the tub—half-filled with warm water—and bathed him with her herbal shampoo. In fact, he seemed to enjoy the attention, cuddling in her lap afterward as she toweled him off, then used her blow-dryer, set on low, to finish his grooming.

Cleaned up, he looked kind of cute. And it took no urging at all to get him to eat the stew she offered him. He licked the bowl clean—peas, carrots, potatoes and all—took a long drink of water from another bowl, then trotted over to the door and yipped politely to be let out.

Wondering if he would take off now that he had been fed, Madelyn opened the door for him. But he did his business quickly, then trotted back inside without any urging. In fact, as she closed and locked the door again, he made a beeline for her bed, managed to hop onto it despite his short stature, and proceeded to curl up on the comforter.

Not having the heart to shoo him off, she washed her face, brushed her teeth, changed into her nightgown, then crawled under the covers. Within moments, he had crept up to snuggle by her side.

Reaching out to stroke his silky head, Madelyn smiled slightly. For the first time since arriving in Santa Fe, a sense of contentment settled over her. Caring for the little dog had taken her mind off her own problems. Not only had she felt useful, but also appreciated. And the loneliness that had nagged at her a little more with each passing day suddenly seemed to have dissipated.

Too bad he was someone else's pet, as he surely had to be. She could have gotten used to having him around. But whoever owned him would want him back. And it would be up to her to help him find his way home.

In the morning, she would take him out again and see if she could find someone who recognized him. If that failed, she would put up a note on the bulletin board at the library—the acknowledged information center regarding most happenings around town.

And if he still went unclaimed?

Madelyn wasn't sure what she would do. She doubted Gabriel would allow her to keep him. He didn't have a dog of his own, so he probably preferred not to have one around.

But she wouldn't worry about that tonight. She would enjoy her good fortune, such as it was.

Easing him closer, she bent and nuzzled his furry neck. He sighed deeply, evidently as pleased as she that they had stumbled upon one another.

He might only be a little lost dog, but he had helped to restore her flagging self-confidence. With that, she could get through the coming weeks, head held high, regardless of what Gabriel Serrano chose to believe about her.

She wasn't going to allow one man's opinion of her to drag her down. She was a decent human being—always had been and always would be. She had just needed a little reminder. And she had gotten one in the nicest way possible.

''Thanks, little buddy,'' she murmured.

Finally closing her eyes, she drifted slowly off to sleep.

Chapter 5

Late Thursday afternoon, Gabriel sat in his office at Nuestra Junior High School, drumming his fingers on the pile of papers spread across his desk as he gazed out the window at a patch of gray sky. There would be snow that night, but the weather was the last thing on his mind.

Earlier in the day, Gloria Munoz, one of the hardest-working, not to mention all-but-irreplaceable teachers on his staff, had called to advise him that her doctor had ordered her to bed for the remainder of her pregnancy.

Gabriel knew how much the baby meant to Gloria and her husband, and he wanted whatever was best for her, first and foremost. But having to find a teacher with the credentials necessary to take over her remedial math and basic science classes—classes she patiently taught in Spanish as well as English to further aid those students who had fallen behind because of language difficulties— had been a task he'd dreaded.

He had sincerely doubted there was a qualified teacher

on the substitute list who would also willingly commit to working until the end of the school year. Teachers with Gloria's background were a rarity. In addition, most substitutes preferred to work only a few days or a week at a time. And with students like the ones in Gloria's classes, a substitute teacher of any ability usually lasted no more than a day or two.

Still, Gabriel had put in a call to the district office. He'd had no choice. There simply wasn't anywhere else he could go to get the help he needed. Which he'd suspected would probably turn out to be whatever help was actually available.

He had hated the idea of filling Gloria's position with one less-than-enthusiastic warm body after another. But the teacher's aide who had tried to supervise the morning classes had ended up in tears by lunchtime. In desperation, Gabriel had asked his vice principal, Eileen Duggan, to take over the afternoon classes. After a lot of drawer banging, door slamming and audible muttering in her office next door, *she* had left at the end of the day without speaking to him.

As Eileen had stormed past his door, his fax machine had whirred to life, spewing out the district's response to his request. The résumé now on his desk was that of a recent addition to the substitute list, a woman with several years' experience teaching remedial math and basic science at the junior high school level who also happened to be fluent in Spanish. The perfect candidate....

Unfortunately, there was one small problem—the woman happened to be Madelyn St. James.

Granted, the problem was his, personally. Her credentials were impeccable. Had she been almost anyone else, he would have hired her on the spot.

But Gabriel simply wasn't sure how he would handle

having her on his staff. She would be at the school five days a week, not only teaching Gloria's classes, but attending meetings, as well. Meetings *he* supervised. She'd also have free run of the teachers' lounge, and if she was willing, she could help out with any extracurricular activities she chose. Which meant that giving her a wide berth, as he had been determined to do after Tuesday night, would be impossible.

As seemed to happen whenever they were together, she had unknowingly stirred up a welter of emotions deep inside him then. Finding out just how ill Ethan had been, Gabriel had run the gamut from pain and anger, to grief and disbelief. Then finally, most devastating of all, he had been overcome by a longing for something he could never have.

He had even tried casting Madelyn in the role of evil woman in an effort to deny that she had done what *he* should have done—*would* have done if only Ethan had trusted him enough to come home. But she hadn't let him get by with it.

Instead, in her own quiet way, she had made sure he understood that she'd stayed with his brother until the end for no other reason than that she had truly cared for him. Cared enough to let him sell her photographs as his own while looking after him with what had to have been selfless devotion as he became more and more infirm.

In the end, Gabriel had found himself wishing there were some way he could inspire that kind of loyalty from her. At the same time he acknowledged, yet again, that Ethan had been a hard act to follow once, and once was enough for him.

So, he had made the decision to avoid her altogether. A decision he had stuck to yesterday, leaving the house with Brian early in the morning, then not returning until well into the evening, after treating his son to his favorite fast-food restaurant after his visit at Donny's house. Even Henry Martin had cooperated. He'd agreed to see Madelyn as they'd arranged, thus making it unnecessary for Gabriel to relay a message to her when he finally did get home.

But if he asked her to take Gloria's job—

The buzz of the telephone on his desk interrupted Gabriel's reverie. Surprised that anyone would be calling the school so late, he sat forward in his chair, lifted the receiver and offered a brisk hello.

"Gabe? Henry Martin."

"Hey, Henry, I was just thinking about you."

"Good thoughts, I hope."

"Always. What's going on?"

"I wanted to thank you for sending Madelyn St. James to see me. Her work is spectacular. I've already sold one of her black-and-white photos and have one of the market scenes on hold for another customer, and they've only been on display half a day."

"I had an idea you'd like her style," Gabriel replied, pleased for both his friend and Madelyn.

"That's putting it mildly. I told her I'd take anything she has to offer."

"Thanks, Henry. I appreciate your helping her get started here in town."

"Well, thank *you* for making sure she didn't go to the competition first."

"You have the best reputation in town, and I know you'll be fair with her."

"That I will," vowed his friend.

They made plans to meet for lunch the following week—something they hadn't done since the holiday season—exchanged a few more pleasantries, then said good-bye.

Staring out the window again, watching as twilight drifted down, Gabriel now found himself wondering if Madelyn would even be interested in taking over Gloria Munoz's classes. With money already coming in from her photographs, she might not want to be tied to a teaching job after all.

He wasn't sure if he was relieved by that possibility, or gravely disappointed. But he did know he was going to set aside his reservations and ask her to take the job, just as he'd known he would have to do all along.

He owed it to the students to try to secure the best possible replacement for their teacher. And if that meant dealing with the emotional turmoil having her around on a daily basis might arouse in him, then he would find a way to do it.

He would talk to her just as soon as he got home. Brian was already with her. His son probably wouldn't appreciate having his father barge in on their visit. But if Madelyn wasn't interested in the job, then Gabriel would have the rest of tonight to consider alternate arrangements.

Or so Gabriel told himself as he gathered his papers together and stuffed them into a desk drawer. He was hurrying home to see her so he could discuss a job opening with her, not for his own gratification. Had duty not demanded it, he wouldn't have gone anywhere near her.

He arrived at the house just after five o'clock. He thought about changing clothes first, then reminded himself that he was approaching her with what amounted to a business proposition as he strode purposefully from the garage straight to the little cottage.

Amazing how the place drew him, he mused. For years, he had rarely given it more than a glance whenever he came or went. Now it seemed to beckon him, whether early in the morning or late at night, whether it stood dark and still, or hummed with the hidden life of lights in the windows and smoke swirling from the chimney, the sound of classical music playing on the radio and the scent of something wonderful baking in the oven as it did just then.

Even more astonishing, he had also stopped thinking of it as Ethan's cottage. Madelyn had transformed the place so completely that he found it almost impossible to conjure up painful memories while he was there. For that, if nothing else, he would always be grateful to her.

Tonight she answered his knock on the door within a second or two, not bothering to turn off the radio. As she had previously, she greeted him with a warm, welcoming smile, albeit a little less so than on his previous visit.

At the rate he was going, before too long she would be scowling at him whenever he came to the door, and he certainly didn't want that to happen. He liked feeling that she was honestly glad to see him. In fact, he could get used to—

From somewhere around his ankles, Gabriel heard a long, low, decidedly menacing growl. Glancing down, he caught sight of what had to be the ugliest little dog he had ever seen. Teeth bared, wiry coat bristling, the creature pressed close to Madelyn's leg, eyeing him with obvious hostility.

"Oh, sorry," Madelyn said, bending to scoop the dog into her arms.

Temporarily sidetracked, the animal licked her chin affectionately, then fixed its beady gaze on him again.

"Who's there?" Brian asked, sidling next to Madelyn in the doorway.

"Your dad," she replied, looking at Gabriel nervously.

"Guess what, Dad? Madelyn found a little dog when she was out walking Tuesday night. He followed her home. And guess what else? We're gonna call him Buddy."

Frowning, Gabriel glanced at his son as he stepped into the cottage. In addition to calling Madelyn by her first name, the boy had said a couple of things that gave him pause.

He had indicated that she'd been out alone late Tuesday night, walking the streets—something he would have to warn her not to do again. While Santa Fe was reasonably safe, she had been taking a chance wandering around on her own after ten o'clock.

Brian had also said *they* had decided to name the dog, which had to mean she was planning on keeping it. He had no real objection to her having a pet—although he would have preferred one that didn't dislike him on sight—but he would have appreciated her asking him first.

However, seeing the excitement in Brian's eyes, and the trepidation in Madelyn's, Gabriel didn't have the heart to reprimand either one of them, at least not as sternly as he probably should have.

"*Ms. St. James,*" he said, emphasizing his point by meeting his son's gaze directly.

"She said it was all right if I called her Madelyn. So, can I, Dad? Can I, *please?*"

"In that case, yes, you *may.* Now, about the dog—"

"He really did follow me home the other night," Madelyn cut in. "I spent all day yesterday trying to find his owner, but didn't have any luck. I posted a note on the bulletin board at the library, and also put an ad in the weekend paper, but if no one claims him—"

"You're welcome to keep him as long as you want," Gabriel assured her hastily.

"That's great, Dad," Brian piped up. "Because I don't think anybody else is gonna want him. He's kinda weird."

Gabriel had to hide a smile at the injured look on Madelyn's face. He agreed with his son. The mutt had a face, a body *and* a temperament only a mother could love— or a softhearted woman with an apparent penchant for picking up strays.

But he didn't dare say as much to her. She seemed quite attached to the creature, and he didn't want to hurt her feelings. Not when he was about to ask a favor of her. A favor he suddenly found himself wanting her to grant for the very reasons that had caused him to hesitate earlier.

He didn't want to go two days without seeing this woman again unless he had no other choice. Nothing had to come of it. Nothing probably would. But why deny himself the pleasure of her company just because Ethan had known her first? They could be friends, after all. Just friends…

"Henry Martin called to tell me he'd sold one of your photographs and was holding another for a customer. Congratulations," he commended her, steering the conversation to a less inflammatory topic.

"I'm trying not to let it go to my head," she admitted, smiling. "But thanks. And thanks for the recommendation, too."

"I guess you're going to be pretty busy now."

"Since I have a place to sell my photographs, I really should get to work," she admitted.

"She was just showing me how to use one of her cameras. And on Saturday, we're gonna take some pictures together," Brian said, adding almost as an afterthought, "As long as it's okay with you."

"Of course," Gabriel replied.

"Good." Brian exchanged a pleased glance with Madelyn, then looked back at his father, frowning slightly when Gabriel moved toward the sofa. "It's not five-thirty yet, and you said I could stay until then."

"I know."

He took off his overcoat, tossed it over the back of the sofa, sat down and started to loosen his tie.

"You don't have to stay, too," Brian said as he and Madelyn—still holding the dog—paused in front of him. "I can find my way home."

"I know that, too."

Gabriel glanced at his son, then at Madelyn. Neither of them seemed all that happy to have him there, and the dog looked as if he were ready to tear him limb from limb. Normally, he would have taken the hint and made himself scarce. But he had a good reason for staying, so the three of them would just have to put up with him for a few minutes more.

"Well, then *why*—?" Brian began.

"I have something I'd like to discuss with Madelyn."

"What?" Brian asked, eyeing him with sudden concern.

Madelyn said nothing, but her grip on the dog seemed to tighten and her expression grew wary.

"Something to do with the junior high school," Gabriel replied.

"Oh." Looking relieved, Brian turned his attention to Madelyn. "Do you think I could decorate the cookies while you talk to my dad?"

"Sure." She set the dog on the center cushion of the

sofa, now covered with the afghan, then added for Gabriel's benefit, "We've been baking gingerbread men."

"I was wondering what smelled so good."

"Let me get Brian set up with the icing and cinnamon hearts, and I'll be right back."

Gabriel watched her cross to the kitchen with his son, then looked down at the dog. The mutt sat at attention, watching *him,* obviously waiting for him to make a wrong move.

"Chill out, Buddy," he muttered. "I'm one of the good guys."

Unimpressed, the animal growled low in his throat.

"Buddy, be nice," Madelyn admonished as she joined them once again.

To Gabriel's dismay, the dog whined pathetically, then crawled into her lap. Immediately, she began to coo over him, totally unaware of the sly look he sent Gabriel's way.

I've got your number, you little faker, Gabriel thought. *And one of these days…*

"You wanted to talk to me about something to do with the school?" Madelyn prompted.

Though she seemed guarded, she also appeared interested in whatever he had to tell her.

Heartened, Gabriel explained the situation as concisely as he could, making sure she understood exactly what she would be getting into if she agreed to take Gloria Munoz's place. At the same time, he also tried to let her know how much he would like her to join his staff.

What he couldn't bring himself to do was back her into a corner by laying a guilt trip on her.

"I know your situation has changed somewhat since you put your name on the substitute list. I realize, too, there's a good chance you're no longer interested in teaching," he said in closing.

She had listened attentively to all he had to say, a thoughtful expression on her face as she petted the little dog curled up in her lap. Now, seeming to consider his proposition, she looked away, focusing her gaze on the fire burning brightly in the fireplace.

Aware that she might be feeling obligated in some way due to the fact that she was living on his property, he added, "I'll understand if you'd rather not commit to a long-term assignment like this."

"What long-term assignment?" Brian asked, plopping down between them on the sofa.

"Your dad has asked me to teach at his school," Madelyn explained.

"He has?" The boy looked up at her, wide-eyed, then grinned. "Cool. Are you gonna do it?"

Mentally crossing his fingers, Gabriel gazed at her questioningly, as well.

She hesitated a few moments more, then nodded decisively. "Yes, I am."

Gabriel was pleased with her response. For the space of a heartbeat, he wanted to grab her and hug her. Luckily, with his son and the dog between them, he was forced to limit himself to an appreciative smile.

Brian, on the other hand, gave a boyish whoop, then sobered suddenly.

"But what about *us?*" he demanded. "Will we still be able to do stuff together?"

"Of course we will," she assured him, reaching over to squeeze his hand.

"And your photography," Gabriel added. "Are you sure you'll have enough time for that, too?"

"I don't see why not. I taught school, worked on my

photography and helped out with my nieces and nephews when I lived in St. Louis," she stated pragmatically. "In fact, I prefer to stay as busy as possible. Otherwise, I tend to get lazy and start feeling sorry for myself. The more I have to do, the more I seem to get done, and the better I feel."

"Well, then, by this time next week you should be on top of the world," Gabriel teased.

"I'm going to hold you to that," she replied, her eyes twinkling merrily. Then, on a more serious note, she asked, "When would you like me to start?"

"Tomorrow?" he suggested hopefully. "Unless you've already made other plans."

"Tomorrow will be fine. Where and when?"

"Nuestra Junior High School." He pulled a pad of paper and pen from his shirt pocket and jotted down directions. "School starts at eight-fifteen, so why don't you plan to be there about seven-thirty? That will give me a little extra time to show you around the school and introduce you to the faculty."

"Should I contact the district office, too?"

"I'll take care of that for you along with the paperwork for administration."

He was tempted to tell her she could ride over to the school with him in the morning, as well. But he realized that would probably be more togetherness than either one of them wanted.

He was glad that she had taken the job and that he would be seeing her every day. However, maintaining some distance between them still seemed like a wise thing to do.

"What about lesson plans?"

"Gloria has them prepared for each of her classes through the end of February," Gabriel replied. "That should allow you to ease back into the classroom without too heavy an initial workload.''

"That *will* be a help," Madelyn agreed.

"And we can still take pictures together on Saturday?" Brian pressed.

"How about meeting me here at two o'clock? Weather permitting, of course."

"Okay."

"I'll have the cameras loaded," she promised.

Aware that they had taken more than enough of her time considering the busy day she had ahead of her, Gabriel stood and reached for his overcoat.

"Better get your jacket, son," he said. "It's almost six o'clock, and I don't know about you, but I have homework."

"Me, too." Brian sighed, hopping off the sofa and heading, reluctantly, toward the door where he'd left his jacket hanging on a peg.

Madelyn shifted the dog off her lap and stood, too.

"Give me a minute, and I'll wrap up some of those gingerbread men for you to take with you," she said.

By the time Gabriel and Brian had buttoned themselves into their coats, she had a foil packet of cookies ready for them. She handed it to Brian, then followed them to the door.

His hand on the doorknob, Gabriel paused, meeting her gaze.

"Thanks again for taking the job. I'll be looking forward to seeing you in the morning," he said, hoping she realized how much he meant it.

She nodded, then ruffled Brian's hair. "And I'll see *you* Saturday afternoon."

"Yeah, see you Saturday," the boy replied.

As the cottage door closed after them, Gabriel slipped

an arm around Brian's shoulders. His son leaned against him with a sigh, clutching the packet of cookies in both hands.

"She's really nice, isn't she, Dad?"

"Yes, she's really nice."

"I like her a lot."

"I do, too."

"And I like her dog, too."

"Now that's where we part company. But then, he doesn't growl at you the way he growls at me, does he?"

"No," Brian admitted.

"I wonder why that is?"

"Maybe he doesn't like having you around, so he was trying to chase you away."

"Well, he's not going to succeed," Gabriel muttered with determination. "I plan to be around *a lot*. Whether *he* likes it or not."

"I was hoping you'd feel that way," Brian said, smiling enigmatically.

"Oh, really? Why?"

"Because I think Madelyn needs a special friend, and you do, too, Dad. So you're perfect for each other."

Gabriel had serious doubts about *that*. But all the same, he wasn't letting any ratty-looking little mutt run him off. Even though he would probably end up wishing he had.

With a weary sigh, Madelyn tossed her pen aside and sat back in her desk chair, aware that the chatter of students on their way home for the weekend, punctuated by the slamming of locker doors and the shuffle of sneaker-clad feet, had finally faded into relative silence.

After her first full week on the job, she couldn't help but wonder what had possessed her to agree in such a cavalier manner to Gabriel Serrano's request that she take over Gloria Munoz's classes. She *had* wanted something more than her photography to occupy her time. And while she had earned several hundred dollars on the photographs Henry had sold, for the time being she had liked the idea of having a more dependable source of income, as well.

What she had failed to remember was how hard teaching could be. She'd been reminded soon enough, of course. And with that reminder had come the fear that she'd gotten in over her head—at least temporarily.

Yet she simply couldn't bring herself to admit as much to Gabriel.

For one thing, she was too proud to renege on their agreement. She had taken the job knowing she'd be expected to work until the end of the school year. And she would, regardless.

She had also realized almost immediately just how much both Gabriel and the students in Gloria's classes needed her. Abandoning either of them was simply out of the question.

Finally, she had to admit—in her calmer moments— that within another week or two she would hit her stride, and thus, settle into a comfortable routine. She would know most, if not all, of her students by name, and be accepted as a colleague by most, if not all, of the other faculty members. She would have acquainted herself with the textbooks she was using. And with Gloria's lesson plans as a guide, she would have begun developing her own ideas of how she could best impart the knowledge required for course completion in her various classes during the last few months of the school year.

However, being aware of all that didn't make her feel any less overwhelmed at the moment. Or any less alone.

For some strange reason, she had expected Gabriel to

be more supportive. Not that she wanted to be singled out for special attention. But he seemed much more friendly toward the other teachers, greeting them with more than the curt nod he offered *her* when they passed in the hall, laughing and talking with them in the lounge before and after school as well as at staff meetings and sitting with them in the cafeteria.

Though she hadn't made a big deal of it, he had to know she'd taken Gloria's job as much as a favor to him as anything. A little appreciation on his part didn't seem like too much to ask in return.

He had been cordial enough when he'd come to the cottage to ask for her help. In fact, he had seemed to set aside whatever animosity he'd felt toward her as a result of her relationship with Ethan. But since then, he had treated her as if she had the plague.

Normally, Madelyn wouldn't have allowed his loutish behavior to bother her. She had been as busy as she wanted to be, she had the yet-to-be-claimed Buddy to keep her company in the evening, and visits from Brian to brighten her Monday, Thursday and Saturday afternoons.

They'd had a wonderful time last weekend, shooting black-and-white photographs all around town. And tomorrow she was going to show him how to develop the film.

But she was tired today, more tired than she could remember being in quite a while. Obviously, the long hours she'd been putting in had worn her out. And that, in turn, had her feeling not only sad and lonely, but also slighted.

Shifting in her chair, Madelyn glanced out the window and saw that it was snowing again as it had the past Friday. Though she didn't have far to go, she decided to head for home. Driving on icy streets, even for a short distance, still made her extremely nervous.

With another sigh, she began to gather the test papers atop her desk into her tote bag. The scores hadn't been as good as she had expected, so she was going to have to come up with another way to impart the basic principles of photosynthesis to a classroom full of eighth-grade children barely able to read at the fourth-grade level.

But that could wait until tomorrow. Tonight she was going to start a fire in the fireplace, take a long hot bath, order a pizza and curl up with the mystery novel she had bought the other day. Maybe a little personal TLC would get her past the blue funk she'd been—

"You're here late again," Gabriel said, his deep voice cutting across her thoughts unexpectedly.

Startled, Madelyn glanced up and saw him standing in the doorway of her classroom. In black wool slacks, a white shirt, paisley tie and gray tweed jacket, he looked very professional. But she had a feeling he hadn't come to see her on school business.

He was smiling a smile she recognized all too well from past encounters. The one he dredged up whenever he wanted something from her—something that would benefit *him* much more than *her*.

What now? she wondered grimly, pressing her lips together.

She had already agreed to put her life on hold indefinitely while he tried to come up with the money he owed her. And she'd agreed to take a teaching job that he had to have known would be more of a challenge than he'd led her to believe.

With her luck, he probably wanted her to baby-sit Brian so he could go out on a hot date. Not that she would mind looking after the boy. But it was the principle of the thing...no pun intended.

"I was just getting ready to leave," she said, her tone polite but cool, her gaze unwavering.

"I wasn't trying to run you off." He moved toward her, then paused halfway down an aisle. His expression changed to one of concern as he leaned a hip against one of the desks. "Hard day?"

"Not really," she hedged, lifting her chin a notch.

Considering how studiously he had seemed to be ignoring her, Madelyn was surprised he'd noticed either the long hours she'd been putting in or the resultant toll they'd taken. But she wasn't about to make a play for his sympathy. She was more than capable of adhering to her side of their bargain, and she refused to say anything that might lead him to believe otherwise.

"You look tired," he pressed, a frown creasing his forehead.

"So do you," she shot back. Then, aware that she was on the verge of being extremely rude to her boss, she added with a slight smile, "But I guess that comes with the territory, doesn't it?"

"Yeah, I guess it does. So how about a little antidote?" he suggested, smiling once again.

"What kind of little antidote?" Sitting back in her chair, Madelyn eyed him uncertainly, wondering what he was up to.

"I thought if you hadn't made other plans yet, you might like to join Brian and me for pizza and a movie."

More than anything, Madelyn wished she could believe his invitation wasn't just the means to another end for him. But her past experience with Gabriel Serrano had taught her to be leery. He could be so charming, but only when it suited his purpose.

Just like Ethan, she thought, though Gabriel would no doubt be appalled by the comparison.

"What do you *really* want?" she asked instead, flattening her hands on her desk.

"Just what I said," he replied, looking honestly bewildered. "To take you out for pizza and a movie."

"Oh, sure." Still unwilling to take him at his word, Madelyn refused to be swayed. "You hardly have two words to say to me all week, and now, all of a sudden, you want to take me out to dinner and a movie? Why don't you just tell me what you really want and save yourself some time and money? By now you must realize what a soft touch I am. I don't have to be bribed."

"Whoa, back up a minute," Gabriel said, his surprise and dismay equally evident. "I said more than two words to you this week. Granted, I thought it best to be reserved about it, but only so the rest of the faculty wouldn't come to the wrong conclusion about you.

"They all know you're living in my cottage, and that you were hired to take Gloria's place at my insistence. What I would also like them to know is that you're a highly qualified teacher who has already become an asset to our school—something they wouldn't have had time to realize if they'd been busy resenting you because I seemed to be giving you special attention."

"Oh," Madelyn murmured, the heat of a blush creeping up her neck and spreading across her cheeks.

She had done to him the exact same thing that had angered her so when the tables had been turned. She had misjudged him completely, assuming the worst, then throwing it in his face when, in reality, she had been way off base.

That was bad enough. But what made her feel even

worse was that Gabriel didn't seem angry. Rather, he seemed hurt.

"And I wasn't trying to bribe you," he continued, straightening his shoulders and shoving his hands in his pockets. "You've been working hard all week, and I thought you might enjoy a night out with me and my son. I know treating you to pizza and a movie isn't much considering all you've done for me as well as for Brian. But I wasn't sure how else to show my appreciation."

"I'm so sorry, Gabriel." She stood, hands clasped in front of her, wanting to go to him and beg his forgiveness. But she had given him more than enough reason to rebuff her, and coward that she was, she stayed behind her desk. "I don't know what I was thinking. Pizza and a movie sound wonderful. That is, if the invitation is still open," she added, giving him the out she owed him.

He didn't reply at once. Instead, he met her gaze consideringly, allowing the momentary silence to stretch between them.

Deeply ashamed, Madelyn finally looked away. Her hands shaking ever so slightly, she tucked the last few papers into her tote bag.

The one man whose company she had been craving had come to her in friendship, and what had she done? She'd lashed out at him ruthlessly, as if he were her worst enemy.

No wonder she was twenty-eight years old and still a spinster. She had all the social savvy of a warthog—

"I'll follow you back to the house," Gabriel said, his deep voice cutting through her mental flagellation. "That way we can pick up Brian and go together in my truck. As long as that's all right with you."

"Oh, yes," Madelyn hastened to assure him. "That's fine with me."

He waited while she put on her coat, then together they walked through the quiet halls to his office so he could collect his things. They seemed to be the only ones left in the building aside from the custodians. And for that Madelyn was grateful. Now that Gabriel had pointed out how their being overly friendly toward each other could work against her where the other faculty members were concerned, she would rather not be seen leaving with him.

Although they were anything but a jolly pair, she thought as he held the door open for her wordlessly.

Why couldn't she have kept her mouth shut and taken his invitation at face value? All she had done was spoil what could have been a delightful evening out.

Gabriel certainly didn't seem overjoyed with the prospect of her company. But rather than admit he'd changed his mind, he was being chivalrous. After the way she had spoken to him, she really should have had the good grace to let him off the hook.

In fact, she still could, she realized as they made their way to the parking lot through a flurry of featherlight snowflakes. All she had to do was—

"You look like you're on your way to your own execution," Gabriel muttered, halting beside her car. "Are you sure you want to go with us?"

"Only if *you're* sure you still want me along," she replied, glancing at him dubiously. "I wouldn't blame you if you'd rather not include me, after all."

"I would have said so if I didn't."

"But I was so rude to you—"

"I can distinctly remember being fairly uncivil myself on one or two occasions when we've been together." He reached out and caught her by the hand, then added with a hint of a smile, "So, what do you say we call a truce, let bygones be bygones and try to have a nice time to-night?''

''All right,'' Madelyn agreed, cheered by the warmth of his touch.

Although forgiving herself would take a while, she was more than willing to start fresh with Gabriel. From now on, she would *think* before she made rash assumptions or accusations, and she hoped Gabriel would do the same.

She hadn't come into his life with a hidden agenda. Nor was she out to hurt him or his son in any way. More than anything, she wanted to believe he would be honest with her, too, and wouldn't intentionally cause her any harm, either.

Even feeling remorseful, as she did, Madelyn enjoyed her night out with Gabriel and Brian. They ate at Brian's favorite pizza parlor, sharing a giant pizza loaded with just about everything. As if by mutual agreement, she and Gabriel kept the conversation light.

After dinner, they caught the early evening show at the theater on San Francisco Street—an action-adventure movie with a minimum of violence and a pleasing hint of romance, at least in Madelyn's opinion.

At Brian's suggestion, they strolled to the sweetshop on the Plaza for ice cream and cappuccinos when the movie was over, then finally headed for home.

Father and son walked Madelyn to her door and wished her good-night. Brian also mentioned their date the following afternoon, just in case she'd forgotten.

She assured him that she hadn't. Then, for one long moment, she considered inviting Gabriel to join them. But Brian had seemed to want to talk about Ethan when they were together, and she wasn't sure how well that would go over with Gabriel. Now that he seemed to be

accepting her, she didn't want to rock the boat by reminding him of who had sent her there and why.

As she readied herself for bed, then curled up under
the covers with Buddy beside her, Madelyn wished she
had met Gabriel in some other way. But she would have
never left St. Louis, much less decided to make a home
for herself in Santa Fe, if it hadn't been for Ethan. Too
bad the animosity Gabriel had felt toward him seemed to
occasionally encompass her, as well.

Although that might not happen again now that they'd
had a pleasant evening together....

Still, Madelyn wasn't about to push her luck. Being
with Gabriel and Brian had been wonderful. She had felt
like part of a family—the kind of family she would like
to have for herself someday.

And she would. Not with him, of course. But with
someone else—someone who wouldn't mind that she'd
once worked for Ethan Merritt as she was afraid Gabriel
always would.

No matter how he vowed to let bygones be bygones....

Chapter 6

Humming along with the vintage rock-and-roll music playing on the truck's radio, Gabriel pulled out of the district administration building's parking lot and turned toward Nuestra Junior High School.

Despite the unusual amount of wrangling that had gone on over allocation of funds at the monthly budget meeting, he was in a surprisingly good mood. Eventually, he had gotten the money he needed to upgrade his school's language lab, but that wasn't the only reason he was feeling so lighthearted.

It was Friday, and for the third week in a row, he and Brian and Madelyn would be spending the evening together. After the rocky start they'd had the first time he'd asked her out, he had been hesitant to suggest it again. Though they had all enjoyed themselves, he hadn't wanted to push his luck.

Luckily, Madelyn hadn't had similar qualms. The following Wednesday she had invited him and Brian to join her for dinner at the cottage Friday night. Afterward, they'd played a rowdy game of Scrabble, and again, they had all had a good time together. It had seemed only natural to invite her to dinner and a rematch at his house tonight—an invitation she had readily accepted.

He would have never guessed they would fall into such a pleasurable routine. Not after the way she had greeted his initial overture. He had been confused and hurt by her erroneous assumptions that Friday afternoon. Gradually, however, understanding had dawned on him.

Looking back, he realized he *had* given her cause to question his motives, albeit unintentionally. Yet he'd also known that she must have harbored some friendly feelings for him, or she wouldn't have taken his avoidance of her so deeply to heart.

Knowing that had pleased him more than he could say. And it had also given him hope. For what, he wasn't quite sure yet. But he liked the upbeat feeling all the same.

Thankfully, whatever minor disgruntlement there had been among the other teachers over his hiring of her had dissipated completely. Most of the staff had begun to accept Madelyn on her own merits, welcoming her gladly into their fold.

That, in turn, had made it possible for him to be more cordial to her at school without arousing any animosity. However, they were still fairly reserved with each other when they happened to cross paths.

Gabriel had been studiously avoiding certain issues, and he sensed Madelyn had been doing likewise. Neither of them mentioned Ethan when they were together, and whenever Brian did, one of them swiftly, yet skillfully, changed the subject. Also, while Madelyn had to be curious about how he had come to be raising Ethan's child, she had yet to introduce the subject. Of course, they were rarely alone for more than a few minutes. But Gabriel doubted she was the type to pry into such a private matter in any case.

Initially, Madelyn's reticence regarding Brian's paternity had been a relief. Lately, however, Gabriel had found himself wondering how she would react if he told her the truth about Ethan and Lily.

He'd had good reason to bear a grudge against his half brother all these years, and he was beginning to think Madelyn ought to know it. Yet he didn't want her feeling sorry for him.

Despite all the heartache he had suffered ten years ago, Gabriel knew he had been the lucky one. And with that knowledge had come a certain amount of forgiveness.

He wouldn't have traded the joy of having Brian in his life for anything. Nor would he have turned Ethan away if he'd chosen to come home to die.

The anger and bitterness he'd felt toward his brother—the same anger and bitterness he had directed Madelyn's way on their first meeting—had gradually begun to dissipate. After seeing the photographs she'd taken of Ethan, Gabriel found it hard to hang on to his hatred. He had also realized how much she must have done for Ethan. He had been glad that she'd been with Ethan at the end, and he had begun to understand, at last, why his brother had chosen to reward her in such a generous way.

Oddly enough, Gabriel wanted her to know *that* most of all. Now all he had to do was find the words to tell her. Along with the words to tell her that he still hadn't had any luck getting a loan to cover the entire sum he owed her.

But that was a whole other story—one he would rather postpone going into as long as possible. Luckily, she hadn't mentioned Ethan's will or the money she was due since he had told her he would need more time, so—

Frowning, Gabriel scanned the cars lined up in the school parking lot as he pulled into his space. Madelyn's sporty little compact wasn't among them. And a glance at the clock on the dashboard told him it was much too early for her lunch break.

So where was she?

Had she come to school as usual, only to be called away? And if so, why?

Her car had still been in the garage when he and Brian had left, but they'd departed earlier than usual because of Gabriel's meeting at the administration building. He was sure the lights had been on in the cottage, though.

Considering how cold it had been that morning, she could have had trouble starting her car. Since he'd already been gone, she would have had to take the bus, or maybe hitch a ride with someone else. Which was no big deal. Though he was still bothered by it.

Inside the building, Gabriel detoured out of his way, walking by Madelyn's classroom just to assure himself she'd gotten to school all right. But through the glass panel in the door he saw Eileen Duggan standing in front of Madelyn's fourth-period, eighth-grade math class.

Worried now, Gabriel walked hurriedly to his office.

"Where's Ms. St. James?" he asked, pausing by his secretary's desk. When she glanced up at him, a puzzled expression on her face, he added, "I saw Eileen in her classroom as I came in."

"Oh, she called in sick this morning. Ms. St. James, that is. Although I have a feeling Eileen isn't going to be feeling too good by the end of day, either," Trisha replied with a knowing smile.

"Probably not," Gabriel agreed.

More concerned than ever about Madelyn, he continued into his office, hung his overcoat on the coat tree and reached for the telephone as he sat in his desk chair.

She had been looking tired for the past couple of weeks. He had mentioned it to her twice, but each time she had fluffed it off. Maybe she had simply worn herself out by trying to do too much. He certainly hoped that was all it was. But in reality, he feared it might be something more than that.

What if she, too, had contracted some sort of virus while she'd been out of the country? Or what if she was pregnant with Ethan's child?

Neither possibility was completely out of the question. Over the past two years, she had traveled throughout Central and South America with Ethan. She could have easily, and unknowingly, picked up some sort of virulent bug along the way.

As for the other...

Ethan had died in mid-November. It was now the first week in February. Which meant she could be almost three months along—

Cursing under his breath, Gabriel dialed his home number. He found the thought of Madelyn carrying his half brother's child more distressing than he would have ever imagined, for reasons he absolutely refused to consider. Unlike Lily, she was really only an acquaintance.

Of course, that didn't mean he would let her struggle on her own. He would do whatever he could to help her. Whether she was pregnant—as he'd much prefer—or dying of some dreaded disease.

After two rings, Millie answered with a businesslike "Serrano residence."

Gabriel had forgotten she would be at the house today

and would probably pick up before Madelyn had a chance.

"Millie, this is Gabriel. Would you do me a favor?"

"Of course."

"Go over to the cottage and check on Ms. St. James for me. She called in sick this morning, and I just want to make sure she has everything she needs."

"Do you want to hold on or shall I call back?"

"Call back," he instructed as Trisha appeared in his office doorway with Ricky Montoya slouching sullenly beside her.

Apparently, the boy was in trouble yet again.

Gabriel had just enough time to lecture Ricky on the perils of shooting rubber bands instead of paying attention in class when the telephone on his desk finally buzzed. He sent the boy back to class with one last warning to shape up or spend the following week at the district's alternative learning center—a fate that would incur his mother's wrath and cost him the new skateboard he'd been promised if he stayed out of ALC for the rest of the semester. Then he grabbed the receiver.

"Your housekeeper's on line one," Trisha told him.

Gabriel thanked her, then punched the appropriate button.

"How is she?" he asked without preamble.

"Well, I don't rightly know," Millie replied, her concern evident. "I knocked on the door several times without getting any answer. Then I checked the garage to see if she'd gone off somewhere, but her car's there. 'Course, she could have been sleeping and just didn't hear me."

"Yes, that's possible."

"I can try again in an hour or so."

Gabriel thought for a moment, trying to decide what to do next. He didn't want to upset Millie, and he certainly didn't want to disturb Madelyn if she was resting. But after the way his imagination had been working overtime, he didn't think he could wait another hour or more to find out if she really was all right.

"I think I'll stop by the cottage myself in a little while," he said, making up his mind. "I was planning to run errands on my lunch hour anyway."

"I'll be here at the house," Millie stated. "Let me know if you need me for anything."

"I will, thanks."

Grabbing his overcoat, he strode out of his office just as the bell rang.

"I'm going out for a while," he said as he passed his secretary's desk. "I have several things to do, so I'm not sure when I'll be back."

"Don't worry. I'll hold down the fort for you," Trisha promised. "Although I may not have much luck running interference for you with Ms. Duggan."

"You know, I think I might actually be gone the rest of the day," he amended, grinning as he glanced back at her.

"Can't say I blame you."

With Trisha's laughter trailing him out into the noisy hallway, Gabriel dug the keys to his truck out of his coat pocket. Moving as quickly as he could through the teeming mass of students, he headed for the nearest exit, barely faltering when he heard his vice principal's strident voice calling his name.

He made the drive home in record time, pulled into the driveway behind Millie's ancient station wagon and went straight to the cottage. In the brilliant late-morning sunlight the place appeared to be deserted. The blinds on the windows were shut tight and not a wisp of smoke drifted from the chimney.

Gabriel rapped sharply on the door, waited what seemed like an eternity as the blasted dog snuffled and growled on the other side, then knocked harder, calling Madelyn's name in a voice that sounded frantic to his own ears.

Somewhere in the back of his mind, he realized he was on the verge of going off the deep end over a woman who should mean little or nothing but trouble to him. Yet sometime during the past month she had begun to stir up emotions in him as no woman had, including his ex-wife.

He kept forgetting that she had once been under Ethan's spell, and that surely *he* must pale in comparison. Instead, he had allowed himself to enjoy her company and to believe that she enjoyed his, as well. And though he had avoided dwelling on the possibility that she would ever be more than just a friend, he couldn't deny that desire lurked deep inside him, often surfacing at the oddest, most unexpected moments.

Now, perhaps not surprisingly, had also come a longing to protect and care for her that, more than likely, she wouldn't welcome—

"Who's there?"

"Gabriel," he answered, his concern deepening at the weak, raspy sound of her voice.

"Gabriel?" The lock clicked and she opened the door only partway, squinting at him in obvious confusion as she shushed the dog. "Why are you here?"

She was dressed in rumpled sweats and she did not look good. Her hair was a tousled mess, her eyes bleary, her face pale except for the bright spots of red high on each cheek.

"I was worried about you," he admitted, setting aside his pride. "They told me you'd called in sick this morning, and when I asked Millie to check on you, she couldn't seem to rouse you.''

Unable to stop himself, he reached out, resting the back of his hand against her forehead. She seemed startled, but stood still as he shifted his hand to the side of her face.

''You're burning up,'' he muttered.

''Mmm,'' she murmured. ''I was afraid of that. My throat's really sore, too.''

''What about headache and nausea?'' His hands on her shoulders, he turned her around, gave her a gentle push into the cottage and followed after her, ignoring the little dog's yap of protest.

''Yes, both.''

''Sounds like strep throat to me. Where's your coat?''

''Closet.'' She gestured with one hand. ''Why?''

''I'm taking you to the emergency medical clinic.''

''You don't have to do that,'' she protested.

''Oh, yes, I do. You're too sick to take yourself,'' he retorted. ''You'll never get well without antibiotics, and I want you well as soon as possible. Eileen Duggan had to take your classes today, and from what Trisha told me, she is not a happy camper.''

''Ah, I was wondering if you provided this service for all your teachers, but I see you have an ulterior motive,'' she teased, a slight smile curving the corners of her mouth as she let him help her on with her coat.

''Hey, cut me some slack. The woman scares me.'' Grinning, he led the way to his truck. ''She'd never agree to take your classes two days in a row. Then what would I do?''

''I'm not sure, but it's certainly nice to know I'm needed.''

"Believe me, you are," he said, realizing he meant it on more than one level.

Fortunately, they didn't have to wait long for Madelyn to see the doctor. His diagnosis matched Gabriel's, and after an injection to help stem the infection, he called in a prescription for her, then sent her on her way with strict orders to take it easy the rest of the weekend and not return to work until she'd been free of fever for at least twenty-four hours.

At the nearby pharmacy, Gabriel made her stay in the truck with the motor running while he ran inside to pick up her medication. Though greatly relieved that she hadn't been suffering from morning sickness or a fatal disease, he was still concerned about her well-being.

In fact, the thought of leaving her to fend for herself alone in the cottage made him so uneasy that by the time they arrived back at the house, he had decided she would be much better off staying in his guest room. However, when he broached the subject as they pulled into the driveway, Madelyn was anything but enthusiastic.

"I really appreciate the ride to the clinic, but I couldn't impose on you that way," she insisted.

"You wouldn't be."

"But I'm probably contagious. I don't want you and Brian getting sick, too."

"It's too late to worry about that. We've both been exposed to everything that's going around at school already."

She tipped her head back, closed her eyes and sighed wearily, a good indication he was wearing her down.

"All I'll probably do is sleep," she muttered.

"I know, but I'll feel a lot better knowing you're here with Millie the rest of the afternoon, then here with me and Brian tonight," he pressed.

She hesitated a long moment, then slanted a glance his way. "What about Buddy? I can't leave him in the cottage all alone overnight."

"Let me get you settled inside, then I'll bring him over to keep you company," he replied, wondering if she had any idea what a concession he was making.

He and the mutt had yet to find friendly common ground.

"All right," she agreed with what sounded like relief.

Leaving Madelyn in Millie's capable hands, Gabriel walked across to the cottage, said a few, brief, laying-down-the-law words of warning to the dog, gathered a few of Madelyn's things for her, then returned to the house.

Buddy trotted along beside him suspiciously until he spied Madelyn, already tucked into bed, asleep, in the guest room, and happily hurried to join her.

Watching as the creature hopped onto the bed and curled up beside her, Gabriel experienced a pang of jealousy. He wouldn't have minded doing the same thing. But he didn't think he'd be anywhere near as welcome as the dog.

He could just imagine Madelyn staring at him in consternation, wondering what he was after.

More than the obvious, he thought. Much more…

Turning away reluctantly, he walked back to the kitchen, said a few words to Millie, then headed out to his truck feeling unaccountably lighthearted considering he'd decided to go back to school and face Eileen Duggan, after all.

He would rather deal with her this afternoon than put it off until Monday. Then he wouldn't have *that* hanging over his head to spoil the weekend. He could look after Madelyn and personally see to it that she got well again.

Not the most exciting way to spend two days off, but he certainly didn't mind. And for some reason, he didn't think she would, either. Of course, he could be wrong, but he hoped not.

Although she was fairly sure it was Saturday, Madelyn had no idea what time it was when she first awoke and realized she was feeling better—*much* better. With the blinds on the windows drawn and the door closed, the guest room in Gabriel's house was more dark than light and very quiet.

But when she turned onto her side, she spied a slim shaft of sunlight that had somehow breached the barrier to slide across the floor. And off in the distance, faint but recognizable, she heard Brian's young voice punctuated by the playful yips and growls of her adopted dog.

Glancing at the clock on the nightstand, she saw that it was nearly twelve o'clock. Which meant she'd been sleeping on and off for almost twenty-four hours. She could never remember indulging herself so luxuriantly when she had been ill in the past. But then, living in St. Louis she'd had too many responsibilities—dictated by the wants and needs of her parents, brothers and sisters-in-law—to consider herself first. Luckily, she had rarely been as sick as she'd been yesterday.

Just being able to stay home and nurse herself back to health would have been a blessing. But having Millie, then Gabriel and Brian looking after her had been truly wonderful. She hadn't even had to remember when to take her medication. All she'd had to do was rest, and apparently that was just what she had needed most.

Rolling onto her back again, Madelyn stared at the shadowy ceiling. Her throat was no longer raw, her head no longer ached and the thought of putting something in her stomach besides the orange juice Gabriel had insisted she try to drink was downright appealing. But first she wanted to shower, wash her hair and change into fresh clothes.

Pushing herself up on her elbows, she noticed a pair of her flannel pajamas and her flannel robe laid out on the chair near the bathroom doorway, and realized all three were possible.

Bless Gabriel. He really had thought of everything. He must be as anxious to get her back to work as he'd said he was. Yet she couldn't believe that was the only reason he had been so concerned about her.

Or maybe she just didn't want to.

Imagining herself as someone he thought of in any special way was just plain silly. Aside from taking Gloria Munoz's job at the junior high school, she had caused him more problems than anything else since she'd shown up on his doorstep in Cullen Birney's company, claiming to own half of his home.

But Gabriel had proven to be a responsible man with a streak of kindness that he probably couldn't help but extend toward anyone who seemed in need of help. Considering the way she had looked when she answered the door yesterday, he would have had to be much more hard-hearted than he was to abandon her.

Talk about seeing her at her very worst. It was a miracle he hadn't turned tail and run.

Grinning at the thought, Madelyn finally crawled out of bed, and after a moment's dizziness, scooped up the clothes on the chair and walked into the bathroom.

Thirty minutes later, she felt almost herself again. With her robe belted tightly at her waist, a pair of thick, wool socks on her feet in lieu of slippers and her hair pulled back with a clip she'd found in her purse, she ventured down the hallway toward the sounds and luscious scents emanating from the kitchen.

Pausing in the doorway, Madelyn caught sight of Gabriel standing by the stove, his back to her, stirring a steaming pot. Through the French doors she also saw Brian and Buddy frolicking on the wide patch of grass just beyond the patio in the sunny courtyard.

There was such a warm, homey feel to the scene that for just an instant, she felt tears prickle at the back of her eyes. How she would love to be a permanent part of their lives instead of a barely welcome visitor being shown a little charity.

To live here with a good man like Gabriel and bright young boy like Brian would be her own very personal dream come true. She'd had all the adventure she ever wanted working with Ethan. She had come to Santa Fe to make a home for herself and hopefully to have a family, never suspecting she would find exactly what she wanted—*needed*—so close, yet so very, very far away.

"You're looking a lot better," Gabriel said, drawing her attention back to him.

Madelyn wondered how long he had been watching her watch his son and the dog, then realized it didn't really matter. Blinking the moisture from her eyes, she pasted a smile on her face as she sat in one of the chairs by the table.

"I'm feeling a lot better, too," she replied. "Thanks to you."

"I didn't do all that much."

"You took me to the doctor and gave me a place to rest without interruption. You also made sure I took my pills and drank lots of juice. Lots and *lots* of juice. And I appreciate it."

He nodded, acknowledging her thanks with a smile of his own, then said, "I bet you're hungry."

"*Very* hungry," she admitted with a grin.

"How does homemade chicken-noodle soup and hot biscuits sound?"

"Wonderful." She gestured toward the cabinets. "Tell me where you keep the dishes and I'll set the table."

"Stay put. I'll have Brian do it when he comes in."

As if on cue, the door opened and both boy and dog scampered inside on a gust of frosty air. Seeing her, Buddy made a beeline across the tile floor, his nails clicking, then bounded into her lap and licked her chin excitedly.

"Are you feeling better now?" Brian asked as he shrugged out of his denim jacket and hung it over a chair.

"Lots," she assured him as she laughingly held the dog away from her.

"Good." He grinned at her, then went to the sink to wash his hands. "We can play Scrabble after lunch, then watch the movies my dad rented. We saved them so you could see them, too."

Madelyn glanced hesitantly at Gabriel. Having lunch with them was obviously expected of her. Beyond that, she didn't want to wear out her welcome. Especially now that she wouldn't have any trouble managing on her own back at the cottage.

"Don't forget—you promised us a rematch," Gabriel reminded her. "And I lucked out at the video store. They had two new releases I think we'll all enjoy."

"Sounds good to me," she agreed at last, glad that he had made it all but impossible for her to cut and run when she really did want to stay.

What difference did it make if she left after lunch or

before dinner as long as they were happy to have her around?

By the time they had finished their game and watched one of the movies, it was almost dinnertime. Gabriel ordered pizza and they settled in to watch the second movie. When it ended, Gabriel hustled Brian off to put on his pajamas while Madelyn gathered up their plates and cups, loaded the dishwasher and wrapped the leftover pizza in foil.

As Gabriel joined her in the kitchen again, she took a last swipe at the counters with the dishcloth, then folded it neatly over the faucet.

"You didn't have to do that," he said, filling the coffeemaker with water.

"After all you've done, it was my pleasure," she assured him.

"Want some coffee? I'm making decaf."

"I really should be going," she demurred. "It's getting late—"

"And risk catching a chill? No way," Gabriel stated in a manner that left little room for argument. "You're staying the night."

Madelyn knew he meant as a guest sleeping in the extra bedroom. But for the space of a heartbeat, she found herself imagining what the night might have held for her if he had actually intended her to share his bed.

Would he have been tender with her?

Oh, yes, she believed he would—

"Now that's settled, do you want coffee or not?" he prodded.

"Yes, I'll have some," she hastened to reply.

Embarrassed by her lascivious thoughts, she fiddled with the belt on her robe as Gabriel scooped coffee into the filter basket. For her emotional well-being, she knew she shouldn't stay. But he was right. Going out into the cold night air wouldn't do her any good. And she certainly wasn't as ready to leave the warmth and coziness of the house or to give up Gabriel's company as she knew she ought to be.

"Why don't you go on back to the living room? I'll have the coffee ready in a few minutes."

Madelyn tuned in the local news on the television, then settled into one of the overstuffed chairs, drawing her legs up under her. Buddy, snoozing by the fire, opened one eye to check on her, but didn't budge otherwise.

He didn't seem to have any problem with staying another night in Gabriel's house, either. Maybe the two of them were finally becoming friends. Although she couldn't say she had seen any real signs of it yet.

If Madelyn hadn't known better, she would say they were vying for her affection. With Buddy, that was quite possible. He had obviously been abandoned at least once already. As a result, he would need her constant reassurance that it wouldn't happen again. But Gabriel was another story altogether. While his animosity toward her had faded, he'd given no indication at all that he wanted anything more from her than cordiality.

Gabriel followed almost immediately, the glass carafe full of steaming coffee in one hand, two white china mugs in the other. Brian, dressed in red pajamas covered with blue and green spaceships, was right behind him, lobbying to stay up a little longer.

When his father refused to be swayed, the boy yawned, smiled sleepily and wished her good-night. Then he and Gabriel headed back to his bedroom.

Madelyn poured the coffee and watched the news until Gabriel returned. He sprawled in the chair across from her, took the mug she offered him and sat back with a sigh of obvious contentment.

"He was asleep before I left the room," he said.

"He looked tired."

"Sometimes he goes until he can't anymore. I wish I had that kind of energy."

"He's a good kid," Madelyn said, taking a sip of her coffee. "Really well adjusted."

"Considering his real father never acknowledged him, his mother abandoned him when he was only a year old and I've been raising him alone ever since?" Gabriel asked.

Though there wasn't any hint of sarcasm in his voice, Madelyn stared into her mug, her cheeks burning with embarrassment.

"That's not what I meant," she murmured.

She had made the comment innocently enough, and wished Gabriel had taken it that way. Instead, he had brought up the one subject she would have never mentioned herself—Brian's parentage.

"I know you didn't, but it's still true," Gabriel stated as he picked up the remote and switched off the television.

Madelyn wasn't sure what to do—plead weariness and escape to the guest room, sit quietly and hope he would choose something else to talk about or use the opening he had given her and satisfy her curiosity. Excusing herself would be the wisest thing to do, but then, she would probably never have another chance to find out how Gabriel had ended up raising his half brother's son.

"He thinks of Ethan as his uncle, and for the time being, there's nothing wrong with that. As for his mother, he's never mentioned her to me," she ventured at last, her tone tentative.

"He's seen pictures of her, but he was just a baby when she left me, so he doesn't have any real memory of her. I'm not sure whether he misses her or not. He hasn't talked about her much since he started preschool. That's when he first realized most children had mothers living at home.

"He asked what happened to her then, and I tried to explain as best I could that her leaving had nothing to do with him. She just needed something more than I could give her."

"What about Ethan?" Madelyn demanded, the anger she felt on Gabriel's behalf getting the better of her. "Something tells me *he* was more to blame for her unhappiness than you."

"That's quite possible, but I couldn't very well tell a four-year-old boy that the man I'd always referred to as his uncle was really his father," he retorted.

"But you'll have to one day."

"Yes, I know."

"Are you going to paint yourself as the bad guy then, too?" she goaded.

"How do you know I wasn't?"

He shot her a challenging look that she met with surprising steadiness.

"I don't. At least not for sure. And I won't…unless you tell me what happened," she added.

She never would have thought she'd have the nerve to confront him in such a brash manner. But he had been the one to set the course of their conversation, and now she wanted to hear what he had to say.

"It's not a very pretty story."

"No, I don't imagine it is."

He looked away from her, staring into the distance.

"Ten years ago, my mother and father, Ethan's stepfather, were killed in an automobile accident,'' he began. ''Ethan came home for the funeral. He seemed as devastated as I was, at least about our mother, and since he was between assignments, he decided to move into the cottage and stay awhile.

''I was living in an apartment, teaching and going to graduate school at the time. I was also engaged to a girl I'd met in Albuquerque. Lily and I were planning to marry that summer after she graduated from college.

''To make a long story short, Ethan and Lily really hit it off. At first, I was glad. Then, gradually I began to wonder if they were more than just friends. Ethan was always around, and all of a sudden, Lily had one excuse or another why we couldn't make love. I kept telling myself they wouldn't do that to me. Until I found them in bed together in the cottage.''

''Oh, Gabriel—''

''I was furious,'' he cut in. Blatantly ignoring her sympathetic murmuring, he finally met her gaze. ''I told Lily the engagement was off. I also made it clear I never wanted to see her again. I knew Ethan was leaving in a few days, and I figured he would take her with him.''

''Only, he didn't,'' Madelyn said.

''No. That hadn't been part of his plan. But I didn't find out until two months later. Lily showed up at my apartment. She wanted me to help her track down Ethan. She was carrying his child and she was sure he would come back for her once he knew. Ethan, however, couldn't have cared less about *her* problem, and didn't hesitate to let both of us know it.

''So I offered to marry her. I still cared for her, and fool that I was, I thought she'd eventually get over him. I couldn't have been more wrong. She waited for him to come back, and when he didn't, she stuck around until she found someone equally exciting—her words, not mine. Said she wasn't cut out to be a wife and mother, after all.

"She moved back to Albuquerque with her new boy-friend, and I filed for divorce. I also sought sole custody of Brian. She signed the papers without a murmur of protest, and I haven't seen or heard from her since."

"I always wondered why Ethan never mentioned any-thing at all about his family," she said. "Now I know. To seduce his brother's fiancée, then abandon his own child—"

Madelyn now understood why Ethan hadn't considered returning to Santa Fe when he realized he was dying. After the havoc he had wreaked, coming face-to-face with Gabriel again would have taken more nerve than even he'd had.

"Obviously, I didn't know either one of them as well as I thought I did," Gabriel admitted.

He stood, paced across the room and paused by one of the windows. Opening the blinds, he stared into the darkness.

"Lily was young and impressionable, and Ethan was not only older, but more worldly-wise than I could have ever hoped to be. I was trying to work and go to school and deal with my parents' deaths. I didn't have much time for either of them. I imagine they were bored, and unfortunately, one thing obviously led to another."

"But that doesn't excuse what either of them did to you. *They* were the ones at fault, not you," Madelyn protested.

"In the end, they were also the ones who lost out," Gabriel replied quietly as he returned to his chair. "I have a wonderful son who means more than anything to me.

Because of him and the happiness he's brought me, I've been able to set aside most of my anger.''

Most, but not all, Madelyn thought. Ethan had betrayed Gabriel in the one way most men found unforgivable. And then, he had betrayed his brother again from the grave by leaving his half of the house to her.

She still couldn't quite grasp why he had done it. The Ethan she had known had been no choirboy. But he hadn't been unconscionably cruel, either. Surely he had realized how her arrival in Santa Fe would affect Gabriel.

Though she had considered Gabriel's behavior boorish when they first met, knowing what she did now, Madelyn marveled at the control he had managed to display. In fact, she found it nothing short of a miracle that he had been able to be as kind to her as he'd been since then.

Turning away, she stared at the embers glowing faintly in the fireplace.

"I'm not sure I could be that generous," she murmured as much to herself as to him.

"I have to admit I wasn't, either. Until recently," he replied. "But knowing how he died…I wouldn't have wished that on anyone."

"No, you wouldn't have, would you?"

"I'm glad you were with him at the end. I owe you for that, Madelyn."

Not really, she thought. Not when there was a good chance Ethan had taken his own life because she had failed to read the signals he'd been giving off, and thus hadn't gotten him the help he needed.

For that, she deserved nothing but Gabriel's disdain. Not the quarter of a million dollars Ethan's half of the house was worth.

As Madelyn had known almost from the moment she'd first seen Brian, she was going to have to tell Gabriel she didn't want the money, after all. What he had told her about Ethan and Lily only made it that much more imperative.

And she would, she vowed. But not just yet. She wanted a little more time in the cottage, a little more time with Gabriel and Brian, before she finally forged ahead on her own.

"I didn't do anything more for him than anyone else would have done in the same situation," she said.

"I'm not so sure of that. Ethan could be a demanding, self-centered bastard," Gabriel stated bluntly. "And I have a feeling you're often much too nice for your own good. I doubt he found it all that hard to take advantage of you."

"He wasn't all bad," Madelyn protested.

"I never meant to imply that he was. For you to have cared for him as much as you did, he must have developed some redeeming qualities."

Again, Gabriel seemed to be assuming that she and Ethan had been lovers.

Madelyn wanted to set him straight, but it was late and suddenly she was very tired. What good would it do anyway? She could deny it all she wanted, but there was only one way she could prove it to him—by making love with him and letting him find out for himself that she was still a virgin. But she couldn't do that without his cooperation. And after all he'd told her, she doubted that would be forthcoming.

"Yes, he did," she agreed simply, then stood, coffee mug in hand. "And, on that note, I think I'd better call it a night."

By the fireplace, Buddy scrambled to his feet and trotted over to her. Gabriel, on the other hand, stayed in his chair, looking up at her, his expression unreadable.

''Sleep as late as you want in the morning,'' he said.

''I probably will.''

With the little dog trailing after her, Madelyn headed for the kitchen. Although she sensed Gabriel watching her, she didn't glance back.

She couldn't risk staying in the same room with him a moment longer. The temptation to bare her soul to him had grown too strong, and doing so would only signal the beginning of the end of her right, however small, to a place in his life.

And that she wasn't about to give up. Not until she had no other choice.

Chapter 7

For a long time after Madelyn went to bed, Gabriel sat in the living room, thinking about the conversation they'd had. All day, he had been waiting, subconsciously, for an opportunity to tell her about Ethan and Lily. He'd had no idea how she would respond, but he had wanted her to know about that part of his past.

Considering the kind of relationship he assumed she'd had with Ethan, her anger at the injustice she seemed to feel *he* had been done had been quite a surprise. Gabriel had expected her to come to Ethan's defense. He had never imagined she would take *his* part instead.

Gabriel had also thought that talking about Ethan and Lily would be much more painful, but it seemed his wounds really had begun to heal. He had even been able to acknowledge—for the first time—that he hadn't been completely blameless himself.

Lily had been a self-absorbed, frivolous young girl. But that hadn't mattered to him. He had been attracted to her giddy, fun-loving ways. She had seemed ideally suited to counterbalance his own more serious nature. Foolishly, he had never suspected that when the going got rough for him, she would seek out a good time somewhere else rather than stand by him.

A good time that Ethan, for whatever reason, had been more than willing to provide.

His brother had obviously recognized Lily for what she was, and had set about making sure Gabriel did, too—proving himself the smarter man, and thus, the better man, yet again.

Finding them together had been no accident, but rather a setup of Ethan's engineering. He had insisted Gabriel meet him at the cottage, and he'd been specific about the time. Finding Ethan and Lily in bed together had shocked and sickened him, but Gabriel couldn't say he had been taken by surprise. As he had told Madelyn, he'd had his suspicions. Especially when Lily had lost interest in sleeping with him. Yet he had chosen to avoid a confrontation until Ethan finally forced his hand.

But that was all in the distant past. And he *had* come out ahead in the end. He had gotten over Lily once and for all, he had a wonderful son whom he loved deeply and now he also had…Madelyn. In a way.

She was a strong, sensible woman, good and decent and kind, and lovely, quite lovely in more ways than one. A woman who had believed in him *fiercely* despite the fact that by all accounts her first loyalty should have been to Ethan.

As he had caught himself doing more and more lately, Gabriel wished he'd met Madelyn St. James under other circumstances—circumstances that precluded her ever having known Ethan Merritt.

Of course, her prior relationship with Ethan hadn't

caused her to look upon him unfavorably yet. And she'd given no indication it ever would. So maybe, just maybe, she might not be all that averse to the possibility of their going beyond friendship. Quite a ways beyond…

After Lily, Gabriel had been certain he would never marry again. Now, however, he found the idea of taking Madelyn St. James as his lawfully wedded wife very appealing. In fact, he couldn't believe he was just now thinking of it.

If he married Madelyn, he would be able to keep the house without going deeply into debt. In addition, he would finally be able to give Brian the kind of mother he deserved. She obviously cared for the boy, and she knew the truth about his paternity. Knew and understood, as well as accepted that one day he would have to be told everything.

Instinctively, Gabriel knew that Madelyn would be more than capable of easing whatever anguish the boy might experience when that time came.

And being married to Madelyn St. James would be no great sacrifice on his part, Gabriel mused with a slight smile. Just the thought of bedding her aroused him in such a profound way that denying how much he desired her physically would have been laughable.

He would have to court her, of course. Slowly, yet inexorably, until she found marriage to him an appealing alternative to the single life-style she seemed intent on leading. She deserved that much from him. And the thought of wooing her filled him with a sense of anticipation, not to mention excitement, the likes of which he hadn't experienced in years.

Of course, the attraction would have to be mutual. Otherwise, they would never survive together over the long haul.

Gabriel wanted that stability. He also needed it—not only for himself, but for Brian, as well. He had tried to be the best possible father he could, but he knew the boy had missed having a mother. A mother he could count on to be there for him through good times and bad. A mother who would provide a kinder, gentler, more sensitive role model for him as he grew into manhood.

Granted, Madelyn might find the idea of acquiring a ready-made family totally repugnant. But what could it hurt to explore certain possibilities? If she wasn't receptive, then so be it.

Though it was probably no more than wishful thinking on his part, Gabriel had a feeling she wouldn't reject him out of hand. She had made no effort to hide the fact that she enjoyed their company. Nor had she made a secret of her fondness for Brian. As far as he knew, there wasn't anyone else in her life, either. And he wasn't exactly pond scum.

He would be good to her. Good and faithful and true. And he would do his best to see that she had everything she wanted.

Unfortunately, what he couldn't do was fall head over heels in love with her. He'd gone down that road before, and it wasn't for him.

Gabriel doubted that would be a problem. Because Madelyn probably wouldn't be inclined to fall head over heels in love with him, either. After Ethan, he imagined she was just as gun-shy as he about that kind of emotional involvement.

However, that didn't mean they couldn't still find some measure of happiness together. As much happiness as two people could share after all that Ethan had put them through....

Inordinately pleased that he had come up with such a

mature and thoughtful analysis of the situation, Gabriel stood and switched off the lamp. From long practice, he easily made his way across the darkened living room toward the hallway leading into the kitchen. Guided by the night-light above the stove, he crossed to the French doors and checked the lock, then headed for his bedroom.

As he did every night, he stopped first in Brian's room. Standing over his soundly sleeping young son for several moments, he marveled yet again at how lucky he had been. Without Brian to love and care for, he might very well have turned into a truly bitter, angry man. But the boy's innocent joy in all life had to offer had been irresistible, and for that, Gabriel would be forever thankful.

Gently he ruffled Brian's hair, tugged the comforter around his shoulders, then moved back into the hallway. He did no more than glance into his office. He had stacks of paperwork waiting to be done, but he wasn't about to tackle that tonight. He'd only end up aggravated, and the day had been too nice to spoil in such an unavailing way.

However, at the partially closed door to the guest room, Gabriel paused again. Intending to close the door completely so he and Brian wouldn't disturb Madelyn in the morning, he reached for the knob. Then, against all rules of propriety, he eased the door open and silently stepped across the threshold.

In the darkness, he could just barely see her, curled on her side beneath the bedcovers, facing toward him. She appeared to be deeply asleep, so deeply asleep, he didn't think he would disturb her by moving a little closer to the bed, then a little closer still.

After the trail his thoughts had taken earlier, he had to admit it was only natural he'd be drawn to her. But at the same time, he was honest enough to acknowledge that he had no right to be there. She was a guest in his home, and for all intents and purposes, he was invading the very privacy he had promised she would have there.

Apparently, Buddy was in total agreement. Immediately alert to Gabriel's presence, the little dog sat up where he'd been sleeping at the foot of the bed—beady eyes glaring, wiry hair bristling—and emitted a low, throaty growl.

"Don't worry, mutt," Gabriel growled back, his voice equally low and throaty. "I'm keeping my distance."

"Gabriel?"

With a quiet sigh, Madelyn shifted onto her back and blinked up at him sleepily.

"Sorry, I didn't mean to wake you," he murmured.

"Is something wrong?"

She pushed up on her elbows, eyeing him with such concern that he wanted to stretch out beside her, gather her into his arms and assure her everything was actually *quite* all right. But he couldn't. Not without scaring her half to death.

Until she understood that his intentions were honorable, he intended to mind his manners. He was a patient man. He could wait to satisfy the longing that suddenly burned deep inside him until she willingly invited him into her bed.

"No, not at all," he said, then added hastily when her expression grew wary, "I was just checking to make sure you were resting comfortably."

"Oh."

Still meeting his gaze uncertainly, she sank back on her pillow.

"Need anything?"

"Not that I can think of." A soft smile played at the corners of her mouth.

He knew he should get out of there fast, but he

couldn't keep from lingering a few moments longer. She looked so appealing snuggled into the bed, her hair tousled, her eyes drowsy, her luscious lips slightly parted.

"Did you remember to take your pills?"

"Yes."

"Well, then, I'd better let you get some rest."

"Yes," she repeated, her smile widening ruefully.

Gabriel wondered if she had any idea what torture it was for him to act like a gentleman rather than give in to the base instincts she stirred in him. Probably not. She wasn't coming on to him. She was just being her own sweet and, more than likely, unknowingly sexy self.

Which made it even more imperative that he maintain some semblance of self-control. The last thing he wanted to do was upset her.

"As I said earlier, sleep as late as you want."

"I will."

With a nod of acknowledgment, Gabriel strode out of the room, pulling the door shut after him, then headed straight to his bedroom without the slightest hesitation. After a quick, cold shower that did little to ease his aching need, he crawled into bed, futilely hoping he'd be able to get some sleep.

Much to his dismay, none of the relaxation techniques he normally employed seemed to work. Giving up, he allowed his mind to wander back to Madelyn and the decisions he'd made concerning their relationship. Since he couldn't sleep anyway, he figured he might as well start working on a plan of action.

He would have to begin his campaign as soon as possible. But he would have to go slowly, and the less obvious he was about it, the better. Asking her out all of a sudden—without including Brian—would more than likely arouse her suspicions. Yet he couldn't initiate a courtship if they were constantly part of a threesome.

What he needed was an innocent as well as acceptable reason to spend a little time alone with her—

With a slow smile, Gabriel thought of the Valentine's dance at the school the following Friday night. Talk about the perfect opportunity.

The entire faculty was expected to chaperon, so both he and Madelyn would have to be there. Brian, on the other hand, wouldn't. In fact, arrangements had already been made for him to stay the night with his best friend, Donny.

Gabriel could casually suggest that she hitch a ride to the school with him, and take it from there. The dance was scheduled from seven until ten. They'd be anything but alone then. Afterward, however... Even stopping somewhere for coffee and dessert would be a start.

After that, casually inviting her out to dinner would follow quite naturally, as would other excursions, occasionally sans Brian. With luck, they would be as compatible as he hoped, and eventually, he would be able to convince her to be his wife.

He couldn't promise they would live happily ever after, but he *would* vow to give it his best shot. Once he'd determined she was willing to do likewise.

With a good deal more reluctance than the situation warranted, Madelyn gathered her things together to finally return to the cottage late Sunday afternoon. She had known all along her stay in Gabriel's house was only temporary, but she had enjoyed being there with him and his son more than she liked to admit.

Glad that they had seemed in no hurry to see her go, she had lingered over a late breakfast and the Sunday papers. Then, at Brian's eager invitation, she had joined in yet another game of Scrabble.

When the game ended, she had insisted it was time for her to go. Gabriel had urged her to wait until after dinner, but she had remained firm in her decision, pleading work to be done in preparation for her return to school the next day.

After eliciting her agreement to leave all tidying up of the guest room to Millie, who would be at the house the following day, he had acquiesced to her wishes. Then he'd gone ahead to start a fire in the fireplace for her.

Now, with a wave to Brian, she crossed the shadowed courtyard, carrying her few belongings in her tote bag, Buddy happily scampering along beside her.

Back to reality, she thought sadly, acknowledging how easily one got used to a little pampering, especially when it was so generously given.

Having been alone more often than not in her free time, she had also appreciated Brian and Gabriel's company. Not once while she'd been at the house had she felt the least bit lonely. In fact, she had quickly realized there was nowhere else she'd rather be than there with them.

Even discussing Ethan, as she and Gabriel had done late Saturday night, seemed right in retrospect. Talking about the past hadn't been easy for Gabriel, yet he had shared more about himself with her than Madelyn imagined he had ever shared with anyone else.

She wished she had the courage to be equally honest with him. But as she'd known last night, that would probably signal the end of their relationship. Much as she hated the idea that Gabriel was being kind to her because he believed he owed her something, she wasn't ready to walk away just yet.

Moving back to the cottage was proving to be difficult enough. She couldn't bear the thought of being cut off completely from Gabriel and Brian. Surely wanting to avoid that anguish for a few more weeks was only natural. And she wasn't really hurting anyone by allowing Gabriel to think kindly of her for a little while longer.

Nudging the cottage door open, Buddy trotted inside with a proprietary air. Smiling, Madelyn followed. The little dog had turned out to be a real character. She sincerely hoped no one would ever claim him, because she wasn't sure she could part with him.

Ignoring Gabriel, Buddy hopped onto the sofa and flopped down with a contented sigh.

"Looks like he's glad to be home," Gabriel said, glancing at the dog, then at her as he adjusted the fire screen.

"Probably not as glad as you are to be rid of him," Madelyn replied as she set her tote bag on the floor and unbuttoned her coat.

"I can't say we're the best of friends yet, but maybe one day...."

"Yes, maybe one day," Madelyn agreed with a wistfulness she couldn't quite hide.

"Are you sure you're going to be all right over here?" Gabriel asked as he started toward the door.

His concern for her was as evident now as it had been the night before when she'd awakened to find him standing beside her bed. At first, she hadn't known what to think, but after a few moments she had realized how seriously he'd taken his self-imposed job of looking after her.

Now, as then, her heart warmed with a sense of gratitude she hadn't the words to adequately express.

"I'll be just fine," she assured him. "My fever's gone and I'm feeling a lot better."

"What about dinner—?"

"I'll heat up some leftovers if I get hungry."

"You don't *have* to come in tomorrow," he reminded her for the umpteenth time. "If I can't get a substitute, Eileen can take your classes."

"Unless I have a major relapse, which I doubt will happen, I'll be there."

Standing at the door, Gabriel gazed at her, a surprisingly speculative gleam in his dark eyes. Madelyn had only a moment or two to wonder what he had in mind before he spoke again.

"If you're determined to teach tomorrow, then at least let me give you a ride to school. I can drop you off at the door so you won't have to tramp across the parking lot and risk catching another chill."

"I appreciate the offer, but I'm not sure that's such a good idea," she hedged uncomfortably. "The others might think you're playing favorites."

"They already know you're living in my cottage and that you were hired at my insistence," he reminded her. "They also know you're a darn good teacher who's worked wonders with some of our most problematic students. And, thanks to Eileen Duggan's muttering, they know you were out sick on Friday.

"Personally, I don't think they'll begrudge my giving you a lift to help keep you healthy. Especially if it keeps Eileen happy, as well."

Put that way, Madelyn couldn't argue with him. It would be easier on her to let him do the driving. But only tomorrow, she vowed.

"All right, what time should I be ready?"

"Seven-thirty."

"I'll see you then."

"Yeah, see you then."

With a nod and a truly enigmatic smile, Gabriel let himself out of the cottage.

As the door clicked shut quietly, Madelyn joined Buddy on the sofa. The dog immediately climbed into her lap and rolled onto his back so she could rub his belly. Petting him, she stared into the fire, wondering again what Gabriel was up to.

Maybe her imagination was working overtime, but it seemed to her he'd been quite taken with the idea of giving her a ride to school. More so than such a simple favor warranted.

Try as she might, though, she couldn't come up with any viable ulterior motive he could have. Finally she gave up, shifted the dog off her lap and crossed to the table where she'd left her books and papers.

Much as she hated to admit it, her respite was over. She really did have work to do—a lot of work. Still, as late afternoon turned to early evening, her mind wandered more than once to thoughts of Gabriel standing by the cottage door, looking much too much like a cat who'd caught the canary.

What Madelyn had meant to be a onetime occurrence turned, instead, into a daily ritual, thanks to Gabriel's quiet insistence. Claiming he should have realized sooner how silly it was for both of them to take their cars to school, he somehow managed to convince her that riding with him and Brian was not only wise, but also economical.

She didn't put up much of an argument since she did enjoy their company on the relatively short commute. And, to her credit, she did offer to take a turn at driving.

However, since Gabriel often needed his truck during the day for trips to the school's district office, they agreed switching off wouldn't really be feasible.

None of the other faculty members seemed to notice their new arrangement, or if they did, no one seemed to take exception to it. After several days, meeting Gabriel and Brian outside the garage at seven-thirty in the morning had become almost routine, pleasantly routine.

Unfortunately, parting with them when they returned in the afternoon wasn't quite as gratifying. Much as she loved the cozy comfort of the little cottage, she would have much preferred to spend her evenings at the house with Gabriel and Brian. Having had a taste of what living with them would be like, she wasn't as happy, or as satisfied, as she'd once been on her own.

Of course, she was careful not to let them know that. She refused to impose on Gabriel more than she already did. Not when she was afraid she was pushing her luck as it was. And since Brian came to visit at the cottage as usual on Monday and Thursday, she wasn't exactly isolated.

In all honesty, what she missed most was just sitting in front of the fire, talking with Gabriel as they'd done Saturday night. They had shared a closeness then that she longed to rekindle. Although, given a choice, she would rather not discuss Ethan again.

While he had been their link at the outset, eventually, when she mustered the courage to tell Gabriel what she believed to be the truth about his death, he could also prove to be the wedge that ultimately drove them apart.

However, their relationship with Ethan certainly wasn't all they had in common. Given the opportunity, Madelyn was sure they would find lots of other things to discuss. Like what Gabriel was building out in his workshop, or the series of photographs she'd taken of Santa Fe now on display at Henry Martin's gallery, or school, or Brian, or even Buddy—

"You're awfully quiet," Gabriel said. "Not starting to feel sick again, are you?"

Drawn from her reverie, Madelyn glanced at Gabriel and smiled reassuringly.

"Not at all," she said.

They were in the truck, headed home from school late Friday afternoon after dropping Brian off at Donny Murphy's house. Since she and Gabriel would be at the school's Valentine dance all evening, he had arranged for his son to spend the night with his best friend.

"That's good. I wouldn't want you to miss out on all the fun tonight," Gabriel teased.

"Actually, I'm looking forward to it," Madelyn admitted.

"Then you've obviously forgotten how chaotic riding herd on a gymnasium full of preteens surging to the beat of the latest grunge rock and hip-hop can be."

"That's true. But then, I haven't gotten out much lately."

"You haven't, have you?" Gabriel said as he pulled into the driveway. Then he added casually, "But we can certainly change that."

Disconcerted by his use of the word *we,* Madelyn said nothing as she gathered her tote bag and purse. She hadn't intended her comment as a play for sympathy. Nor had she been angling for a date. But how could she explain that without looking more foolish than she already felt?

Seeming totally unaware of her embarrassment, and apparently expecting no reply, Gabriel hopped out of the truck, walked around to the passenger door and opened it for her.

"Got everything?" he asked.

"Yes."

Avoiding his gaze, she took his proffered hand and stepped onto the driveway.

"I guess we'd better try to leave around six-fifteen. Even though the dance isn't supposed to start until seven, there will be the usual early arrivals."

"We're going together?" Madelyn eyed Gabriel questioningly, wondering if she'd understood him correctly.

She was going to the dance, but as far as she knew, not with—

"Yes, together. No sense in your driving there alone," he stated matter-of-factly.

Somehow it had never occurred to Madelyn that he expected her to go with him. He hadn't said anything until just now. But then, they'd been riding back and forth to school together all week. Unlike her, he had probably just taken for granted they'd do the same tonight. And since she couldn't think of any reason why they shouldn't, she agreed quite happily.

"No, no sense at all."

"I'll stop by the cottage for you at six-fifteen, then."

Though Madelyn kept reminding herself that Gabriel was just being pragmatic, she flitted around the cottage— Buddy close at her heels—thoughts of the evening ahead filling her with anticipation.

One would have thought he was whisking her away to a romantic rendezvous rather than to a preteen dance at the local junior high school where they would more than likely spend most of the time apart. But to Madelyn that was infinitely more appealing than spending another night alone.

To ensure that as many students as possible attended, dancing to music provided by a disc jockey was actually only one of several activities planned by the PTA for the evening. A cakewalk, bingo game and a variety of carnival booths along with a refreshment stand had been set up in the gymnasium, and dress had been designated as casual.

Standing in front of her closet, Madelyn mulled over what to wear. Originally, she had planned to don tailored slacks and a sweater. But when she reached into the closet, her hand latched on to the simple black wool dress she hadn't been able to resist buying while she'd been in St. Louis.

The slim sheath accentuated her slender curves, while the white satin collar and French cuffs added a modest touch of elegance. She would probably be just a tad over-dressed in it. But if she tied her hair back at the nape of her neck with a small black bow and wore her gold-and-pearl stud earrings, she'd still look relatively subdued.

Her mind made up, she headed for the kitchen, fed the dog, heated some soup for herself, then retreated to the bathroom for a relaxing soak in the tub.

By the time Gabriel knocked on the door, she was dressed, but not necessarily ready to go. Eyeing herself critically in the mirror, she wished she had settled for the slacks and sweater, after all. Chaperoning a mass of preteens at a school dance didn't really call for such preening on her part, and she wasn't really going *with* Gabriel, just riding along in his truck.

However, it was much too late to change.

Hoping she wouldn't look too out of place, she shushed the dog, then quickly slipped into her black wool coat and grabbed her purse.

"I'm not early, am I?" Gabriel asked as she opened the door.

"No, not at all," she assured him, stepping out into the cold, clear, smoke-scented night. "You're right on time."

Seeing that he wore a dark suit, white shirt and tie beneath his open overcoat, she felt somewhat relieved. Apparently, "casual dress" didn't necessarily apply to the faculty. Since the school principal was dressed as formally as she, Madelyn figured she wouldn't stand out like a sore thumb, after all.

"Hope you had a chance to relax," Gabriel said as he started the truck and backed down the driveway. "We're going to have a busy evening ahead of us."

"I did."

"What about dinner?"

"A bowl of soup."

"That's all?" Frowning, Gabriel glanced at her.

"I wanted to save room for nachos and a hot dog," she admitted, smiling ruefully. "I love that kind of stuff, and I haven't had either in ages."

"Well, then, we'd better see that you have time to hit the refreshment stand before everything's sold out," he teased.

Liking the way he again used the word *we,* Madelyn readily agreed.

"Just save room for coffee and dessert later," Gabriel added as he pulled into the school's parking lot.

"Are the PTA members serving that, too?"

"No, I thought we'd stop at the café on the Plaza afterward. To wind down. If you'd like…"

"Oh, yes," she hastened to reply, not only surprised, but quite pleased by his suggestion. "I'd enjoy that very much."

"I would, too." In the semidarkness of the truck's interior, Gabriel look over at her, smiling as he met her gaze. "So, it's a date?"

"Yes, it's a date," Madelyn murmured, noting that, once again, he had a rather speculative gleam in his dark eyes.

A *pleasingly* speculative gleam that made her heart beat a little faster.

Sure that she had read way too much into Gabriel's glance, Madelyn walked into the school building with him.

Although thirty minutes remained until the official start of the dance, most of the faculty and PTA members were already arriving, along with a smattering of students. Everyone seemed to know Gabriel, and as they headed toward the classroom that had been set up as a coat-check stand, he exchanged numerous greetings along the way.

Madelyn smiled and nodded, speaking to the few people she recognized. There was a noticeable curiosity about her among the others, but since everyone also seemed friendly, she wasn't discomfited by it. She was still the new kid in town, and she *was* arriving with the principal, so some interest in her was to be expected.

With gentlemanly courtesy, Gabriel helped her out of her coat and handed it, along with his, to the parent in charge of checking them. When he turned back to her, he paused and looked at her, head to toe and back again, his eyes widening with such obvious appreciation, the heat of a blush warmed her cheeks.

"Where are you scheduled to work first?" he asked, though she had a feeling that wasn't really what he'd wanted to say to her.

Unfortunately, they were surrounded by at least a dozen other people, all vying for his attention.

"Hallways and rest rooms," she replied.

For security reasons, as well as general crowd control, parents and teachers had been assigned a different area of the school for each of the three hours of the dance.

"Followed by?"

"The front door, then the gym."

"I'll bring you some nachos once the first rush is over," he promised.

"Thanks."

He reached out and gave her arm a quick squeeze, then turned to talk to the PTA president, a slightly overweight, middle-aged woman wearing a bright red, satin-and-lace dress at least one size too small.

Reluctantly, Madelyn moved away from him, joining the other teachers, most of whom had brought along spouses or dates. They welcomed her into their midst, making introductions and light conversation until the time came for them to take up their various stations.

As good as his word, Gabriel sought her out as she walked along a far hall, checking for stragglers. Falling into step with her, he handed her one of the soft drinks he carried along with a plate of nachos. They shared the crispy, cheese-coated chips, not saying much. Then, at Eileen Duggan's behest, he was off again to break up a minor altercation between two girls who wanted to dance with the same grinning, couldn't-care-less boy.

Except at a distance, Madelyn didn't see Gabriel again until the dance was almost over. On duty in the gym, she had just polished off the hot dog she'd been craving when the disc jockey, in deference to the baby-boomer parents and teachers, slowed down the tempo with a Motown golden oldie.

As the velvet-voiced male vocalist sang about his girl, Gabriel appeared out of nowhere and halted beside her.

"May I have this dance?" he asked, sliding a hand under her elbow and urging her toward the dance floor.

"I have a feeling you're not taking no for an answer," she replied lightly.

"You're right. I'm not," he said, pulling her close.

Though she was somewhat disconcerted at being singled out thus, Madelyn didn't think their sharing one dance would cause too much of a stir. She had seen Gabriel on the dance floor with several of the other teachers, some of the parents, even a few of the bolder students.

Granted, he hadn't danced slow dances with them. But then, none had been played until now. Which made her feel rather special, no matter how she tried to convince herself that she really had no reason to.

Gabriel was an excellent dancer, and Madelyn easily followed his lead, giving herself up to the sensual rhythm. She also marveled at how well they fit together as she savored the warm, solid feel of his arms around her.

"I don't think I've told you how lovely you look tonight, have I?" he asked, his mouth close to her ear, his voice low, his breath tickling her neck.

Startled by such a personal compliment given in such an intimate way, Madelyn jerked back, stumbling a bit as she looked up at him. He met her gaze, his eyes steady, his expression serious. At a loss for words, she shook her head as she once again fell into step with him.

"Well, you do."

"Thank you."

Unable to decipher what, if any, underlying meaning there might be beneath his softly spoken words, she lowered her gaze. Almost imperceptibly, his arms tightened around her, and for just a moment, as the music faded, she rested her head on his shoulder.

Surely he hadn't been coming on to her, had he? But the way he'd looked at her, the way he'd held her, the words he'd spoken, all seemed to add up to something more than a casual exchange between two friends of the opposite sex.

A few minutes later, as she quieted a rowdy bunch of students cutting up in line at the refreshment stand, Madelyn told herself she was being silly. With Gabriel across the gym, his back turned to her, she found it easy to believe she'd been letting her imagination run wild.

Certainly nothing else he had said or done since their first meeting several weeks ago indicated he had any personal interest in her. He had been kind and helpful to her, but she had gradually come to realize that Gabriel Serrano was generally kind and helpful to anyone in need.

And, in his mind, he would always couple her with Ethan, the brother who had caused him so much grief. More than likely, he thought of her as he had Lily ten years ago. To him, she was another abandoned woman in need of aid. And, regrettably, all used up.

She wished there were some way she could tell him that Ethan had never engaged her emotions in quite the way Gabriel suspected—that, in truth, she hadn't loved anyone until now—without running the risk of sounding like a desperate fool.

By ten-thirty, the last of the students were on their way home, the PTA cleanup crew had set to work and the faculty was finally free to go.

Having talked some sense into herself, Madelyn chattered inanely about nothing in particular on the walk to Gabriel's truck, the ride to the café on the Plaza, even over the steaming cups of cappuccino and slices of decadently delicious raspberry cream cake they ordered.

Gabriel eyed her curiously, making only a token effort

to hold up his end of the conversation until Madelyn finally ran out of chirpy comments. Sitting beside him in the truck as they neared home, she plucked nervously at the fabric of her coat as a discomfiting silence suddenly stretched between them.

Unexpectedly, Gabriel's hand settled over hers, and she swung around to face him.

"Did you have a nice time tonight?" he asked, keeping his eyes on the road.

"Very nice," she murmured.

"But you're upset about something." He made it a statement rather than a question.

"No, I'm not," she said, then added when he glanced at her skeptically, "really."

"Am I making you uncomfortable, then?"

"No."

At her all-too-hasty reply, he favored her with another dubious look.

"I'm just a little wound up from all the excitement," she hedged. "And that second cup of cappuccino probably isn't helping any, either."

"Because I wouldn't want you to think I would ever knowingly do anything to upset or embarrass you," he continued as if she hadn't spoken.

"I know that, Gabriel."

Looking away, she stared out the window, more confused than ever.

"Good."

He gave her hand a gentle squeeze, then released her so he could maneuver the truck into the driveway. After parking in the garage, he walked with her to the cottage door.

With a full moon shining high overhead, the courtyard was bathed in a shimmering, silvery glow. Key in hand,

Madelyn turned to thank Gabriel for a lovely evening. As she did, he moved a step closer to her and took the key from her,

"Let me get the door for you," he said, reaching around her to fit the key into the lock.

Unable to move away from him with the door at her back, Madelyn fixed her gaze on the top button of his overcoat and willed her heart to stop racing.

Say thank you and good-night, then go inside, she ordered herself. But somehow she couldn't seem to follow those oh-so-simple instructions. Instead, her gaze drifted upward to Gabriel's mouth, snagged and held as she found herself leaning toward him, wondering how it would feel to be kissed—

"Maddy?" he muttered.

Just her name, shortened in an achingly intimate way.

She met his gaze and saw her need mirrored in his eyes for an instant before he bent his head and brushed his lips ever so gently over hers.

With a sigh, she rested her hands on his chest, tilted her head and brazenly demanded more. Acting purely on instinct, she nipped at his lower lip, then traced it tenderly with the tip of her tongue. Obviously needing no further urging, Gabriel took her mouth with a low groan as he gathered her close in his arms. Secure in his embrace, Madelyn parted her lips, savoring the masterful glide of his tongue over hers, as she sank against him, surprise and sheer delight humming through her.

She was breathless by the time he finally raised his head, yet she couldn't stop her murmur of protest. She felt as if she'd been waiting forever for this magic moment, and she didn't want it to end, even though she knew it must.

"You'd better go in," Gabriel muttered, his voice rough.

He pressed a quick, hard kiss on her forehead, another on her cheek, then another at the corner of her mouth.

"Yes," she admitted, though without enthusiasm.

Vaguely, she was aware of Buddy, alternately whining pitifully and snuffling just inside the door. The little dog had been alone hours longer than usual, and needed attention, too. But the last thing she wanted to do was let go of Gabriel.

"This isn't something we should…rush," he said.

"No," she agreed reluctantly.

He was right, of course. Their relationship had changed rather quickly and, for her, unexpectedly. While she was sure of her feelings for him, she didn't want him to have any regrets.

"But just so you know, I'm not the type to start something I don't plan to finish. Eventually…"

"Is that a promise?" she asked, her tone light and teasing as she stepped away from him.

"Oh, yes, Ms. St. James. That *is* a promise."

He put his hands on her shoulders, hesitated as if uncertain, then turned her around and gave her a firm yet gentle push into the cottage.

"Good night, Madelyn."

"Good night, Gabriel."

She glanced back at him for a long moment, resisted the urge to reach for him again, then slowly closed the door.

As his footsteps faded across the courtyard, she bent and picked up the little dog, holding him close, afraid she was dreaming. Buddy, squirming delightedly as he lapped at her chin with his warm, wet tongue, assured her she wasn't.

She was wide-awake. She was also happier than she could ever remember being. But niggling at the back of her mind was a sense of dread, as well.

What would Gabriel think of her once she told him that his brother had more than likely taken his own life because she hadn't been paying attention? Gabriel seemed to think she was some kind of saint. But as she was going to have to admit before they went much further, she had turned away from Ethan at the very moment when he'd needed her most.

Chapter 8

Alone in the quiet house, Gabriel wandered from the kitchen to the living room, shedding first his overcoat, then his suit coat and tie along the way.

The evening had gone better than he had expected—much, much better. Offering to take Madelyn to school each day had been a stroke of genius, making it possible for him to assume, as he'd done, that they'd go to the dance together. After that, everything else had followed quite naturally. At least to his way of thinking.

He had definitely made some progress in changing their relationship, and he had enjoyed the effort enormously. Not that anything he'd done during the time he'd spent with Madelyn had been a *chore*.

He had been proud to be paired with her, however informally. And the dance they'd shared had left him wanting so much more. After holding her close, swaying to the sensual music, he'd had a hard time letting her go.

He'd wanted to grab her hand, drag her to a dark,

secluded corner and have her all to himself. Unfortunately, that hadn't been possible, which was probably just as well.

His sudden, amorous attention had taken Madelyn completely by surprise, and although she had denied it rather vehemently, he knew he'd made her nervous. In fact, from the way she had talked nonstop about nothing in particular from the moment they'd left the dance until they were almost home, he'd been afraid he'd scared the living daylights out of her.

But then, as they had stood close outside the cottage, she'd looked up at him with such longing that he couldn't have stopped himself from kissing her to save his soul.

Just a tender, good-night kiss, he'd vowed, determined not to frighten her again. He hadn't anticipated how fervently she would respond, nor how her response would shatter his own resolute self-control.

Until the moment she ever so lightly, ever so invitingly, traced the tip of her tongue along his lower lip, he had been following almost step-by-step the well-orchestrated plan he'd devised to reach his ultimate goal of wedded bliss.

But in the space of a heartbeat, she'd had him throwing caution to the wind, ravishing her luscious mouth with a hunger that had astonished him. That still astonished him as he stood before the fireplace, staring at the charred wood and ashes in the grate.

There had been nothing calculated about that kiss— not on his part, and certainly not on hers. She'd been just as stunned as he, and just as sorry when he had finally forced himself to break away.

He would have much preferred to carry her into the cottage, toss her on the bed and take her so hard, so fast, that all memory of anyone else who had ever had her would be permanently wiped from her mind and heart.

However, common sense, coupled with his basic decency—not to mention a hearty measure of concern that he was on the verge of getting in way too deep—kept him from giving in to that all-too-carnal desire. He couldn't afford to lose control that way, couldn't afford the risk inherent in letting Madelyn have that kind of power over him.

This time, *he* was calling the shots. He had trailed after one woman like a lovesick puppy. He wasn't doing it again. He was going to remain as detached as he possibly could.

Wanting her sexually was not only understandable, but completely acceptable. Falling in love with her—so in love that he no longer had the upper hand—was totally out of the question.

As he'd told her, he had every intention of finishing what they'd started tonight, to her satisfaction as well as his, but in his own good time. He could marry her, sire her children and enjoy a long and happy life with her, all without enslaving himself to an emotion that had only led to pain and disillusionment in the past.

He could, and he *would,* he promised himself as he finally headed for his bedroom, allowing himself only the slightest glance at the cottage as he passed the French doors along the way.

The cottage that beckoned to him from across the moonlit courtyard so enchantingly that he nearly forgot all his good, safe, *sound* intentions. Nearly…

Despite his renewed state of arousal, Gabriel slept soundly and awoke only a little later than usual, feeling both rested and relaxed. Once he was up and dressed, however, he found himself standing at the French doors, eyeing the cottage hopefully, looking for some sign that Madelyn, too, was awake. However, none was forthcoming.

With a negative shake of his head and a muttered curse, he grabbed his jacket, tucked his wallet and keys in the back pocket of his jeans, and so as not to be tempted any further, let himself out the front door. A brisk walk to the Plaza in the cold morning air, followed by breakfast at Tia Sofia's, would do him a world of good.

Then, at ten o'clock, he would pick up Brian at the Murphys' house as scheduled, and take him to the mall to get the new shoes his son had mentioned he needed. The mall in Albuquerque, he decided. That way, they could make a day of it—a day away from the house, the cottage *and* the cottage's occupant—so he could regain his equanimity.

Gabriel didn't want to *want* to see Madelyn again so badly. He would much prefer to be able to take or leave her company at *his* discretion. And he would once he got his mind off that treacherous kiss they'd shared.

The walk to the Plaza was invigorating, and at the restaurant, he ran into a couple of school board members and their spouses. He gladly accepted their invitation to join them, then lingered awhile on his own, reading the paper, after they left.

Back at the house, he went straight to the garage, hopped into the truck and backed down the driveway, thus avoiding the possibility of getting more than a glimpse of the cottage.

Brian was ready and waiting for him at the Murphys' house. However, when Gabriel suggested they drive to Albuquerque, he wasn't the least bit agreeable.

"I'd rather go to the mall here," the boy insisted.

"Otherwise, I won't be able to have lunch with Madelyn, then go to Mr. Martin's gallery with her. She wants to show him some more of her Santa Fe photographs, and she said I could go with her. Plus I have to give her the valentine I made for her at school yesterday."

"All right, we'll go to the mall here." Gabriel relented, unwilling to spoil his son's plans without good reason.

He could certainly find something to keep his mind occupied at the house. He had piles of paperwork to sort through, and the bookcase he was building for Brian was ready for a second coat of varnish.

"Did you have fun at the dance?" Brian asked, obviously happy with Gabriel's decision.

"Yes, I did."

"What about Madelyn? Did she have fun, too?"

"I think so, but you'll have to ask her to be sure."

"Did you give her a valentine?"

"No," Gabriel admitted ruefully, thinking that *would* have been a nice touch. Then, after several moments of consideration, he added casually, "But I kissed her goodnight."

He knew how much Brian liked Madelyn, but he wasn't sure how his son would take to the possibility of her becoming a more permanent part of their lives.

They had fended for themselves, just the two of them—with some housekeeping help from Millie Richards—for eight years now. And during those eight years, Brian had had Gabriel's undivided attention.

Now he thought it might be best for Brian to gradually get used to his changing relationship with Madelyn. Since he had made his first move in that direction, he figured this was as good a time as any to introduce the idea of her possibly becoming a member of their family sometime in the near future. As long as Brian was agreeable, of course.

"You did?"

Bright blue eyes widening with surprise, as well as what looked a lot like delight, the boy turned to stare at his father.

"Yes, I did," Gabriel said, grinning proudly.

"Did she kiss you back?"

"Oh, yes."

"So does that mean she's gonna be your girlfriend now?"

"Well, that depends. I haven't exactly asked her yet. I wanted to find out how you felt about it first," he admitted.

Brian thought for several seconds, his expression serious. Then he answered at last, "I feel pretty good about it, so hurry up and ask her before somebody else does, okay?"

"Okay," Gabriel laughingly agreed.

To himself, he also acknowledged how savvy his son was. With Madelyn's looks and personality, it *was* a wonder no one else had made a play for her yet. Luckily, he was the only single male at the junior high school, and so far, she'd spent most of her time there or alone in the cottage. But gradually, she would be getting out more, especially once the weather warmed up.

Now, with Brian's blessing, Gabriel could set about seeing to it that she understood she was already spoken for. By *him.*

"Can she live in the house with us, then?" Brian asked enthusiastically.

"Not just yet," Gabriel hedged.

"Why not? It was so much fun having her there last weekend."

"I know, Brian. But for now it's best that she stay in the cottage."

"Because you're not married yet?"

"Yes," Gabriel agreed, relieved that his son seemed to understand the situation so well.

"But you're gonna *get* married, aren't you?" the boy prodded.

"Well, I hope so. But we haven't even talked about it yet. We will, of course. Talk about it, that is." He hesitated a moment, then added carefully, "However, in the meantime, I'd rather you didn't mention it to her yourself. Okay?"

"Okay," Brian replied rather dejectedly.

"We want her to have a chance to get to know us a little better before we pop the big question, don't we? So she'll be sure to say yes."

"You'd better kiss her a lot, too. On the mouth," Brian advised so seriously that Gabriel had to bite his lip to keep from laughing out loud. "I think it's pretty yucky, but ladies seem to like it, don't they?"

"Yes, ladies do seem to like it. And one day, my young son, you will like it, too," Gabriel replied, smiling as he tweaked the boy's chin.

"Not me. I'm *never* gonna like kissing, *especially* on the mouth," Brian vowed.

As they wandered from store to store in the shopping mall south of town, Gabriel wondered if he had been wise to discuss his feelings for Madelyn to the extent he'd done with Brian. He had meant only to prepare the child for what *might* happen in the coming months. He hadn't suspected Brian would be several steps ahead of him.

Now, as relieved as Gabriel was that his son had no objections to his courting Madelyn, he hoped Brian wouldn't jump the gun by blurting out something that could disconcert her. She was skittish enough as it was. And Gabriel needed more time to get used to the idea himself.

He didn't want to give in too quickly, too completely, to his desire, and let his increasing ardor for her get the better of him. Should that happen, holding a part of himself separate—as he knew he must—could very well prove to be impossible.

He hadn't been so attracted to a woman since he'd first met Lily. Looking back, however, he realized that had been more youthful infatuation than true love. With Madelyn, the feelings he seemed to be experiencing had the potential of being infinitely deeper, not to mention ultimately more binding, and considering his track record, unnerving in the extreme.

Brian found the shoes he wanted—brown leather-and-suede hiking boots with sturdy soles and a price tag that made Gabriel wince as he pulled his credit card from his wallet. Then the two of them headed back home.

Once there, however, Gabriel's plan to keep his mind occupied with something other than thoughts of Madelyn quickly fell apart.

As he pulled into the driveway, Brian caught sight of her walking toward the house along the sidewalk, a camera slung over her shoulder and Buddy, on a leash, trotting along ahead of her. The boy waved to her and she waved back, and after parking in the garage, Gabriel decided it would be rude not to wait for her in the courtyard along with his son.

"We're still having lunch together, aren't we?" Brian asked as he bent to scratch the little dog's scraggly ears.

"We certainly are," Madelyn assured him.

When she'd first joined them in the courtyard, she had seemed to be avoiding Gabriel's gaze. But now she directed a look his way as she added, "You're welcome to join us, too. We're having Brian's favorites—tomato soup and grilled-cheese sandwiches."

"Sounds good to me," Gabriel replied, throwing caution to the wind despite his better judgment.

"Can he go to Mr. Martin's gallery with us, too?" Brian piped up as they started toward the cottage.

"Sure." Madelyn glanced at him shyly. "Unless you have something else to do."

"Not a thing," he stated easily, experiencing only the merest twinge of guilt at his prevarication.

He had a lot to keep him busy, but nothing that seemed more important to him at the moment than spending the afternoon with Madelyn and his son.

Though Madelyn seemed more interested in Brian than in him—thanking the boy profusely for the lovely valentine and admiring his new hiking boots—Gabriel thought she seemed quite comfortable having him around, as well. She put him to work setting the table while Brian stirred the soup and she grilled the sandwiches. And after they'd eaten, she welcomed both his and Brian's help with the dishes, laughing as she scooted around them in the narrow confines of the tiny kitchen.

Twice while they were in the cottage he turned to say something to her and found her staring at him, an odd expression on her face. She looked as if she were bemused by the whole situation. But not distressingly so.

Her swift, almost sheepish smiles convinced Gabriel that while she might not fully understand the sudden shift in his demeanor, she considered it wholly acceptable.

Because the weather was so nice, they decided to walk to the Plaza. Brian held Buddy's leash, Gabriel carried her leather portfolio and Madelyn strode along between the two of them, her camera slung over her shoulder once again.

At the gallery, they parked the dog on a bench just outside the door, then Gabriel and Brian joined the other browsers milling about while Madelyn and Henry pored over her most recent series of photographs.

The tone of Henry's murmured comments left no doubt in Gabriel's mind of how much his friend appreciated not only Madelyn's work, but Madelyn, as well. The temptation to invent some reason to interrupt what was essentially a business meeting almost got the better of him. Only by reminding himself that Henry was a very happily married man did he manage to resist.

Henry selected several of Madelyn's photographs to display in the gallery and, to her obvious delight, also handed her a check. Grinning ear to ear, she bid Henry farewell then hurried to join Gabriel and Brian.

"He sold *three* more of my photographs," she said, waving the check excitedly.

"That's really great," Brian crowed.

"Congratulations," Gabriel added.

Without thinking, he put an arm around her shoulders and gave her a proprietary hug, wanting her to know how pleased he was for her. Startled, she glanced up at him but didn't move away. After a long moment, she relaxed and leaned against him as naturally as if she really did belong right there by his side.

"This calls for a celebration," she stated, folding the check and tucking it into the back pocket of her jeans. "How about ice-cream sodas at Woolworth's—my treat?"

"How about *my* treat?" Gabriel suggested.

"But I'm the one who just got paid," she teased.

"You're also the one who did a lot of hard work. Let me honor that by spoiling you just a little, okay?"

"Put so gallantly, how could I refuse? But I must warn you, I intend to pig out."

"Me, too, Dad," Brian said.

"I guess that makes three of us, then," Gabriel replied, not only surprised, but also very pleased when Madelyn slid her arm around his waist as they left the gallery.

They did, indeed, indulge themselves on the tallest, richest, chocolate ice-cream sodas to be had at the store's lunch counter while Buddy once again waited patiently just outside the door. Then they walked up Canyon Road, taking a more roundabout route back to the house as the sun began to dip toward the western horizon.

Obviously intrigued by the play of sunlight and shadows, Madelyn uncapped the lens on her camera and, stopping at odd moments, proceeded to take several shots of Brian, followed by several more of Brian and Gabriel together.

Wanting to try out his skill, Brian begged to take a couple of pictures of Madelyn and Gabriel. When the boy, grinning broadly, urged them to stand closer, Gabriel readily complied, putting his arm around her shoulders again. Then, since it only seemed natural that he offer to take some shots of Madelyn and Brian, he gladly did that, too.

"They won't be nearly as good as yours. Probably not even as good as Brian's," he said. "But I'd really like to have some prints of them—all of them."

"I'll be more than happy to make them for you," she promised.

All too soon they arrived at the house. Gabriel wasn't anxious to part company yet, but Madelyn and Brian both looked tired. And since he'd played all day, he knew he really ought to spend the evening catching up on school-work. Otherwise he was going to end up falling impossibly far behind.

They'd had a pleasant afternoon together. Leaving it at that seemed the best thing to do. They would have lots of other opportunities to be together in the days and weeks ahead, with Brian, as well as on their own. He intended to see to it. But there was no sense looking overeager now.

In fact, he'd probably be wise to get away with Brian tomorrow—just the two of them. They hadn't been skiing in several weeks, and conditions at the Santa Fe Basin were excellent after the snowfall they'd had lately. They could get up early and stay all day.

Putting a little distance between himself and Madelyn couldn't possibly do any harm. As it was, they'd be seeing each other at school all next week, anyway. Then maybe next weekend they could plan an activity all together again. Or maybe he could arrange for Brian to spend Friday or Saturday night with a friend so he could have Madelyn all to himself.

He would have to see what worked out best. In the meantime…

Halting in the courtyard halfway between the house and the cottage, Gabriel handed Madelyn the portfolio he'd been carrying.

"Thanks for inviting me along," he said, smiling as he met her gaze. "I had a good time."

"Me, too," Brian agreed as he unfastened Buddy's leash and handed it to her, as well. "A really, *really,* good time."

"I'm glad you decided to come along." She shifted uncertainly from one foot to another, seeming at a loss for what to say next. Finally she looked away as she added, ''Well, I'd better go in. See you....''

''Yeah, see you....''

''Tomorrow?'' Brian asked hopefully.

''Probably not,'' Gabriel stated briskly.

Trying not to let himself be thrown off course by the longing he heard in his son's voice—a longing he felt deep in his own heart, and if he wasn't mistaken, saw in Madelyn's eyes—he put a hand on his son's shoulder and guided him toward the house.

''But *Dad*—''

''Good night, Madelyn,'' he called out a little too loudly, hoping to override his son.

''Good night, guys,'' she replied, much more softly, almost sadly.

Unable to stop himself, Gabriel glanced over his shoulder, but, head bowed, she was already letting herself into the cottage.

Just as well, he told himself, as he hustled Brian through the French doors. Even though deep down inside he couldn't really say he believed it was.

In the two weeks following the Valentine's dance and her Saturday afternoon with Gabriel and Brian, Madelyn began to feel as if she were riding a rather rickety roller coaster.

Some days she would find herself thinking—as she had that Friday night and Saturday afternoon—that Gabriel's interest in her went beyond the bounds normally dictated by simple friendship between two adults, one male and one female.

He would slip an arm around her and hug her close, or catch her hand in his as they walked along on their way to one place or another, usually with Brian, and often even Buddy, in tow. Just like they were a family.

Twice, too, when they had gone out to dinner together at *his* suggestion—without Brian—he had kissed her outside the cottage door with a passion unmistakable even to someone as inexperienced as she. A passion that had left her breathlessly wanting something more, something she hadn't the confidence or the courage to ask for.

Better to follow his lead. Especially when she had serious doubts as to how deserving of his admiration and affection she really was.

She had done what she could for Ethan, but not as much as Gabriel seemed to give her credit for. Otherwise, Ethan would still be alive. Gabriel had a right to know that before they got any more involved than they already were.

But would they be getting any more involved? Madelyn wondered as she mixed chemicals at the bathroom sink on a snowy Thursday night at the end of February.

She had finally finished mounting and framing the photographs Henry had chosen for the gallery and was now ready to print the roll of film she and Brian and Gabriel had shot together that Saturday afternoon.

Gabriel had sworn he wasn't starting something he didn't intend to finish. Yet each time they seemed to reach a new level of closeness, he backed off, treating her more like a good buddy than the love of his life.

While he was still amiable and easygoing, Madelyn would sense that he was trying to maintain a certain distance between them, sometimes only for a day or two, sometimes longer. After including her in an outing with Brian or inviting her to dinner, he would keep to himself, saying little as they drove back and forth to school, and busying himself with other activities while Brian came to visit her at the cottage.

Madelyn didn't really blame him. He and Brian had been on their own for a long time. Having a third person around, even temporarily, had to take some getting used to. But she really wished he wouldn't tease her with the possibility of happily-ever-after if that wasn't what he had in mind.

If he wanted sex without any strings attached, why didn't he just say so? They were both adults, after all. And whether or not she chose to enter into that kind of relationship with him, at least she would know what was expected of her.

Why give the impression that he was wooing her, then retreat as if he were afraid he was on the verge of making a big mistake?

Probably because, in his more rational moments, he *was,* she thought as the first print—a close-up of Gabriel and Brian—came up in the developer.

He had been badly hurt by his ex-wife's involvement with Ethan, and here *she* was, supposedly fresh from what he obviously believed had been an intimate affair with the same man.

From what Gabriel had said, ten years ago he hadn't felt that in Lily's eyes he measured up to his half brother. Quite possibly, he thought the same might very well prove true with *her.* And she simply didn't have the knowledge or the expertise to convince him otherwise.

She had only her virginity, and she simply wasn't brave enough to blatantly advertise that asset. What if he laughed in her face incredulously? Or worse, what if he pitied her?

Poor Madelyn, on the far side of twenty-something and never been touched.

More than likely, he'd assume—wrongly so—that it was from lack of opportunity. Ethan hadn't been the first to suggest a sexual liaison. But she had been waiting for the right man to entrust with her love. A man like Gabriel Serrano...

Now that she had found him, it saddened her to think there was a good chance he'd consider *her* all wrong.

By the time Madelyn finished printing two sets of the photographs—one for herself and one for Gabriel and Brian—it was past midnight. She tidied up the bathroom, then put on her coat and took Buddy out one last time.

As the little dog snuffled around on the patch of snow-covered grass behind the garage, she gazed at the shadowed house, wondering where her relationship with Gabriel would eventually lead. She also wondered if she should stay around long enough to find out.

She had seen his love for his son reflected in the photographs she'd developed. Her own fond feelings for the boy and his father were also equally evident. But in the photographs Brian had taken of her and Gabriel, she hadn't been able to determine what *he* thought of *her.*

Gabriel had had his arm around her and he'd been smiling happily enough. However, while she had been captured on film looking up at him with her heart in her eyes, he had been gazing off in the distance, as if he couldn't have cared less that she was standing by his side.

Watching as Gabriel's obviously indifferent image materialized on the contact paper had been hard enough. Did she really want to hear him *say* that she would never mean anything to him?

She had money coming in now. More than enough to pay rent on an apartment and buy groceries. And with Spring Break coming up in mid-March, she would have time to find another place to live. Then she could tell

Gabriel she'd changed her mind about accepting Ethan's bequest, and why.

She would still see him at school, of course. But at least she wouldn't be living in his back pocket. And any responsibility he felt for looking after her would finally be nullified, along with any indebtedness she'd allowed him to believe he had to her.

If he wanted to see her socially after that, at least she would know it wasn't simply out of force of habit.

Having come to such a sensible conclusion, Madelyn was sure she'd sleep soundly. Instead, she tossed and turned restlessly. Finally she dozed off, only to be awakened too soon by the buzzing of her alarm clock.

Not sure whether she wanted to lay her head down and cry or hurl her coffee cup against the wall, she somehow managed to wash, dress, take the dog out, gather her books and papers together, and meet Gabriel and Brian at the usual time. That they were both in high spirits, frolicking in the fresh snow as they waited for her to join them, only soured her mood all the more.

She sat in the truck silently, staring out the side window as father and son bantered back and forth. She sensed Gabriel shooting her questioning glances, but she studiously ignored him. However, after they'd dropped Brian at the elementary school he finally mentioned her taciturn behavior.

"You're awfully quiet this morning," he stated abruptly. "Something bothering you?"

"Not really," she responded, her tone waspish.

"Doesn't sound like it to me," Gabriel murmured.

"I was up late developing some photographs. Then I had a hard time falling asleep," she admitted grudgingly. "When I finally did, the alarm went off and I guess I got up on the wrong side of the bed."

"Maybe you ought to take the day off," he suggested kindly. "I'll turn around at the next corner and take you back home."

"I'm not sick, just…crabby," she insisted, trying to blink back the hot tears stinging her eyes. "But don't worry. I promise not to take it out on the kids."

"I never thought you would," he admonished as he reached over and gave her shoulder a reassuring pat. Then, hesitantly, he added, "I guess you'd rather forget about tonight, though."

She would, and yet she wouldn't.

This happened to be her week to host their Friday night get-together. Gabriel and Brian were supposed to come for dinner, and since she still didn't have a television, Brian had suggested they play Monopoly afterward. In preparation, she had made a pot of stew. It was in the refrigerator, ready to pop in the oven when she got home. If they didn't come for dinner, she'd be stuck with enough leftovers to last six months.

Also, early tomorrow morning, Brian was going on an overnight camping trip with his Scout troop. Canceling tonight meant she wouldn't get to spend any time with him, and probably Gabriel, as well, all weekend.

"No, not really," she replied, lightening her tone considerably as she risked a look in his direction. "I was looking forward to it. And I'm sure I'll feel better by the end of the day, if only because it will also be the end of the school week."

"Well, if you change your mind, please tell me. I'm not sure what we'll do about dinner, and we won't have nearly as much fun playing Monopoly without you. But I suppose we'll manage somehow," he muttered woefully, though his dark eyes twinkled merrily when he met her gaze.

She barely controlled the urge to slug him in the arm. He was doing it again. Being sweet and kind and funny after three days of curt nods and a few casual words. And she was lapping it up like a cat with a bowl of cream.

Of course, she was also feeling one hundred percent better by the time they pulled into the school's parking lot.

No matter how she tried to harden her heart toward him, he still had that effect on her. All he had to do was act as if he cared about her, and she was putty in his hands.

But not for much longer, she told herself. Sometime in the very near future, he probably wouldn't care about her at all anymore. So why not enjoy it while she could?

The day turned out to be no worse than most. On the ride home, she assured Gabriel she would be expecting him and Brian—who was at a precampout Scout meeting—at six o'clock as originally planned.

She had time for a short nap before they arrived. Then, showered and dressed in faded jeans and a pullover sweater, she was almost feeling her old self again.

While she fixed the salad, Brian and Gabriel pored over the prints she'd made for them, teasing each other about who had taken the best shots. They finally agreed *she* had, but Gabriel conceded his son was a close second.

Madelyn wondered what he thought of the photographs of the two of them together. Unfortunately, she wasn't close enough to get a glimpse of his expression as he studied them. She could only hope he hadn't noticed how adoringly she'd been looking up at him.

During dinner, Brian chattered nonstop about his camping trip. Normally, Gabriel, along with most of the other fathers, would be going along, too. But space in the rustic cabins where the troop would be staying was limited, so there was room for only the leader and co-leaders. Thus, Brian was especially excited about going off on his own, more or less, for the first time.

However, by the time they'd finished eating and cleaned up the kitchen, the boy was yawning and rubbing his eyes. When his father suggested they save Monopoly for another night, he readily agreed.

"Hope you're not too disappointed that we're leaving so early," Gabriel said, sending a smile Madelyn's way as he slipped into his jacket.

"Well, maybe just a little," she teased back, then clapped a hand over her mouth to cover a yawn of her own.

"How about I make it up to you tomorrow night?" he suggested. "We'll do something special."

"Like what?" she asked, her heart beating a little faster in eager anticipation.

"I'm not sure yet, but I'll think of something. Wear that pretty black dress of yours, why don't you? And let me surprise you."

"All right," she agreed, intrigued by the glimmer in his eyes.

"I've got several things to do after I drop Brian off at his Scout leader's house tomorrow. I'll probably be gone most of the day. So why don't we plan to leave about seven o'clock?"

"I'll be ready."

Saturday dawned bright and clear, but by late afternoon, heavy clouds had rolled in from the north, promising snow by early evening.

Taking a break from working on lesson plans for the coming month, Madelyn stood by one of the windows, wondering how Brian was enjoying the camping trip.

Probably quite a bit. Along with the other boys, she figured he was also hoping they'd get snowed in. Although the campground was less than two hours away, a heavy snowfall in the mountains tonight could make delaying the drive back until Monday necessary.

She hadn't caught so much as a glimpse of Gabriel all day. But then, he'd said he would be gone. And except for a noontime walk with Buddy, she'd been cooped up in the cottage.

Now, however, she noticed that the lights were on in the house across the courtyard, though she was too far away to see if Gabriel was in the kitchen or breakfast room. Not that it would make any difference. She had no reason to go over there, and they weren't due to leave on their mystery date for almost three hours yet.

As she had on and off since they'd parted last night, Madelyn wondered what he had decided they would do. The Santa Fe Symphony Orchestra had a program at the Sweeney Center, and the new movie they'd talked about seeing was playing at the theater on San Francisco Street. Or perhaps Gabriel intended to take her to Albuquerque. If so, maybe they, too, would get snowed in, she thought.

Madelyn wasn't exactly sure how she would feel about that. But the fact that she caught herself smiling as she eyed the lowering clouds left her reasonably certain she wouldn't be all that upset.

Gabriel was such a gentleman, she doubted anything untoward would occur. Still, they would have more time together, and just being with him platonically gave her great pleasure. Since they would soon be going their separate ways, she wanted to make the most of whatever opportunities she had left.

She hadn't changed her mind about moving into her own apartment, and she didn't think she would. Unless—

From where she stood, Madelyn saw one of the French doors shoot open. Gabriel, struggling into his denim jacket, strode out, then halted abruptly to close the door. His mouth set in a grim line, he continued across the courtyard, heading straight for the cottage.

Her heart fluttering in her chest, Madelyn hurried to the door. Something about the look on his face sent a shiver of fear racing up her spine. What had happened to send him flying out of the house as if he had the hounds of hell at his heels?

Before she reached the door, his knock rang out, loud and demanding.

"Maddy, are you there?" he called out in a voice filled with anxiety.

Hushing the dog, who had leapt off the sofa, barking wildly, she fumbled with the lock and swung the door wide.

"Gabriel, what is it? What's wrong?" Reaching out, she drew him into the cottage, her trepidation growing.

He halted just across the threshold and took her by the shoulders, as if he desperately needed to ground himself by touching her. His face was unnaturally pale and his hands trembled ever so slightly.

"It's Brian. He's been hurt," he explained, his voice breaking.

"Oh, Gabriel, no," she murmured, clutching his arms. "How badly—?"

"I don't know for sure. His Scout leader called to tell me he'd taken a fall. He was on a cellular telephone and the line kept breaking up. All he was able to add was that a helicopter had been called to ferry him to the hospital here in Santa Fe. He should be there within the next ten or fifteen minutes." He paused, made a valiant effort to steady himself, then added, "Come with me, Maddy. Please. I need you...."

"Let me get my coat while you start the truck," she responded, forcing into her voice a dispassion she wasn't anywhere near feeling.

She had always considered Gabriel to be unflappable, but at that moment, unaware of how seriously injured his son might be, he was dreadfully close to falling apart. Yet he had come to her, seeking her help. She couldn't let him down. She had to be strong for both of them, no matter how frightened she was.

He had said he needed her with him, and she would be there for him, every step of the way.

Somehow managing to stay within the speed limit, Gabriel made the drive to the hospital south of the city in record time. While waiting at a stoplight, he reached over and took her by the hand. He didn't let her go until they arrived at the hospital.

The helicopter was already on the ground, but there didn't seem to be anyone in the immediate area. Gabriel headed for the emergency room at a run, and Madelyn followed as quickly as she could.

In the waiting area, they were directed to a room down a short hallway where a doctor and two nurses hovered over a stretcher. Her heart in her throat, Madelyn halted beside Gabriel in the doorway.

One of the nurses turned to look at them, and as she did, they caught a glimpse of Brian, propped up in a half-sitting position. His left arm, cocked at an odd angle, was elevated on a pile of pillows, but although his face was deathly pale, his bright blue eyes were wide open and alert.

"Hi, Dad. Hi, Madelyn," he said, his young voice a

shade higher in pitch than normal. "I slipped and fell and broke my arm."

His relief palpable, Gabriel put his arm around Madelyn's shoulders, then sagged against the door frame. She clung to him, her worry equally assuaged by the boy's stoutheartedness. He had to be in pain, but he was gamely attempting to maintain his composure.

"Are you his father?" the doctor asked, glancing at Gabriel.

"Yes." His arm still around her, Gabriel finally moved toward the stretcher. "How is he?"

"Except for his left arm, he's just fine. And we'll have the arm fixed up good as new in no time."

Giving Brian an encouraging smile as she took his right hand in hers, Madelyn listened as the doctor explained how he intended to set the fractures displayed on the X rays that had already been taken.

Because both bones just above the boy's wrist had not only been broken, but had also crossed over each other, general anesthesia would be necessary so the best possible realignment could be attained.

The doctor, an orthopedic surgeon on call, advised that he had an operating room on standby. Once Gabriel signed the necessary papers and Brian had been prepped, he would begin the surgery. The boy would then have to remain in the hospital overnight, but if no complications arose, he would be discharged Sunday afternoon.

"I'm really sorry, Dad," Brian said as Madelyn and Gabriel walked alongside the gurney on the way to preop thirty minutes later. Now dressed in a hospital gown, he looked small and scared, though he seemed determined to keep up a brave front. "I was trying to be careful, but I stepped on a patch of ice."

"Hey, don't worry about it. You had an accident, a

relatively *minor* accident, and you're going to be just fine once the doc straightens out your arm. And since it's your left arm, you'll still be able to do your schoolwork.''

"Oh, wow, that's a *big* relief," the boy replied ruefully.

As a nurse sent them off to the waiting room, Gabriel and Madelyn exchanged a smile, reassured that he really was going to be all right.

In the long narrow room, empty except for the two of them, Gabriel paced the entire forty-five minutes it took for the doctor to set Brian's arm. Madelyn left him to it, sensing the constant motion helped to keep him calm.

Every few minutes, he stopped beside her where she stood by one of the windows, watching the snow drift down. He would put an arm around her shoulders and stand beside her silently for a few moments, then move away again. At one point, Brian's Scout leader stopped by to check on the boy. Reassured by Gabriel's upbeat attitude, he left almost immediately to rejoin the others while the roads to the campground were still passable.

Finally, the doctor strode in carrying a new set of X rays that showed the bones now neatly realigned.

"We'll have him back in his room in about twenty minutes or so," he told them. "Why don't you go up and wait for him there?"

With the worst over, Madelyn wasn't sure her presence was still necessary, but when Gabriel took her hand and led her to the elevator, she went along with him willingly.

"I know I promised you we'd do something special tonight, but this wasn't exactly what I had in mind," he said, his tone apologetic as the elevator took them up to the second floor.

"I have to admit I wasn't quite prepared for this much

excitement,'' she replied, smiling up at him. ''I'm just glad he's going to be okay. I was so scared....''

''Yeah, me, too.'' He lifted a hand and gently touched her cheek. ''Thanks for being here with me. I'm not sure I could have handled all this on my own. Just walking into the emergency room nearly knocked me to my knees. I kept remembering the last time I was here. It was ten years ago, when my parents were killed. I was so afraid that Brian—''

He leaned back against the wall, eyes closed, a shudder running through his body. Then, as the elevator doors opened, he straightened again.

''I know I'm asking a lot, but will you stay with us tonight?''

''Of course I will,'' she assured him as they started toward Brian's room.

Although she wished the circumstances could be different, Madelyn was more than happy to share his vigil. In a moment of crisis, he had turned to her, and she wasn't about to abandon him now. He and Brian meant so much to her. Maybe too much. But she intended to stay close by as long as she was welcome.

By eight o'clock that night, Brian—his left arm in a cast almost to his shoulder—had recovered enough to express a wild craving for a burger, fries and chocolate shake. Gabriel checked with the nurse on duty, who assured him that was a good sign. Then he took off on a fast-food run that also included a quick stop at the cottage to check on Buddy.

At nine-thirty, his tummy full, the boy dropped off to sleep. Both Gabriel and Madelyn were fading fast, as well. At Gabriel's insistence, she stretched out to rest on the chair that converted into a bed of sorts while he took the wooden rocker in the opposite corner.

Madelyn awoke once, sometime after midnight, to find that Gabriel had joined his son on the bed. Curled protectively around the boy, he dozed peacefully.

In the pale glow of the night-light, Madelyn studied his strong, handsome face, glad that the strain of the afternoon and evening hadn't taken too great a toll on him. Glad, too, that she could be here with him now.

Because she loved him so much—him and his son— so very, very much.

She would never be able to tell them that, of course. But she could show them in little ways like this in the few weeks remaining when she could still be a part of their lives.

Chapter 9

"Mr. Serrano, you're not supposed to be sleeping on your son's bed," the day-shift nurse admonished as she bustled into Brian's hospital room early Sunday morning, waking him from a sound sleep.

"Sorry, I must have dozed off," he muttered sheepishly.

He rolled to his feet and moved out of her way, blinking bleary eyes and stretching stiff muscles. Then, raking a hand through his hair, he glanced at his son. Brian gave him a wan smile.

"How are you feeling?" Gabriel asked as the nurse checked the boy's blood pressure.

"Still sleepy," Brian grumbled. "And my arm kinda hurts."

"We can fix that," the nurse said. Smiling at Brian, she gave him a reassuring pat on the shoulder. "The doctor left orders for pain medication as needed."

As she pressed a button, the bed whirred Brian into a

semiupright position. Then she plumped the pillows elevating his broken arm, and left the room.

As the door whooshed shut after her, Gabriel looked across the room to where Madelyn should have been and realized, with a start, that she wasn't there. The bed of sorts had been converted back to a chair—an empty chair. Even her coat and purse were gone.

"Where's Madelyn?" Brian asked, the concern in his young voice echoing that which Gabriel himself was feeling.

"I don't know," he admitted.

She had said she would stay the night, but the night was over. Had she gone back to the cottage thinking she was no longer welcome? Granted, the worst was over, and she had more than done her part to help him through what had been some truly traumatic moments. But Gabriel still wanted her there with them—still *needed* her there with them.

He wasn't quite sure how he felt about being so reliant on her. After years of depending only upon himself, it seemed strange. Yet, at the same time, having someone he could count on when the going got rough was so… heartening.

When he had gotten the call from Brian's Scout leader yesterday afternoon, Gabriel had known instinctively that Madelyn would help him to bear whatever news awaited him at the hospital. And she had. Courageous woman that she was, she'd gone with him, no questions asked. Because of her grace under pressure, he had somehow managed to pull himself together when all he had really wanted to do was collapse in utter despair.

"Do you think she went home without us?" Brian persisted.

''Maybe—'' Gabriel began, then paused as the door slowly began to open.

Not the nurse, who had yet to return with Brian's pain medication. She had a bad habit of barging in rather than creeping quietly. And surely anyone else would have the courtesy to knock first. Anyone except—

As the door inched open a little more, Madelyn's bent head came into view.

Seeing her, Brian demanded, ''Madelyn, where have you been?''

''Yes,'' Gabriel seconded with equal parts vexation and relief. ''Where have you been?''

''Well, good morning to you, too,'' she said, eyeing them reproachfully for a long moment, then continued in answer to their questions, ''I woke up early and decided to get a little fresh air. I was sure you two would still be sleeping when I got back.''

''Not around here,'' Gabriel retorted. Noting that she had her hands full, he moved around the bed to help her with the door, adding, ''What's that?''

''Juice, coffee, milk for the boy with the broken arm, rolls still warm from the oven and the Sunday papers.'' With a grin, she dangled the bags she carried in front of their noses. ''I thought I'd better run by the cottage to let Buddy out. I borrowed your truck, by the way. Took your keys out of your jacket pocket. I hope you don't mind,'' she said, glancing at Gabriel. ''Anyway, while I was at the cottage, I figured I might as well shower and change clothes. Then I stopped at that little bakery on Grant Avenue on my way back.'' When she met his gaze again, her eyes were filled with uncertainty. ''Was that okay?''

Gabriel took the bags from her, set them on the bed

tray, and unable to stop himself, gathered her into his arms.

"That was definitely okay," he murmured, savoring the warmth of her as he held her close.

Hesitating only an instant, she leaned against him with a soft sigh. Of course, the nurse chose just that moment to return, and while Gabriel was reluctant to let Madelyn go, when she stepped back self-consciously, he released her.

"We were worried about you," Brian announced after he'd swallowed his pill and the nurse left again.

"I'm sorry. I should have left a note, but I thought I'd be back before you guys woke up." She glanced at Gabriel. "I didn't mean to cause you any concern."

"Well, we'll let it go this time," Gabriel advised her with mock severity. "As long as you brought my truck back in one piece."

"Oh, yes, it's in one piece. Only…" Madelyn frowned and ducked her head.

"What happened?" Gabriel asked, suddenly serious again.

"Gotcha," she teased, her eyes glinting with amusement as she looked up at him.

He wanted to put his hands on her, wanted to haul her into his arms and kiss her breathless. Just for starters. But that would have to wait until later. Not too much later, though.

"Yeah, you did," he growled for her ears only. "But your turn's coming. Then I'm gonna get *you*."

As he started to move away, he saw her eyes widen with surprise. Then she smiled slowly, seductively, murmuring, "Promises, promises."

"And I always keep them," he reminded her.

"Always keep what?" Brian asked.

''My promises,'' Gabriel answered lightly, then focused his attention on the bags of goodies awaiting them on the bed tray. ''Now, let's see what we have here. Juice and a carton of milk for you, Brian. And…'' He dug into the second, smaller bag. ''A cinnamon roll. How's that?''

''That's great.''

Managing fairly well one-handedly, Brain started on his breakfast as the two adults helped themselves to juice, coffee and their own buttery cinnamon rolls dripping with icing.

They had just finished eating when Brian's doctor stopped in to see him. Satisfied that the boy wasn't having any unusual problems, he indicated Gabriel was free to take him home at any time. He also instructed Gabriel to see that Brian kept the arm elevated and moved his fingers occasionally to help prevent swelling. And, to Brian's delight, he recommended the boy stay home from school all week. Then, after writing a prescription for pain medication and advising Gabriel to make an appointment with his office for a checkup the following Friday, he bid them all good day.

Anxious to get his son home, Gabriel wasted no time taking care of the paperwork necessary to have him officially released from the hospital, while Madelyn stayed in the room with Brian and helped him to dress.

Looking smug as a little prince, Brian thoroughly enjoyed his ride down to the lobby in a wheelchair. However, once in the truck, his mood deteriorated drastically. He complained that the sling was digging into his neck, that he was too hot, then too cold, and finally, that his arm had begun to ache again.

By the time they reached the house, having stopped to fill Brian's prescription along the way, Gabriel fully expected Madelyn to excuse herself and make a beeline for the cottage. Had he not been Brian's father, he would have opted for a little peace and quiet himself. However, she surprised him by following them into the house.

"Why don't you take a shower, shave and change into fresh clothes?" she suggested as she set her purse on the kitchen table and slipped out of her coat. "I guarantee you'll feel a lot better. And while you're in the bathroom, I'll get Brian tucked into bed."

"I don't want to go to bed," the boy grumbled, scowling as he struggled with his jacket. "I want to sit on the sofa in the living room and watch television. And I'm hungry. I need some lunch. And I want Buddy to keep me company—"

"Brian—" Gabriel cut in, trying for an even-toned voice.

Granted, the boy might not be feeling all that good, but his behavior was way out of line.

"Gabriel, go take a shower," Madelyn directed in a gentle voice.

Meeting his gaze pleadingly, she put an arm around his son's shoulders.

Glancing at Brian, Gabriel realized that his son was very close to tears, and quickly bit back the angry words he'd been about to say. At that moment, the boy was definitely more in need of a little indulgent mothering than stern fathering.

"Sure you'll be all right?" he asked Madelyn, smiling apologetically.

"Just let me get him settled, see that he takes one of his pills and has something to eat, and I think we'll *all* be fine," she replied serenely.

As he headed back to his bedroom, Gabriel certainly hoped so. He had rarely been forced to deal with Brian in a cranky mood, and after all that had happened during the past twenty-four hours, he was too nerved up to cope with a full-blown temper tantrum. Thank heavens, Madelyn seemed as self-possessed as ever.

But then, she'd had her shower already.

Feeling infinitely much better forty-five minutes later, Gabriel called Millie Richards to ask if she could stay with Brian during the coming week. She could. Then, following the sound of the television drifting into the kitchen from the living room, he strode down the hallway purposefully. As he passed the dining room, he halted in midstep, suddenly reminded of the plans he'd made for the previous night. Plans he had completely forgotten until now.

Eyeing the table, covered with a snowy linen cloth and set with china, silverware and crystal for two, as well as an assortment of brass candlesticks holding white candles and a brass bowl full of fresh flowers, he wondered what Madelyn had thought of the preparations he'd made.

He had planned to serve her the gourmet meal he'd picked up yesterday afternoon at the city's premier catering shop and stored in the refrigerator. Then he had intended to see where the remainder of the evening took them.

That it had been Gabriel's hope they'd end up in his bed now made him slightly uncomfortable.

Bringing her to the house last night—with the lights turned down low, soft music on the stereo and both of them dressed in their best—would have set the mood for romance. But in the light of day, with his son hurt and both of them still a bit frazzled…

Gabriel could only hope she hadn't gotten the wrong idea. Though what idea he expected her to get, he wasn't really sure. Seduction *had* been on his mind. He had the newly purchased box of condoms on his nightstand to prove it. But seduction of a *willing* woman only.

He had tried to be patient. Had tried to maintain some semblance of control over himself and the situation he'd found himself in. But going slowly, deepening his relationship with Madelyn at a measured pace while holding back, always holding back, hadn't made it any easier for him to distance himself emotionally. Instead, it seemed he had only fed his desire for her, as effectively as he would have fed a raging fire with dry wood.

In addition, Gabriel had grown increasingly concerned that what he considered a subtle courtship had left Madelyn more confused than anything. He didn't want her thinking he was playing games with her when that wasn't true at all. He intended for her to be a permanent part of his life, and he wanted her to know it. Especially since he'd begun to believe that was what she wanted, too.

After seeing the photographs of the two of them together—photographs in which her fondness for him was more than evident—Gabriel had come to the conclusion that taking Madelyn to bed would be the best thing he could do for both of them.

He would finally be able to gain some surcease from the lustful yearnings that surely could be nothing more than the result of certain…urges being denied all too long. Once he had relieved the sexual tension that now seemed to be holding him in thrall, he knew he would be able to think straight again.

Seeing Madelyn, being with her, talking to her, touching her, would no longer be of such importance to him. His every thought and most every action wouldn't revolve around her as had been the case far too often lately.

As for Madelyn, she would have to realize, once and for all, that his intentions were serious. They would make love, and then they would sit down like the mature adults they were and talk about the future—their future—together.

Considering how she had stood by him yesterday, any lingering doubts he'd had about making her his wife had vanished. She had proven herself worthy of his faith and trust. Now all he had to do was convince her that she belonged there with him, and that, in the years ahead, he would do everything in his power to see that she was content.

He might not be able to promise her love, but then, he wouldn't be expecting that from her, either. He firmly believed a marriage could survive on mutual respect and affection. And unless he was mistaken, they already had that going for them.

Unable to think of any good reason why they couldn't pick up where they had left off yesterday afternoon—with a few modifications for the change in circumstances—Gabriel continued into the living room, a smile tugging at the corners of his mouth. He could set another place at the table for his son, then heat and serve the meal. And after Brian went to bed, he could see where the remainder of the evening took them.

He certainly didn't like the idea of Madelyn going back to the cottage just yet. As a matter of fact, he didn't like the idea of her ever going back there at all. But until they were officially husband and wife—

"Hey, Dad, why's all that stuff on the dining room table?" Brian asked.

He was tucked under a blanket on the sofa, a pillow under his head, another under his arm, the remnants of a sandwich and half a glass of milk on the end table and Buddy snuggled up beside him. He looked and sounded more like his old self.

Gabriel knew he had Madelyn to thank for that. She sat at the opposite end of the sofa, her legs under her, holding a steaming mug of coffee in her hands, her expression slightly amused as she met his gaze.

"Expecting company last night, were you?" she inquired as he hunkered down on the floor in front of her.

"The *stuff* on the dining room table is our best china, crystal and silverware, handed down from your grandmother, Brian. And yes, I was expecting company last night, Ms. St. James. Before Brian's accident, I was planning to fix dinner for you. Now I guess I'll just have to do it tonight."

"But what about me?" the boy demanded. "There's only enough dishes and stuff on the table for two people."

"Well, luckily for you, I just happen to have enough dishes and stuff to set a place for you, too," Gabriel advised. "That is, if you'd care to join us."

"What are you gonna fix?" Brian asked suspiciously.

"Something special."

"Tell me what it is."

"I'd rather surprise you," Gabriel replied, smiling at his son enigmatically.

"Will I like it?"

"I hope so."

"What about Madelyn? Will she like it?"

"I hope so." Gabriel glanced over his shoulder at her. "You will stay for dinner, won't you?"

"As long you're serving the goodies I saw in the refrigerator, *yes,*" she answered, grinning broadly.

"I am, compliments of Mayfair and Vargo," he said, naming the well-known catering service.

"Oh, yum." She held his gaze, her eyes twinkling. "Shall I go home and change into my black dress?"

"How about we just keep it casual?" he suggested.

"Okay."

At that moment, the doorbell rang. Excusing himself, Gabriel went to see who had come to call. He returned a few moments later with the other members of Brian's Scout troop, along with his leader and two coleaders, all come to see how he was doing. The snowfall in the mountains hadn't been as heavy as originally expected, so they had made it back to Santa Fe as planned.

Brian delighted in being the center of attention, offering up his cast for signatures all around, while Gabriel and Madelyn busied themselves serving soft drinks to the boys and welcome mugs of fresh coffee to the men.

By the time they left, it was almost five-thirty. Bidding Madelyn to sit back and relax, Gabriel popped their dinner in the oven, set another place at the table and opened a bottle of wine.

Although the Caesar salad was a bit wilted, Gabriel and Madelyn agreed that, overall, the dinner was delicious. They thoroughly enjoyed the salad, chicken in wine sauce, fresh asparagus and potatoes lyonnaise. After one look at the adult fare, Brian, on the other hand, opted for beans and wieners hot out of the microwave.

After they'd eaten, Gabriel sent Madelyn back to the living room, forbidding her to lift a finger while he helped Brian take a bath and put on his pajamas. However, when he went in search of her so she could help tuck his son into bed, he found her in the kitchen, loading the dishwasher.

"I was going to do that," he chided.

"I know, but I felt kind of foolish just sitting, doing nothing, when I could have been helping out," she replied, her smile endearingly wry.

"You've helped quite a lot already."

"As in helped enough, thank you very much. Now please go home?" she asked, her smile fading.

"As in please stay and let *me* look after *you.*" Reaching out, he touched the back of his hand to her cheek. "Come and give my son a good-night hug. Then we can share the chocolate cake I stashed in the cupboard."

"Mayfair and Vargo chocolate cake?" she asked, following him down the hallway.

"Of course."

"You really went all out, didn't you?"

"I told you we'd do something special. Even postponed a night, the food was still pretty good, wasn't it?"

"Indeed, it was," she agreed. "I've thoroughly enjoyed the company, as well."

Brian looked half-asleep when they joined him in his room, but he perked up momentarily. He was snug in bed, his left arm propped on an extra pillow. Buddy was with him once again, curled up at his side.

Gabriel stood back as Madelyn bent to hug the boy, his heart swelling with an emotion he dared not name. She really did care for his son. The warmth and affection she showed him came naturally, without the slightest hint of pretense.

"Can Buddy stay with me all night?" Brian asked as Madelyn straightened and stepped back.

"I don't see why not," she replied. "He looks perfectly content there with you."

"What about you? Are you gonna stay here tonight, too?"

"I can't, really," she demurred, blushing prettily. "Unlike you, I have school tomorrow, and lots still to do in preparation for my classes."

"Will you come to see me when you get home?"

"I most certainly will. But only if you promise not to run Millie ragged."

"I won't." He smiled sleepily, looking from one to the other of them. "Good night, Madelyn. Good night, Dad."

Avoiding Gabriel's gaze, Madelyn moved away from the bed so he could give his son a hug. Then she walked back to the kitchen with him, suddenly much quieter than she had been earlier.

"You haven't changed your mind about the cake, have you?" he asked, concerned about her sudden shift in mood.

Brian's mention of her staying the night had definitely made her uncomfortable. Though the boy had meant well, Gabriel had a feeling his innocent question had reminded her that she really wasn't a part of their family, a reminder Gabriel would have preferred she hadn't had. While technically true, he already thought of her as one of them and wanted her to feel that way, too.

"Oh, no," she assured him, although she still refused to look at him. "But then I really should go back to the cottage. I have quite a bit of work—"

Not liking the barriers she suddenly seemed intent on erecting between them, Gabriel caught her by the arm and gently turned her to face him. When she ducked her head, he slid a finger under her chin, tilting her face up until she finally met his gaze.

An odd mix of sadness and bewilderment shadowed her gray-green eyes, making his heart ache. She looked so forlorn that he put his arms around her and drew her close.

"Don't go back there tonight, Maddy," he muttered, speaking his heart's desire aloud. "Stay here with me. Please…"

He hadn't intended to be so blunt, to blurt out such an intimate invitation in such a spontaneous manner that he was no less taken by surprise than she. He had meant to lure her into his bed with gentlemanly kisses and caresses, not a few blatant words of wanting, *needing*—

"Are you sure, Gabriel? Are you sure that's what you want?" she asked, resting her head against his chest.

"I can't remember ever wanting anything—*anyone*—more," he answered with absolute honesty.

"You can't?" She looked up at him wonderingly.

"No, I can't."

Taking a step back, he cupped her face in his hands and kissed her with a thoroughness he hoped would erase any lingering doubts she might have. After only the slightest hesitation, she kissed him back with equal fervor, sliding her arms around his waist and pressing her slender body close to his.

Needing no further encouragement, Gabriel shifted one hand from her face to her breast, stroking her gently. She tensed slightly, as if surprised, then relaxed with a quiet sigh. Still kissing her, he rubbed his thumb over her nipple, taut beneath the fabric of her bra and sweater. Again, she seemed startled by his touch. But again she quickly gave herself up to his tender ministrations, her own hands roving over his shoulders restlessly.

Reluctantly he raised his head at last, though he still cupped her breast in his palm.

"Come to bed with me, Maddy," he said, his voice low, his breathing ragged.

Though she didn't speak, she gazed up at him with such longing that he stole another swift kiss from her, then took her by the hand and headed toward the hallway.

A glance into Brian's bedroom as they passed assured him the boy was fast asleep. But just in case he awoke and called out, Gabriel closed his bedroom door only partway.

After turning on one small lamp on the dresser, he led Madelyn to his bed. He kissed her on the cheek, then moved alone to the fireplace where he'd laid fresh wood the day before. Now he struck a match, touched it to the kindling, waited a few moments for the flames to catch and walked back to her.

She had sat down on the edge of the mattress, and as he approached, she eyed him with a hint of trepidation. Kneeling in front of her, he took her hands in his.

"You look a little scared."

"I am," she said, her voice barely above a whisper.

"You're not afraid of me, are you? Because I would never hurt you. Never," he vowed.

"I know." She smiled slightly, but almost immediately her expression grew serious again.

"Then what's bothering you?"

"I…I have to tell you something, and I'm not sure…" As her words trailed off, she looked away.

Gently, so as not to frighten her further, Gabriel reached up, cupped her cheek in his palm, and turned her face until their gazes met again.

"Just tell me, Maddy. Whatever it is, it can't be that bad."

"I…" She blinked once, then again, a blush climbing her neck and spreading across her face. "I'm a…a virgin," she murmured.

"A virgin?" he repeated, sitting back on his heels.

"I've never…been with anyone…not ever."

Stunned, Gabriel stared at her, unable to speak as her words slowly sank into his befuddled brain. She was a virgin. She hadn't ever been with anyone. Not even Ethan.

Yet she was here in *his* bedroom, ready to give herself to *him*.

"I wanted to wait for someone special. Someone I loved, and I—"

"Hush, Maddy. You don't have to explain."

Moving to sit beside her, he turned her toward him and kissed the words from her lips. He didn't want to hear her say she loved him. Not when he couldn't say it back to her.

But he could make these moments special for her. He could *show* her that, as much as he was able, he truly cared for her and always would.

With a soul-deep sigh, Madelyn gave herself up to Gabriel's loving attention. He hadn't laughed at her. Nor had he looked at her with pity. Rather, he had gazed at her with a reverence that made her realize just how much he appreciated the simple gift she was about to give him.

The gift of her deepest love and trust.

"I'll be gentle with you, Maddy," he promised.

"And I'll be gentle with you, too," she said, teasing him lightheartedly.

He chuckled softly, sexily, pressing his lips against her neck, then nibbling at her ear.

"You're sounding awfully feisty all of a sudden."

"Mmm, I'm feeling..." Her breath caught in her throat as his hands found their way under her sweater.

"Yes? You're feeling what?" he growled, releasing the catch on her bra, then cupping her bare breasts in his palms.

"I'm...I'm..." She moaned softly as he gently played first one nipple, then the other, between his thumb and forefinger.

"What, sweetheart?"

"Is it just me, or is it...is it hot in here?"

She was on fire, burning up, every nerve ending in her body tingling with sensation as he tormented her lovingly with his hands and mouth.

"I'm a little warm myself," he admitted, laughing quietly.

To her dismay, he moved his hands away. Then, at her murmured protest, he kissed her on the cheek, adding, "But I have just the remedy for that."

"You're going to stop?"

"Only until I get us out of our clothes."

He did so deftly, kissing away her momentary embarrassment.

"You're so lovely," he said when she finally lay beside him, naked.

"So are you," she admitted, unabashedly admiring the masculine lines of his body, her gaze lingering here and…there.

Tentatively she trailed her fingertips over his broad chest, then his flat belly, finally touching him intimately, mesmerized by the hardness of him and the velvet softness.

"Maddy…" He breathed her name.

Then he was kissing her again and touching her as intimately as she had touched him. She writhed under his hands and mouth, unable to get enough of him, until, at last, he moved away from her just long enough to deal with a condom, then braced himself between her widespread thighs.

"Look at me, Madelyn," he muttered, his hands in her hair.

She did as he asked, falling into the depths of his dark eyes as he entered her ever so slowly, ever so gently. For an instant, she felt only the slightest pinch of pain, and then pleasure. A rolling, undulating, all-encompassing pleasure that built steadily as he moved inside her.

All control seemed to slip away, and suddenly she cried out, coming apart in his arms as he arched back, his own gratification imminent.

"Yes," he growled low in his throat, his gaze, still holding hers, triumphant. *"Yes."*

As their breathing finally slowed, Gabriel eased off her and pulled the bedcovers up over them. Then, lying on his side, he cradled her close, not quite ready to let her go yet. Perfectly happy to stay right where she was, Madelyn curled into his embrace with a sigh of utter contentment.

Never before had she felt so…complete. Always, there had been something lacking in her life. Now she knew that something had really been *someone*—someone to love with all her heart as she loved Gabriel Serrano.

But did he feel the same about her? she wondered, watching the flickering firelight throw shadows around the room. He hadn't said it in so many words, and when she had tried, he'd shushed her with a kiss. Yet why else would he have made love to her so tenderly?

Because they had made love, not simply had sex. She believed *that* with ever fiber of her being. So what if he hadn't actually said "I love you"? He had shown her how much she meant to him—

"I owe you an apology," he said, his deep voice cutting across her thoughts.

Confused, she glanced up at him. He met her gaze steadily, his expression unreadable.

"For what?" she asked.

"For not only assuming you were Ethan's mistress, but also flaunting it in your face. I had no right to denigrate you that way."

"You made a mistake—understandable enough," she said, looking away. "And I didn't really say anything to discourage you."

"You shouldn't have had to defend yourself to me. I should have believed you when you told me you were only his assistant," he insisted.

"Please, Gabriel, don't worry about it anymore."

"You're an honest, decent person, Madelyn. I just want you to know that I know it. Despite the insinuations I made, I think, deep down inside, I always knew it."

Wordlessly, she stared into the distance, aware that she wasn't quite as honest or as decent as Gabriel believed she was. She had kept something about her relationship with Ethan a secret. Something she should have revealed weeks ago. Something that could drastically change how Gabriel thought of her. Something that could end what had only just begun between them.

"I wish I deserved such high praise, but I don't," she said at last.

She rolled away from him and sat up, dragging the blanket up to cover her bare breasts.

Frowning, Gabriel sat up, too.

"What do you mean?" he asked, turning to face her.

"Just what I said." She risked a glance at him, then added, "I haven't been completely honest with you about Ethan...about his...death."

"Are you telling me he died as a result of something other than the virus he contracted?"

"I'm not sure. It's possible the virus caused his death. But..." She paused, glancing at him again. "But it's also possible he committed suicide."

"Suicide?" Gabriel repeated, his confusion evident.

"He wasn't quite as upbeat as I led you to believe those last few days on Roatán. He was unusually quiet, and as our departure drew closer, he became more and more withdrawn. He seemed so…sad. But when I questioned him about it, he insisted he was only tired. I wanted to believe him because…because it was just easier," she admitted. "There was so much to do—finishing the photographs for *Travel International,* packing up our gear. I just wasn't paying attention to the signals he was sending out. Otherwise, I would have known.…

"That last night…he asked me to stay with him. It was a running joke between us—he would hit on me and I'd tell him to get lost. But that night, he really needed me, and I just didn't realize—"

Covering her face with her hands, she began to weep. "I'm so sorry, Gabriel—"

"Oh, Maddy, don't cry," he murmured, putting his arms around her and holding her close.

"I was the only one there with him. If I'd just *thought* for half a minute, he might still be alive."

"But you said you only *suspect* he committed suicide. So that means you could be wrong, couldn't you?"

Sitting back, Gabriel took a tissue from the box on the nightstand and handed it to Madelyn. She accepted it gratefully, dabbed at her eyes and blew her nose.

"Yes, but—" she began.

"Did he leave a note?"

"Well, no. But when I went through his things afterward I found an empty pill bottle. The last time I'd seen it, a couple of weeks earlier, it had been almost full of the capsules his doctor prescribed for pain. Ethan rarely took them. He claimed they made him woozy, and they did. Still, he insisted on keeping the prescription filled just in case he ever really needed them.

"To empty the bottle that quickly, he would have had

to have been using them regularly, and I would have noticed *that.*''

"Even if he was using them at night to help him sleep? Even if, gradually, over time, he upped the dosage on his own because the original dosage wasn't helping anymore?''

"No, not necessarily,'' Madelyn admitted.

Looking away, she considered what Gabriel was suggesting. Ethan could very well have been using the pills at night without telling her. Which meant he could very well have overdosed by accident. Still…

"I should have *known,*'' she insisted.

"Not if he didn't want you to. Remember what you told me a few weeks ago? Ethan was an adult. He made his own choices, choices that, more often than not, were to his benefit. Whether he took the pills inadvertently or intentionally, ultimately *he* made the decision.

"You did what you could for him, Madelyn. But he was dying a slow death, a debilitating death. Even if you'd stayed with him that last night, you would have only been postponing the inevitable. Ethan would have never come back here to live off my charity. Nor would he have allowed himself to be dependent on you for much longer. He was a proud man. He would have rather died first.''

Gabriel took another tissue from the box and blotted the fresh tears trickling down her cheeks.

"Stop blaming yourself, Maddy,'' he pleaded softly. "That's not what he would have wanted you to do. And it's not what I want you to do, either. I want you to see yourself for the good person you truly are.''

"Oh, Gabriel,'' she murmured, going to him gladly when he reached out for her.

She wanted to believe him. What he said made sense.

And if *he* didn't consider her at fault, then surely she hadn't been.

"You did the best you could with what you had," Gabriel assured her, as if aware that she still had her doubts. "That's all any of us can ask of ourselves."

Smoothing a hand over her hair, he bent and kissed her cheek, then shifted so that he could brush his lips across hers. With a ragged sigh, she gave herself up to him again, letting him soothe away the last of her sadness and regret.

Whether Ethan had died of natural causes or by his own hand, she couldn't bring him back. But she could honor him by making the most of the legacy he'd left her. A legacy that had less to do with part-ownership of a five-hundred-thousand-dollar house than it did with his half brother and a little boy named Brian.

They were the reason Ethan had sent her here, she acknowledged with sudden understanding. *They* were his real gift to her. Ethan had known Gabriel and he had known her, and he must have realized that, given a chance, they would see in each other what he had seen in them, and admired, no matter how disdainfully he'd treated them.

As Gabriel worked his magic, kissing her, touching her, Madelyn imagined Ethan looking down on them, smiling that sly smile of his. For just a moment, she smiled, too, sending him a whisper of thanks. Then she focused all her attention on Gabriel.

Her hands in his hair, she tugged his head up.

"I love you," she murmured.

Wordlessly, he met her gaze, then took her mouth in a deep, drugging kiss, shifting her under him, showing her, once more, just how much he needed her.

* * *

Much later, when Madelyn mumbled drowsily about going back to the cottage, Gabriel insisted she stay with him until morning, and she agreed without the slightest hesitation. He checked on Brian, who was still sleeping soundly, set the clock for six, giving her more than enough time to get ready for school, then settled her beside him, an arm looped around her waist possessively.

Feeling more at peace than she had in months, she slept deeply. And when she awoke, not only to the buzz of the alarm, but to the feathery touch of Gabriel's lips on her shoulder, as well, she turned to him with an eagerness she couldn't have hidden if she tried.

It was closer to seven than six when Gabriel and she finally slipped out of the house and headed across to the cottage. He had refused to let her walk back alone despite her protests, and as she waited for him to unlock the door, she was glad that he had.

She didn't want what they had shared to seem furtive. Yet she knew they couldn't be blatant about their sexual relationship for Brian's sake, as well as their own. Gabriel, especially, could be hurt by rumors of misconduct. They would have to be circumspect until they had a chance to make some decisions about the future.

Their future together, Madelyn thought, having no doubt that Gabriel's intentions were honorable. Even if he still hadn't said he loved her....

"We can leave a little later than usual if you think you'll need more time," he said as he opened the door.

"I'll be ready by seven-thirty," she assured him.

"I didn't mean to keep you quite so long—"

"I'm glad you did." Rising up on her toes, she kissed him on the nose. "Now, *please*, go back home before Millie pulls up and catches us out here."

"I'm not thrilled about having to leave you like this."

"Me, neither."

"Well, then, I guess we should do something about it fairly soon, shouldn't we?"

"As long as that *something* involves us being together, yes we should," she agreed with a teasing grin.

She couldn't believe she was being so bold. But after last night, she saw no reason to hide her feelings from him any longer.

"My plan exactly."

He stole a swift kiss. Then, with obvious reluctance, he turned and strode back across the courtyard.

Madelyn stood in the doorway, watching him go, her heart filled with love. At last, aware that time was flying by, she headed into the cottage.

She could hardly believe that her dream seemed to be coming true, after all. But deep down inside, along with her love, she had faith in Gabriel, as well.

Faith that she meant as much to him as he meant to her, and that one day soon, he'd find the words to tell her.

Chapter 10

Almost two full weeks had passed since the Sunday night Gabriel first made love to Madelyn, weeks that had been among the best of his life. They had also been among the busiest he'd had in quite a while, and that was why he hadn't yet had a chance to discuss marriage with her. While they had spent as much time together as possible, the right moment simply hadn't presented itself.

They had both been swamped with school-related work of one kind or another, including various extracurricular activities that first week. Also, Brian had been more demanding than usual of their time and attention as he gradually, and occasionally grudgingly, adjusted to life with one arm in a cast and sling.

Bored and lonely after a week away from school, he had begged to have friends over all weekend, and although it had meant Gabriel and Madelyn would have to be on their best behavior—that is, sleeping separately—Gabriel had agreed. Then three days of regional meetings for junior and senior high school principals had taken him to Albuquerque the past week.

However, as of three-thirty that afternoon, school was officially out for a week so students and teachers alike could enjoy Spring Break. And with Brian well enough to spend the night at Donny's house, Gabriel and Madelyn could finally enjoy some much-needed time alone together. As they would now that their dinner with Henry Martin and his wife, Magda, was over, and they were almost home.

Time to talk about the future. Time, too, to make slow, sweet love.

Rather than assuage Gabriel's desire for Madelyn, the odd moments when they'd been able to slip away together had left him wanting her all the more. And she still dominated his thoughts day and night. Had he not known himself better, he could have been tempted to believe he was besotted with her.

She was so very lovely, and she had honored him deeply with the gift of her virginity. A gift he would cherish all the days of his life.

Her honesty about Ethan had touched him, too. Telling him that his brother had possibly committed suicide hadn't been easy for her. She had blamed herself, and had been afraid he would blame her, as well. Yet she'd had the integrity to reveal what she thought to be the truth, and the consequences be damned.

Knowing Ethan as he did, Gabriel hadn't thought for a moment that she'd been at fault. He had admired her all the more for the strength and courage she had displayed. And he had tried to dispel any doubts she had about her basic decency with what he considered some success.

"Did you have a nice time?" he asked, glancing at her as he reached out and took her by the hand.

They were nearing the house, driving in his truck, and he realized she had been as quiet as he since they had bid the Martins good-night. He wondered if the thoughts she had been thinking had been as heartening as his.

"I had a wonderful time," she admitted, favoring him with a winsome smile. "I'm so glad Henry suggested it. I really enjoyed meeting Magda. She can be so serious, but she also has a great sense of humor."

"Being married to Henry, she has to," Gabriel said. "He's really off-the-wall most of the time."

"We creative types usually are," Madelyn teased. "Which probably explains why I'm so attracted to you. You can be serious, but you have a great sense of humor, too."

"You're attracted to me, are you?" He grinned at her as he pulled into the driveway.

"Oh, please. Don't tell me you haven't noticed?"

"Well, on a few occasions, a *very* few occasions, I've gotten that impression. But a little reminder would be nice."

"Your place or mine?" she asked, arching a delicate eyebrow.

"Mine, I think. That's where we left the dog, isn't it?"

"Yes, I do believe it is," she agreed as they left the truck in the garage and walked across the courtyard.

Since Brian and Buddy had become best friends during the week Brian was home from school, the little dog had been dividing his time between the house and cottage. However, he always spent the night wherever Madelyn would be so neither one of them ended up home alone.

Tonight, Madelyn had brought Buddy over to the house before they left to meet Henry and his wife. Obviously, she had been thinking ahead to this part of the evening—the part they would be spending alone together—just as much as he had.

The dog greeted them—actually, Madelyn—as if he had been left alone for two weeks instead of only two hours. Of course, Gabriel could understand how he felt. He, too, always seemed to want to kiss Madelyn senseless whenever they had been apart for any amount of time.

Laughing, she put the dog down, then shooed him outside so he could take care of his business. Gabriel helped her out of her coat, stealing a quick kiss of his own, took off his coat, crossed to the counter and started to fill the coffeepot.

There would be no better time for them to sit down and talk about the future. And once they had gotten that out of the way—

"What are you doing?" Madelyn asked, her voice whisper soft as she came up behind him, put her arms around his waist and rubbed up against him in sensual invitation.

"Making coffee," he answered, though he set the pot down. "I wanted to talk—"

"No," she stated, rising up on her toes so she could nibble at the back of his neck.

"No?"

"I don't want to talk now. I want to make love."

Turning to face her, Gabriel put his hands on her shoulders, determined to remain firm in his decision that they get certain matters settled first. But one look at Madelyn's sassy smile, one luscious taste of her tempting mouth, one touch of her teasingly provocative hands, and he surrendered to her wishes with a low groan.

Pausing just long enough to let the dog in, then closet

him in Brian's room, Gabriel wasted little time getting Madelyn out of her black dress and into his bed. But then, with the whole night ahead of them, he slowed the pace considerably, doing a good deal of tempting and teasing of his own.

He now knew exactly what she enjoyed most—long, slow kisses all over her delectable body, coupled with tenderly intimate touches—and he delighted as much in giving her what she wanted as he did receiving the darkly sensual, deeply sexual gratification she so willingly offered him in return.

He marveled anew at how freely she gave of herself and how trustingly she came apart in his arms—once, then once again—until he finally yielded to his own breathtaking fulfillment with a shuddering moan.

Afterward, Gabriel held Madelyn close, staring into the darkness as their breathing slowed and their bodies cooled. He wished he could see her face, but he hadn't taken the time to switch on a lamp, much less light a fire in the fireplace.

They would sleep soon, anyway, so they didn't really need a light on. But there was wood on the grate, and the flickering flames would provide just the right atmosphere for the talk he was still set upon having with her.

He eased away from her, shushing her protest with a kiss and a few words of explanation, lit the fire and returned gladly to the warmth of her open arms, all within a matter of minutes.

"Now we're going to talk," he said, plumping up their pillows, then holding her close.

"That sounded rather ominous," she replied, glancing at him, the faintest hint of wariness evident in her eyes. "Is something wrong?"

"Not at all." He gave her a reassuring hug, and she

relaxed against him once more. "I just wanted to be sure I had your attention."

"You do," she purred, her hand trailing down his chest and across his belly. "My undivided attention…"

"Maddy," he chastised her gently, catching her hand and holding it still before she could sidetrack him yet again. "I'm serious."

She heaved an exaggeratedly exasperated sigh. "Okay. I'm listening."

Now that the moment had come for him to say his piece, Gabriel hesitated. He hadn't any doubt that Madelyn would accept his proposal of marriage. She had made no secret of her feelings for him or his son, and from little things she'd said, she seemed to believe their relationship would be a long-term one. But all the same, he was about to lay himself open to her in a way he hadn't with any woman since Lily walked out on him.

Of course, he wasn't going to declare his undying love for her, he reminded himself. He wasn't capable of such profound emotion anymore. As pragmatically as possible, he was going to express his admiration and affection for her, then suggest that marriage would simplify their lives, provide Brian with a two-parent family and be the ideal solution to the problem of their co-ownership of what he considered *his* home.

Thus prompted, Gabriel took a deep breath and began, his voice matter-of-fact.

"You know you mean a great deal to me, Madelyn, and to Brian, as well. Over the past few weeks, you've become like one of the family. We're almost always together, and we enjoy a lot of the same things. So, I was thinking that we should get married. Then we could share a bed without worrying about gossip. You could be a real mother to Brian, too. And best of all, each of us owning half the house would no longer be a problem.''

Having stated his case concisely, Gabriel paused, waiting for Madelyn to reply, but only silence greeted his ears. After several long moments, he looked down at her with sudden concern.

Though she still lay close to him, he sensed a slight stiffening of her body, and she stared at the fire as if she were a million miles away. Not exactly the response he'd been anticipating.

"So, what do you say, Maddy?'' he prodded softly, brushing his lips against her tousled hair. "Will you marry me?''

"Gabriel, I…''. Her expression unreadable, she shifted away from him, putting a little distance between them. "I wasn't expecting…'' She hesitated again, took several rapid breaths, then continued, "I'd really like a little time to think. Marriage is a…a big commitment. I wouldn't want to rush—''

"No, of course not,'' he agreed hastily, his relief almost palpable.

For a while there, he had been afraid she was going to refuse him outright, but she just needed a day or two to get used to the idea. That was understandable. He *had* sprung his proposal on her out of the blue. And he *was* asking a lot of her. He did want her to be sure, absolutely sure.

"I don't think it will take me long to decide,'' she added in a barely audible voice.

"Take as much time as you need,'' he urged, drawing her close again.

He would spend the next few days doing everything he could to convince her to accept his proposal, he decided. He knew they could be happy together, and he wanted her to know it, too.

"I will."

He hugged her again, then yawned sleepily.

"Boy, am I bushed," he muttered, closing his eyes.

"You're going to have a busy day tomorrow. You'd better get some sleep."

"Yeah, I'd better. G'night, Maddy."

"Good night, Gabriel," Madelyn replied quietly, a tear trickling down her cheek.

She swiped at it as surreptitiously as she could, though she doubted Gabriel would notice. He was already sound asleep, snoring softly as if he hadn't a care in the world.

And he hadn't, she thought. Not now that he had found the ultimate solution to his biggest problem—her half-ownership of the house.

No wonder he had never said he loved her. He hadn't. He'd simply wanted what he believed to be his, and he'd found the ideal way to get it back without incurring a major debt.

Of course, she had gone right along with his little plan. She had fallen into his arms like the lonely, love-starved woman she was. And for reasons of her own, she hadn't mentioned the money he owed her.

Now she realized that for reasons of *his* own, Gabriel hadn't, either. Not in weeks—weeks during which he had subtly begun to pursue her.

She had been so sure that he was courting her because he loved her. Truly, deeply, completely. But in reality, she had only meant a "great deal" to him.

Great deal, indeed.

Were she foolish enough to accept his proposal, he would certainly be getting one. An eager bedmate, a mother for his son, and best of all—*his* words, not hers—

the one prize only she had to offer: full ownership of his house.

He could find a bedmate for himself, as well as a mother for his son, almost anywhere. As for the house, he wouldn't have had to marry her to get that, either. Only he hadn't known that.

Along with telling Gabriel about Ethan's death, Madelyn had also intended to tell him she didn't want the money he owed her. But she hadn't had a chance that Sunday night, and she hadn't really thought about it again in the weeks since.

The subject hadn't come up in any of their conversations until tonight, and then, only as part of Gabriel's proposal. A proposal she now realized he wouldn't have made if he'd been aware of her plan to relinquish Ethan's bequest.

Granted, she could awaken him now, and inform him of her decision. But she'd probably blubber like a baby the whole time, and end up looking even more foolish.

It would be much easier on her to wait until tomorrow, call Cullen Birney, tell *him* and let him pass on the good news to Gabriel.

Tomorrow, too, she would move out of the cottage and start looking for an apartment as she'd originally planned. Gabriel and Brian were going to be gone all day, so getting away without a major confrontation would be possible.

Gabriel was supposed to pick up his son at eight in the morning. Then the two of them, along with Donny Murphy and his father, were going straight to a father-son jamboree hosted by the regional Scouting association. They wouldn't be home again until four or five o'clock.

She'd prefer to leave Santa Fe altogether. Unfortunately, that wasn't possible just yet. She had made a com-

mitment to teach until the end of May, and she wasn't
about to go back on her word.

Granted, seeing Gabriel at the junior high school
would be painful. But as long as she had a place of her
own to go to each afternoon, she would be able to tolerate
the situation for the few months remaining in the school
year.

Slowly easing away from Gabriel so as not to disturb
him, Madelyn wiped the last of her tears from her eyes.
She couldn't stay with him any longer, knowing that he
didn't love her, after all. She'd rather go back to the
cottage and start getting her things together.

She could only hope he wouldn't realize she'd left his
bed and decide to come after her. The thought of facing
him in her current state was beyond bearing. Running
into him at school after Spring Break ended would be
difficult enough. But perhaps, by then, she would be capable of facing him without falling apart.

Somehow she managed to gather her clothes and dress.
Then she crept down the hall, opened the door to Brian's
room, scooped Buddy into her arms and hurried to the
kitchen. There, she grabbed her coat, let herself out
through the French door and ran across to the cottage,
hugging the little dog close.

Tears blurring her vision again, Madelyn tried not to
think about Brian. The boy wouldn't understand why
she'd run off without saying goodbye. No matter how
Gabriel chose to explain the situation, he would be hurt
and confused. And he wouldn't have Buddy to keep him
company.

Right now, however, the dog was all she had. She just
wasn't strong enough to leave him behind along with all
her hopes and dreams.

* * *

"Well, Ms. St. James, what can I do for you?" Cullen Birney asked, standing as Madelyn entered his office at ten o'clock Saturday morning.

She had called him just after eight from the hotel room she had checked into around midnight after paying a premium so Buddy could stay with her. Like a woman possessed, she had thrown clothes, camera equipment, photographs, schoolbooks and papers into her car. Then she had grabbed the dog and driven to one of the big, expensive hotels where the desk clerks were used to guests arriving at all hours of the day or night.

The rest of her things—the bed linens, towels, rugs and other odds and ends—she had decided to leave behind until she found an apartment. She didn't think Gabriel would toss the stuff out. But if he did, then so be it. Getting away without being caught by him had been more important to her than just about anything else.

At the hotel, she hadn't even tried to sleep. Instead, she had sat in a chair by the window, watching as the sky faded from black to gray, lightened to orange and gold, then burst into a brilliant blue as the sun crept over the horizon.

Schooling herself to be patient, she had waited as long as common courtesy dictated, then finally called the lawyer, all but begging him to meet with her on what she had termed a matter of urgent business.

"I would like you to draw up papers for me to sign relinquishing Ethan's bequest," she stated simply. "Then I want you to see that Gabriel Serrano gets a copy as soon as possible."

Cullen eyed her quietly for what seemed like forever. Madelyn could only imagine what must be going through his mind. She had no doubt she looked as bad as she felt.

And no matter how she tried, she couldn't seem to keep her voice from wavering.

"Are you sure you want to do that?" he asked at last.

"Absolutely sure," she replied, forcing herself to meet his gaze.

"This seems rather sudden to me." He paused, his expression thoughtful, then added, "Maybe we should discuss your decision with Gabe—"

"*No,*" she cut in fearfully. "There's nothing to discuss. My mind is made up. Just draw up the papers, let me sign them, then see that he gets a copy."

"Have you discussed this with him at all?" Cullen prodded, frowning.

"No."

"Then he'll want to know why—"

"Tell him…" She blinked rapidly, trying to hold back the tears pooling in her eyes as she dragged in a steadying breath. "Tell him I finally realized how important the house is to him. That I know he'd do anything to hang on to it, but what he had in mind won't be necessary, after all."

"You know, Ms. St. James, giving up such a large sum of money seemingly on the spur of the moment is highly irregular. I'm not sure—"

"Please, Mr. Birney," she pleaded. "Draw up the papers. I know what I'm doing."

While she sat in the chair by his desk, clutching her hands in her lap, trying not to cry, the lawyer pulled up what appeared to be a standard document on his computer. He made several additions and deletions, printed three copies and gave them to her to look over.

Satisfied that the property at 15 Alameda Road would now belong solely to Gabriel Serrano, Madelyn signed all three copies, witnessed by two of the real-estate agents from the office across the hallway. After they had gone, she took the copy that was hers to keep, folded it and stuck it in her purse, then stood to leave.

"Thank you, Mr. Birney."

"You're welcome, Ms. St. James." He shook her proffered hand. Then, as he walked with her to the door, he asked, "Will you be leaving Santa Fe now?"

"Oh, no," she replied. "At least not until school's out. I'm teaching at the junior high school."

"Does that mean you'll still be living in the cottage, as well?"

"I've decided to move into an apartment of my own as soon as possible. In the meantime, I'm staying in a hotel."

"I see." He halted at the doorway, and once again eyed her thoughtfully. "Would you mind telling me which one, in case something else comes up regarding Ethan's estate? I'd really like to know where to get in touch with you."

Without thinking, she named the hotel where she was staying. Then, suddenly wary, she added, "But I'd rather you not tell anyone else."

"Certainly," he agreed. "I'll treat that information with the utmost discretion."

"Thanks." She offered him a slight smile, then started out the door.

"Take care, Ms. St. James."

"You, too, Mr. Birney."

Outside, the sun blazed in the bright blue sky and the air carried more than a hint of warmth. A lovely day— so lovely it brought tears to Madelyn's eyes. Tears she shed all the way back to her room at the hotel.

There, she curled up on the bed with her scraggly little mutt, telling herself enough was enough. She had made a mistake where Gabriel Serrano was concerned. But she was a smart woman—a woman who had always learned from her mistakes. She only wished this one hadn't been quite so devastating.

Still, she would get over it eventually, and be a better person for it.

"At least that's some consolation," she muttered.

Beside her, Buddy whined softly, then licked her chin, offering what commiseration he could.

Gratefully, Madelyn hugged him close.

Then, her new resolve apparently not as firm as she'd hoped, somehow she found herself weeping once again.

Chapter 11

"Madelyn's car is gone," Brian said as Gabriel opened the garage door late Saturday afternoon.

"Yes, it is," he agreed, frowning as he eyed the empty space where her sporty little compact should have been.

"Where did she go?" his son asked.

"I don't know."

"When will she be back?"

"I don't know that, either," Gabriel admitted uneasily.

"Maybe she left a message for us."

"Yeah, maybe she did."

Under normal circumstances, there wouldn't have been any maybe about it. As a matter of course, Madelyn would have made sure he knew where she was going and when she planned to return. But there had been nothing normal about the way she had left his bed sometime during the night, then just disappeared.

Gabriel remembered awakening sometime after midnight and vaguely realizing she wasn't there with him.

But he had assumed she was in the bathroom or checking on the dog, and would be right back. He had rolled over and, worn-out from the long hours he'd put in at the regional meeting that week, he had immediately fallen asleep again.

When he awoke a second time to find himself alone in bed, it had been almost seven o'clock in the morning. A quick check of the house had revealed that Madelyn had dressed, taken the dog and, he assumed, gone back to the cottage. He had been confused by her absence, but not unduly upset.

As he had hurried to shower and dress so he wouldn't be late arriving at the Murphys' house, he had convinced himself that she'd just wanted a little time alone to consider his proposal. Time, he acknowledged, that she more than deserved when he took into account the kind of commitment he had asked her to make. She'd been foot-loose and fancy-free for a long time. When she married him, she would be acquiring a ready-made family.

When, not *if*, he had thought that morning, certain of what her answer would be. But his confidence had waned somewhat when he'd stopped at the cottage to see her on his way out.

She hadn't answered his knock on the door, nor had the dog barked as was his habit. Gabriel had thought about going back to the house to get the spare key so he could let himself in. But he had already been running late, and he'd figured she and the mutt were probably just sleeping more soundly than usual.

Until he walked into the garage to get his truck and saw that her car was gone. Then he had suffered his first faint pang of apprehension.

She had known about his plans for the day because he'd told her. Yet she hadn't mentioned any plans of her own at any time that he could recall. And he was sure he would have. Finding her car gone would have jolted his memory, if nothing else.

The father-son Scout jamboree had diverted Gabriel's attention most of the day. Still, at odd moments, he had found himself wondering where Madelyn had gone. Maybe out to breakfast with one of the teachers she'd become friendly with. Or maybe off to the outskirts of town, taking photographs. Nothing out of the ordinary, and surely nothing to worry about.

Only, he grew more and more concerned as the day progressed. She had been so quiet after he'd mentioned marriage. Had he scared her away?

She hadn't seemed frightened by the prospect of becoming his lawfully wedded wife. Nor had she seemed overwhelmed in any noticeable way. She had just been…quiet. Very quiet, and thoughtful. But that wasn't out of character. In fact, her response had been about what he'd expected, although, in all honesty, he had thought she might display a tad more enthusiasm.

Now, arriving home and finding her either still gone, or gone again, Gabriel had to admit her absence seriously troubled him. Frowning, he glanced at the darkened windows of the cottage, then followed Brian across the courtyard.

"Hey, Dad, there *is* a message for you," his son called out as he halted in front of the French doors.

With a surge of relief, Gabriel spied the small white envelope taped to one of the glass panels. However, his relief faded almost immediately when he saw that the handwriting spelling out his name wasn't Madelyn's, but rather someone else's he didn't recognize.

He yanked the envelope off the door, ripped it open and withdrew a single sheet of yellow legal paper. Unfolding it, he scanned down to Cullen's signature, then read what the lawyer had written.

Gabe:
An answering machine is a good investment. Saves lots of time for people—like your lawyer—who are trying to get in touch with you. Anyway, call me just as soon as you get back. I'll be home all evening. I have some good news for you that I'd like to pass on.

Cullen

"Is the note from Madelyn?" Brian asked hopefully.

"No, it's from Mr. Birney."

Gabriel unlocked the door and walked into the house with his son.

Crestfallen, the boy unfastened his jacket and wriggled out of it.

"What did he want?"

"To talk to me about something," Gabriel answered.

"What?"

"He said he had some good news for me. Guess I'll call him and find out what it is."

"Do you think Madelyn left Buddy in the cottage?"

No longer interested in the contents of the note, Brian looked at Gabriel expectantly.

"Why don't I go see?"

Given a good excuse, he set the note aside, took the spare key to the cottage from one of the drawers under the counter and headed back outside.

He didn't really expect to find the dog in the cottage. However, neither did he anticipate the sense of abandonment he felt as he crossed the threshold and switched on a light. For several moments, he looked around, sure that something was missing.

Had the place not been as neat and tidy as usual, he would have sworn a burglary had been committed. Or that Madelyn had moved out—

Frowning, Gabriel stepped forward and closed the door. Most of her things were still in place—rugs on the floor, comforter on the bed, afghan on the sofa, candles and silk flowers on the end tables. Still…

The framed photographs weren't there. Nor were her schoolbooks and papers.

With a sinking feeling in the pit of his stomach, Gabriel crossed to the closet and opened the door. Empty. He moved on to the dresser and chest, pulling the drawers open. Empty, too. Her clothes, her cameras, books, papers, photographs, the dog—all that she would have considered her most important possessions—all gone, along with her.

''Oh, hell,'' he muttered, sitting down on the bed and staring at the sole photograph remaining atop the nightstand—the photograph Brian had taken of the two of them together.

Where had she gone? And, more important, *why?* Because he had asked her to marry him? That didn't seem like a good reason to run away. Not if she loved him as she'd said, and he loved her—

Loved her? But he didn't—

Drawing in a ragged breath, Gabriel closed his eyes as realization washed over him. The realization that he *did* love her, more than he had ever thought possible. Yet he had never told her. He'd been too damned busy denying it to himself.

Still, wouldn't the fact that he'd asked her to marry him—?

Again he swore softly, remembering just how un-
emotionally he had done *that*. The words he'd used, the
practical tone of his voice. He must have sounded as
though he was negotiating a business deal, a business
deal he couldn't blame her for finding completely unten-
able.

She had offered him her truest love, and he'd offered
her an opportunity to service his every need.

"Maddy, I am so sorry," he whispered into the silence
surrounding him.

Too little, he knew. And obviously, much, much too
late.

Although...

He couldn't believe she was gone for good. She had
left too much of value behind here in the cottage, and
she had signed a contract with the school district to teach
until the end of the year. A contract he was almost pos-
itive she would honor.

Which meant she was still somewhere here in Santa
Fe.

Somehow he was going to find a way to track her
down, and then he was going to tell her how he really
felt. He was going to say what he should have said weeks
ago. He was going to say that he loved her, and mean it
with all his heart and soul, then beg her to give him a
second chance.

Somewhat heartened, Gabriel locked up the cottage
and returned to the house. Brian greeted him at the door,
a worried look on his face.

"What's wrong, son?" he asked.

"You were gone so long, I was afraid something happened to you."

"I'm just fine." He bent and hugged the boy.

"I guess Buddy wasn't there."

''No, he wasn't.''

''Well, I'm gonna watch television for a while.'' Dejectedly, he left the kitchen.

Relieved that he wouldn't have to answer any questions about Madelyn just yet, Gabriel let him go.

. He wasn't hungry, but he knew Brian would be wanting dinner in an hour or so. As he stood at the counter, trying to decide what to fix, Cullen's note caught his attention. Gabriel couldn't imagine what kind of good news the lawyer had for him. Unless it had something to do with Madelyn.

He crossed to the telephone, looked up Cullen's home number in the book and punched it into the keypad. Cullen answered after only two rings.

''I got your note,'' Gabriel said, too anxious to bother with a greeting. ''Does this have anything to do with Madelyn?''

''Funny you should ask that—'' Cullen began.

''You mentioned good news,'' Gabriel cut in. ''What is it?''

''Well, I'd rather tell you in person. Unless you have something else to do, I can come over right now.''

''I'll be here,'' Gabriel replied and hung up.

He paced in the kitchen, aware that minutes *did* pass like hours when you were waiting for someone, especially someone who might be able to help you rectify a serious wrong.

When the doorbell finally rang, Brian beat him to the entryway. Gabriel heard him call out ''Who is it?'' in a hopeful tone, then saw him turn away unhappily when Cullen, not Madelyn, replied.

''For you, Dad. Mr. Birney.''

''Thanks, son.''

Gabriel let Cullen in, then led him back to the kitchen

where they could talk in private. As the lawyer took off his coat and sat at the table, he poured mugs of coffee for both of them, then joined him there.

"All right, tell me the good news as it pertains to Madelyn," he insisted, having taken care of the necessary niceties.

"She called me early this morning and asked if I would meet her at my office. Said she had some urgent business to take care of," Cullen stated, then paused to take a drink of his coffee.

"What kind of urgent business?" Gabriel prompted impatiently.

Cullen eyed him consideringly for several moments.

"You really don't know, do you?"

"Damn it, Cullen, if I *knew,* why would I be asking you?"

"You've got a point there," the lawyer agreed, then went on. "As I was saying, she called, and I offered to meet with her at ten o'clock. She was right on time, but I have to admit, I was concerned by her appearance. She was neatly dressed and her hair was combed, but she had a wounded look about her. As if someone had kicked her when she was down. I could tell she'd been crying, too."

"Aw, hell," Gabriel muttered, clenching his hands around his mug.

"I take it you do know something about *that,*" Cullen said.

"Yes, I know something about that," Gabriel admitted.

"Then maybe the rest won't come as a surprise to you."

"The rest?"

Cullen opened his briefcase and took out several sheets of paper.

"She had me draw up a document for her to sign. In it, she gives up her claim to half the value of your property. I have your copy of it here." Cullen handed Gabriel the papers, then sat back in his chair, took another drink of his coffee and added, "I don't know how you managed it, but it looks like you're off the hook. I was assuming that would be good news—"

"I managed it by acting like a Class A bastard," Gabriel replied as he scanned the pages.

"That doesn't sound like you, Gabe."

"Believe me, I did." He tossed the document aside and rubbed a hand over his face. "Not that it's any of my business, but did she happen to mention *why* she decided to do this?"

"From what you've been saying, I thought you knew."

"I have a pretty good idea, but I'd like to be sure."

"She said she finally realized how important the house is to you. That she knew you'd do anything to hang on to it, but what you had in mind wouldn't be necessary, after all," Cullen said, then eyed him quizzically. "So, what were you going to do? Rob a bank?"

"No."

"Then what precipitated all this?"

"I asked her to marry me."

"You did *what?*"

"Oh, it wasn't the hearts-and-flowers proposal she deserved. I didn't want any part of falling of love. I wanted a nice, safe business deal. What I didn't realize until a little while ago is that I *do* love her. But apparently she's gone, and I don't have the faintest idea how to find her, much less how to win her back if I do."

"I know where she is," Cullen stated, smiling slyly over his coffee mug. "I got her to tell me where she was staying just in case I had to contact her regarding Ethan's estate. And since it seems to me that you'd like to discuss related business with her…''

"Tell me where she is, Cullen. *Now.*"

Cullen obligingly gave him the name of her hotel.

"But I don't have her room number," he added.

"I'll find a way to get it," Gabriel assured him.

"Let me know what happens."

"I will."

"You know, I've been wondering…" Cullen mused as he put on his coat and picked up his briefcase.

"What?" Gabriel asked.

"Do you think maybe this is what Ethan had in mind when he left his half of the house to her?"

"I really don't know. Ethan lived by a code of his own. A couple of things I am sure of, though. He must have cared for her quite a bit, and he must have expected me to treat her better than I did, or he never would have sent her here."

"I'd never have guessed you two would end up together. Not the way you sniped at each other that first night."

"Well, thanks to my pigheadedness, we haven't ended up together yet, and maybe we never will."

"Oh, I think there's hope," Cullen said. "But when you see her again, go for the hearts-and-flowers routine, okay?"

"Okay."

After Gabriel saw Cullen to the door, he called Carol Murphy, and pleading a minor emergency, asked if Brian could spend another night at her house. She readily agreed, and within minutes he had his surprised and reasonably pleased son bundled into the truck.

The boy was still concerned about Madelyn's continued absence, but Gabriel told him not to worry, that Mr. Birney had seen her earlier in the day, and she was all right.

"Are you gonna see her now?" Brian asked as they pulled out of the driveway.

"Yes, I am," Gabriel replied, trying to bolster his flagging confidence.

He had no idea how to approach her, but after dropping Brian off at the Murphys' house, he drove on to the hotel where she was staying.

Getting her room number proved to be impossible. He was informed that yes, Madelyn St. James was a guest at the hotel, but they were not allowed to give out any other information about her. However, if he wished to leave a message for her, they would see that she got it. Or he could call her, via the operator, on the hotel telephone in the lobby.

Gabriel considered his limited options, finally deciding to call her. At least then he would know whether or not she was currently in her room.

She answered after three rings, and he quickly hung up with a satisfied nod. He now knew where she was. He also knew that, as per his own schedule, sometime between nine and ten o'clock that night her blessed little mutt would ask to go outside so he could answer one last call of nature.

All Gabriel had to do was find an inconspicuous place to wait for them. When they got off the elevator and went out the lobby door, he would follow them. And hope to heaven she didn't have him arrested before he had a chance to tell her just how much she really meant to him.

"Oh, all right. We can go out," Madelyn grumbled, flicking off the television with the remote control, then rolling off the bed as Buddy wriggled around excitedly by the door of her hotel room.

Had anyone asked, she couldn't have said what she'd been watching on TV. She hadn't been paying any attention at all. She'd been too busy crying again.

A glance in the bathroom mirror made her wince. She really was a mess, and not proud of it. Quickly, so as not to keep the dog waiting longer than absolutely necessary, she washed her face, brushed her teeth and ran a comb through her tangled hair. Then she grabbed her jacket, clipped Buddy's leash to his collar, made sure she had her room key and headed for the elevators.

In the lobby, she hurried toward the door, keeping her head down so no one could get a good look at her puffy eyes and red nose.

Thinking of Buddy's needs, she walked along Sandoval Street toward the little park area that ran along the Santa Fe River at De Vargos Street. Since it was just after nine o'clock, a few people were out and about. Still, she hoped the dog wouldn't tarry too long.

Occasionally, aging hippie types or groups of teenage boys gathered in the park. While she hadn't heard any reports of anyone being accosted, she didn't want to risk running into trouble. Buddy was a tough little guy, but he wouldn't be much of a match against someone set on doing her serious harm.

As if tuned in to her thoughts, the dog glanced over his shoulder, growling low in his throat. Madelyn's heartbeat quickened at the sound of footsteps behind her, but she didn't turn around. Instead, she picked up her pace, now all but dragging the dog along. The dog who suddenly seemed much too interested in whoever was closing in on them. He was now yipping joyfully, as if he actually knew the person.

Finally she risked a glance back, then swiftly turned away again.

Gabriel. How had he managed to find her? Probably through Cullen, she thought. She should have never told him where she was staying.

But why was he following her? He had everything he really wanted now. Didn't he?

"Madelyn, wait. *Please,*" he said, catching up to her and taking her by the arm.

"Let me alone," she snapped as she tried, unsuccessfully, to pull away from him.

"Not until you hear what I have to say."

He halted under a street lamp, and turned her to face him. Looking up at him for a moment, she saw anguish in his eyes. An anguish that sent a stab of fear shooting through her.

"What is it? Has something happened to Brian?" she asked, sure that only his son could stir such emotion in him.

"Brian's fine. He's at Donny Murphy's house. What I have to say concerns us."

"There is no *us,* Gabriel." She ducked her head. "There doesn't have to be. Surely Cullen explained that to you." When he didn't respond, she glanced at him again. "You've seen Cullen, haven't you? And he did give you a copy of the papers I signed—?"

"Yes, but the house wasn't what I was after when I asked you to marry me, Maddy. I realize that I made it sound that way, and I'm sorry, truly sorry, I did. I was afraid to say what was really in my heart. But I'm not afraid anymore."

Taking her by the hand, he led her to a bench and sat her down. She stared at him stupidly, trying to make sense of what he'd been saying.

"Gabriel, I don't understand. The house is all yours. You don't have to—"

"Hush," he said, his voice gruff.

Bending, he brushed his lips over hers. Then he went down on one knee in front of her and took both her hands in his.

As if following Gabriel's lead, Buddy sidled up beside him, sat on his haunches and, cocking his head to one side, gazed up at her, too.

Madelyn looked from one of them to the other, a smile tugging at the corners of her mouth.

"You two—"

"I said *hush*," Gabriel repeated.

Raising her hands to his lips, he pressed a kiss onto each palm, then solemnly looked her in the eye.

"I love you, Madelyn St. James. More than I've ever loved any woman. I want you to be my wife, but more than that, I need you, Maddy. I need you to be a part of my life for always. So I'm asking you, here and now, to do me the honor of accepting my proposal. Marry me, Maddy. Please…"

Madelyn looked into his eyes as a fragile silence stretched between them, and knew, without the shadow of a doubt, that what he had said was true. He did love her. Truly, deeply and completely—

"Go ahead, lady. Make his day," someone among the groups of people standing somewhere on the sidelines instructed.

That was all the prompting she needed.

"Yes, Gabriel, I will marry you."

Standing again, he pulled her into his arms and kissed her with a thoroughness that stole her breath away. Around them, a smattering of applause broke out and the dog began to bark. But for Madelyn, at that moment, there was no one else in the world except the man she loved. Gabriel. Her Gabriel…

Her dreams were going to come true, after all. What had seemed a sad ending only an hour ago had suddenly become the happiest of new beginnings. The beginning of their life together.

Epilogue

On a brilliant day in mid-June, Gabriel walked with his wife and son along a pristine beach on the island of Roatán just off the coast of Honduras.

When he had suggested they make this trip together, in lieu of a more traditional honeymoon, Madelyn had been surprised, then very, very pleased. They hadn't talked much about why coming here was important to them. But now, as they paused under a palm tree and looked out at the crystal blue water lapping against the sand, he knew she had wanted to come here for much the same reason he had.

In this beautiful place, a very special man had spent his last days. A man who had caused them both sorrow, yet had, in the end, brought them together with what Gabriel now believed had been a legacy of love.

Gabriel and Madelyn had been married in a small, private ceremony a week after she accepted his revised proposal. Within days after that, as if it were the most natural thing for him to do, Brian had begun calling her Mom. Both Gabriel and Madelyn had been delighted.

At Easter, they had traveled north to St. Louis so she could introduce him and Brian to her parents, her brothers and their families. Though not overly friendly, the St. James clan had tried to be gracious about Madelyn's change in circumstances, and for her, Gabriel had kept his opinion of them to himself.

Then, just a few weeks ago, as he had held Madelyn in his arms, savoring the afterglow of their lovemaking, she had told him—shyly, sweetly—that she was pregnant.

Gabriel hadn't thought he could possibly be any happier, but her announcement had proven him wrong. Every time he thought of the child growing inside her, he experienced an exhilarating sense of completion.

So much good had come into their lives because of Ethan. It had seemed only right to honor his memory by visiting this place together as the family they had become.

"Do you think he found some peace here?" Gabriel asked, drawing Madelyn close to his side as Brian frolicked in the water.

"I think he found a great deal of peace here," she replied quietly, leaning against him.

"I'm glad."

"Yes, so am I. For that, and for so many other things. I love you, Gabriel. You and Brian, and our baby-to-be."

"And I love you, Maddy. With all my heart, for always."

*   *   *   *   *

SILHOUETTE
SENSATION ®

AVAILABLE FROM 20TH JULY 2001

UNDERCOVER BRIDE Kylie Brant

A Year of Loving Dangerously

Agent Rachel Grunwald's mission was to convince Caleb Carpenter, a man whose reputation was as dangerous and devastating as his looks, that she sho be his bride.

MADE FOR EACH OTHER Doreen Owens Malek

Tony Barringer was an FBI agent sworn to do his duty, but his latest mission him choosing between his career and a woman. The woman he was supposed protect had stolen his heart!

HER FIRST MOTHER Kayla Daniels

Amanda Prentiss suddenly had a second chance to share her adopted daught life, but only if she agreed to a marriage—in name only—to a man who had helped take her child...

DANGEROUS LIAISONS Maggie Price

When they met, it was murder! Police Sergeant Jake Ford was investigating t death of one of Nicole's clients, and the signs all pointed to her being involve But even with blazing desire for Nicole clouding his judgement, somehow Jak didn't think so...

HUNTED Jo Leigh

Once they'd shared a bed, a child, their world, but now their marriage had en However, when police detective Mike McCullough received threats that exte to his ex-wife and son, he swept them away to a safe location, where he could stand guard.

SAVING GRACE RaeAnne Thayne

When a beautiful stranger saved the life of his daughter, Jack Dugan knew h had to find the mystery woman. He also had to find out if there was still a thr to his child.

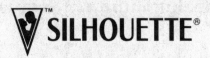

SILHOUETTE

THE MACGREGORS

4 BOOKS ON THIS WELL-LOVED FAMILY

BY

NORA ROBERTS

Book 1 - Serena and Caine - September 2000

Book 2 - Alan and Grant - December 2000

Book 3 - Daniel and Ian - May 2001

Book 4 - Rebellion - August 2001

Don't miss these four fantastic books by Silhouette's top author

0009/ I15 S1-

2 FREE

books and a surprise gift!

We would like to take this opportunity to thank you for reading th
Silhouette® book by offering you the chance to take TWO mo
specially selected titles from the Sensation™ series absolutely FRE
We're also making this offer to introduce you to the benefits of th
Reader Service™—

★ FREE home delivery
★ FREE gifts and competitions
★ FREE monthly Newsletter
★ Exclusive Reader Service discounts
★ Books available before they're in the shops

Accepting these FREE books and gift places you under r
obligation to buy, you may cancel at any time, even after receivi
your free shipment. Simply complete your details below and retu
the entire page to the address below. *You don't even need a stamp*

YES! Please send me 2 free Sensation books and a surprise gi
I understand that unless you hear from me, I will receive
superb new titles every month for just £2.80 each, postage ar
packing free. I am under no obligation to purchase any books ar
may cancel my subscription at any time. The free books and gift w
be mine to keep in any case.

SIZE

Ms/Mrs/Miss/Mr ....Initials................................
BLOCK CAPITALS PLEA:

Surname ....

Address ....

....

....Postcode...............................

Send this whole page to:
UK: FREEPOST CN81, Croydon, CR9 3WZ
EIRE: PO Box 4546, Kilcock, County Kildare (stamp required)